Blossoms in the Eternal Spring

"Seeing my Lord,
I'm wholly in bloom."

To Him
With deepest love and gratitude

Blossoms in the Eternal Spring

Shammi Paranjape

RUPA

Published by
Rupa Publications India Pvt. Ltd 2004
7/16, Ansari Road, Daryaganj
New Delhi 110002

Sales Centres:

Allahabad Bengaluru Chennai
Hyderabad Jaipur Kathmandu
Kolkata Mumbai

ISBN: 978-81-291-0406-9

Second impression 2022

10 9 8 7 6 5 4 3 2

Typeset by Nikita Overseas Pvt Ltd, New Delhi

Printed at Saurabh Printers Pvt. Ltd, Noida

Question Him, for He has come.
He knows. He is the conscious one.
He is to be sought again and again.
In Him are the guidances.
He is the Lord....

Rig Veda

Contents

Acknowledgements

Just a few words to express my gratitude to the wonderful people who helped me in the realization of this book. Apart from my family and friends whose love is a constant source of inspiration in my life, I especially wish to thank Juliana for her wonderful help in typing the manuscript over many months.

I am also grateful to the publishers, Rupa & Company for taking up this project with so much enthusiasm.

An interesting aside to this is that ten years back when I couldn't imagine myself writing a book, Baba came in my dream and told me that I would. In that dream, I take His blessings and touch His lotus feet. Baba tells me that the book would be published from Delhi and Kolkata. Later, thinking over the dream I often wondered, 'why Delhi and Kolkata and why not Bombay?' After this manuscript was completed, without any planning on my part it fell into the hands of the publishers, Rupa & Company. This large publishing house has offices all over India – the main ones being in Delhi and Kolkata!

Preface

"I have come to light the lamp of love..."

Sri Sathya Sai

"Paritranaaya Sadhunaam
Vinaashaya Cha Dushkrutam
Dharma-Sansthapanarthya
Sambhavami Yuge Yuge"

'For the protection of the good, for the destruction of evil forces and for the firm establishment of dharma or right conduct, I am born in every age.'

This divine assurance is from the *Bhagawad Gita.* Hindu belief incorporates the concept of the avatar – the descent of divinity into a form. However, for all the sanctity attached to scriptural truths, one doesn't imagine that one will meet an avatar in one's lifetime! By and large – over many thousands of years – one doesn't. And even when one meets – one may not recognize. It is my belief that I have, by His grace alone, met the avatar of the age – Sri Sathya Sai Baba. This belief rests on my direct perceptions and experience, and my intuition. Also, the epic scale of the work accomplished by Baba speaks for itself. One doesn't have to look beyond that.

This Sai avatar, has a unique speciality being a 'triple avatar' covering three incarnations – Shirdi Sai, Sathya Sai and Prema Sai. Sathya Sai Baba has given the exact birthplace and time of the third incarnation – Prema Sai – that will take place in the future, to complete this magnificent three-fold avataric mission. However, this book is not about Baba's grand works, the scale of which defies human comprehension, nor does it seek to convince anyone about Baba's divinity. If anything, this book is about the joy of self-discovery – the unlocking of the spiritual treasures that lie within each one of us.

All belief has a starting point. Before my direct experience of Baba's divinity, even I did not believe. It is for each one of us to test and experience for oneself.

Why did I turn to Baba? The answer to that can only be – just because. There was no reason. And yet it happened as the strongest, most undeniable experience of my life. This book is an attempt to trace the path that brought me here.

My reference to Him throughout is naturally as to the Highest. At different places, I refer to Him as Baba, Sai, Swami, the Lord – for He is all this to me. Baba's many followers from around the world will be able to easily relate to the style and content of the book. But, for those who may be new or at the threshold, or just curious, I have included an introductory chapter –*The Ambrosial Saga* – on His early life to mark out the unusual aspects that made it extraordinary. This is just to give a background to those who may have none. It is like cupping the ocean in one's palm. May His grace do the task.

I would like to add that He alone has guided me all the way. Even the title of the book, the two exquisite invocatory prayers at the start and three poetic messages, were given to me by Swami Himself in one of the many innumerable ways He has of communicating with His devotees.

There are millions of devotees and each one has a story. That is the wonder. This is mine...

Shammi Paranjape

All the italicized quotes in the book are Sri Sathya Sai's.

Prayer

Oh Lord Ganesha, *the remover of obstacles, I pray to Thee to don my intellect and work through my thoughts to enable me to weave the lyrics of an enchanting melody, enlivening the glory of my beloved Lord Sri Sathya Sai.*

Bless me so that my mind overflows with an unending stream of words suffused with ambrosia. And grant me the wisdom to understand this lilting song of Lord Sai so that it may fill my whole being with the light and the sweetness of divine love.

I surrender myself at Thy Lotus Feet. Thou art the Doer. Make me Thy instrument.

✦

Oh Goddess Saraswati, *the beautiful glorious One, I pray to Thee, to encompass my intellect with Thy sweetness and beauty so that this garland of divine love is strung with the sweetest of words and purest of thoughts.*

Bless me so that Thy beauty shines forth through each verse and Thy fragrance wafts through each word.

Grant me the vision of Thy presence within me so that I can give my best to this celestial music.

The Ambrosial Saga

This glorious saga began in the dusky little village called Puttaparthi, when a celestial babe was born to Easwaramma and Pedda Venkappa Raju, two simple pure souls in the wee hours of 23 November 1926. Little did they realize that their darling babe was going to usher in a golden era, by drawing millions to the dusky little village and encompass the world in the sweet nectar of his divine love.

It was a blessed dawn, moving on paths of gold, that broke quietly over the village. It was a moment, keenly awaited by pious and knowing ones; hymns of praise and adoration of that event of birth were waiting to be sung; flowers for adorning the cradle of the babe were coming to bloom and scent- laden breezes were stirring to blow over the brow of the babe. Mother earth was rising up, as it were, to greet that dawn. It was the answer to the earnest prayers of sages and saints – an event that according to Hindu belief comes but once in an entire yuga – the birth of an avatar. A little distance away, in His ashram, the sage Aurobindo was given the realization that His intense prayers for a saviour to come on the earth had come to holy fruition. Accordingly, Sri Aurobindo went into mystic seclusion on 24 November 1926. Before doing so, he made the stunning declaration that the holy day had seen, "the descent of Krishna into the physical. A power infallible shall lead the thought, in earthly hearts kindle the Immortal's Fire, even the multitude shall hear the voice!"

There was, of course, nothing explicit to reveal the glory of that birth, just then. Two thousand years ago, when a babe was born in a humble manger, few could have known the amazing grace of that event. Even those pure souls, who were given an inkling of the holy nature of that birth, could not have imagined the full extent of its grandeur. So it was in the tiny, inaccessible village of Puttaparthi. When, not only the village but the entire world should have been rejoicing, there was just the ordinary jubilation that marks any new birth. However, there was an extra note to the celebrations alright, because of some strange and wondrous occurrances that preceded this birth.

Few months prior, when the chosen mother Easwaramma (who had spent countless hours in prayer propitiating the deities for a son) had gone to fetch water from a village well, she had a mystifying experience – a ball of blue ethereal light approached and entered her causing her to go down in a swoon. The pravesa or Immaculate Conception had taken place but there was no way for that simple, pure hearted lady to know that. Following that episode, and upto the time of the birth, there was an uncanny occurrence in the Raju household. The musical instruments would burst forth into spontaneous melody with no human hands touching them. This was disturbing to the inmates of the house who felt that some evil spirits were at work. The distraught father, Pedda Venkappa Raju even sought an astrologer's counsel and was partly consoled on being told that it was a highly auspicious sign that announced the birth of a great soul. To add further to the mystery, immediately after the birth, a cobra appeared from nowhere to briefly swing the baby from beneath, as it lay swaddled in its bedclothes. It disappeared as mysteriously as it had come. Everybody was startled, but the matter was soon forgotten in the excitement of the celebrations of the birth.

How was that simple household to know that the child, born to promote the joy of mankind had come and that His virtues would nourish and foster the entire length and breadth of the land? Yes, their child was luminous looking and had a noble brow, but did not all fond parents think so? that their child is the fairest one?

An auspicious day was quickly fixed for the name-giving ceremony after appropriate consultation. When the bright day dawned, the humble abode buzzed with festive activity. Mango leaf festoons were strung on doorways and rice rangoli patterns decorated on the floor. Delicious savouries for guests were prepared in the kitchen and auspicious lamps were lit. The baby's crib was decorated with all manner of flowers and with loving care, the baby too was adorned. Not that it was needed. For, more enchanting than a blue lotus, he adorned His surroundings!

And finally, the moment came for the name to be whispered, as according to custom, into the child's ear. It was – Sathyanarayan Raju. Was it imagination or did the baby smile? Much afterwards, the passage of time would reveal that the baby had every reason to smile. Sathya means Truth and Narayan means God. A more truthful name could not have been given!

On top of the small hillock, a tamarind tree quivered. The boy, Sathya stood under it holding a rope-swing hanging from its branches. His playmates stood at a distance keenly watching. They knew anything could happen. If they were lucky to be there, so was the tree, for it pleased the boy, Sathya (Raju) to transform it into a kalpataru – wish fulfilling tree! Whichever fruit His companions wanted –apples, mangoes, oranges – were plucked from that tree by Sathya. Fruits of all kinds and from all seasons, from the same tree! His young companions did not express wonder at this nor did they try to analyse. Hadn't Sathya proved it time and again that he was different? That he defied analysis? They simply and unquestioningly accepted Him as their guru. Those simple village children were the trailblazers. How could they know who and what their 'guru' was?

Lilas abounded. Once, Sathya swang merrily on the swing. And time itself swung back 5,000 years! In a brilliant vision, suffused with light, the stunned onlookers saw murali-lola Krishna, the Lord of the flute swinging on the flower-bedecked swing! Some fainted, others just stared with open mouths. The vision over, Sathya lovingly chided them, saying, "Now you know why I don't give such visions!"

In another charming episode, he asked a couple of His friends if they wanted to hear the notes of Krishna's flute some 5,000 years after they had actually been played. Of course, they did. With eager faces they awaited their next cue. Sathya pressed their ears against His heart and said, "listen..." They did. And nearly swooned as much at the sweet sound of the notes as the manner in which they were hearing them.

With things like this happening with regularity, it became more and more difficult to view Sathya as an ordinary boy. Yet, on the other hand, he maintained the delicate balance by behaving and acting like any normal boy too! Here, the maya factor would come in – on the one side, there were the lilas and on the other the cloaking over with maya. It is said that when an avatar takes birth, maya or illusion walks hand in hand with Him. This role of maya is ordained and designed by the Lord Himself, because without it there can be no world and no play (lila). The challenge for the spiritual seeker ever is to overcome the maya and see the resplendent reality of the one non-dual God behind the veil. Even in Krishna's time, for all His miraculous deeds, after the 'event', most, including His mother, Yashodha would slip back into the comfortable delusion that he was an ordinary boy with some extraordinary qualities. Even Jesus often scolded His disciples for wanting proofs of divinity again and again. Sathya's childhood too was both ordinary and extraordinary. It was a slow and measured build up. He was preparing the ground for the much greater things to follow.

As a child, Sathya was pure gold. He was an example to all the kids. In the kaliyug, the mischievous divine pranks of a Krishna avatar would hardly hold water. The pure vision required is sorely lacking today. Our own distortions of the mind are projected outwards. So, God plans out His avataric missions on earth with perfect precision and timing. Where, in earlier *yugas*, to attain the vision of God prolonged tapas, rituals, sacrifice, etc. was required; in this age, just taking His Name is enough. It was perhaps foreseen that in these impious times, the greed for money and power would overpower everything else and the mere chanting of the Name would constitute a fair effort to seek communion with the divine.

Sathya's childhood was not easy. He was born in a poor family with humble means. He had to trudge to school on foot everyday, a distance of six miles. He had to fetch water from the village well in heavy pails for the household where he lived. Sathya displayed amazing tolerance and deep compassion for fellow human beings, especially the deprived and homeless. He especially loved animals. He would feed beggars at His door by giving them His portion of food. Once, on His torn shirt, he used a thorn as a safety pin! He bore everything with fortitude and equal mindedness – and bid His time. For, the day was to come when the boy who walked to school, would bring university education to that very village; the boy who trudged for water to the village well would bring the gift of water in taps to hundreds of thirsty villages. And the same boy, who shared His meager meal with others, would feed hundreds and thousands of the poor. Not only that, having once used a thorn to pin His shirt, he would one day be mending the very fabric of humanity.

It was at the age of fourteen, one dramatic day, that Sathya revealed and announced Himself. His simple parents, Pedda V. Raju and Easwaramma were besides themselves with worry and concern about their unusual son. Who was He? Sathya took a handful of jasmine flowers and flung them on to the ground. The white blossoms miraculously formed themselves into the name – Sai Baba. Wonder all around. Who was Sai Baba? The glory of the saint of Shirdi had yet not reached the southern parts of India. Though time would come soon enough, when Shirdi Sai would pervade the country's length and breadth, from Kashmir to Kanyakumari.

Sathya renounced family ties, left school and home and declared that His mission had started. He had His work to do. Sitting on a rock, in a neighbouring garden, Sathya sang the very first bhajan:

Manas bhajare, guru charanam
Dushtara bhava, sagara taranam...

And with that divine melody, all auspiciousness descended upon earth, had one but known it. The glorious boon-conferring feet of the Sadguru were graciously made available to mankind – to those fortunate ones who would reach out and heed the call.

With the declaration of the Advent, the little village of Puttaparthi acquired a luminous status. Word spread and people started coming in increasing numbers. It became a sacred destination for some and for the scoffers and skeptics, always part of the drama, a target for their invective. For every believer, there was a non-believer. And there were the barbs and scorn alongside the praise and adoration. There would be inexplicable phenomena like cures of diseases, etc., and yet, the strong maya was always there. In the history of avatars, the chosen mothers/families have to pay heavily it seems for the boon of having an avatar born to them. Be it Devaki or Kaushalya, chosen mothers pay a heavy price.

When initially people flocked to see the young guru 'Sai Baba', it was mainly for cures and boons relating to worldly life. Baba has said, "I give you what you want, so you may want what I have come to give." By and by, proximity to the divine Sadguru and exposure to His teachings creates the shift from the worldly to the spiritual. Those who gained the precious proximity and received His divine counsel, could not remain unmoved by the experience. They divined that their guru was much more than any reason could fathom even in a thousand years.

That was a charmed time for the devotees lucky enough to be there. Compared to the millions that would come later, they were just a handful. Consequently, they were afforded amazing insights into the unfolding saga of the avatar of the age. They were blessed souls able to witness up-close, beguiling facets of the Lord, something which devotees cannot even dream of today. Every devotee knows too well, that however much the Sathya Sai avatar may be an embodiment of love who showers devotees with ceaseless grace in His person, He is essentially remote, divinely aloof and quite unreachable. It is impossible for even the closest devotee of many many years' standing to take the slightest personal liberty with Baba – it is as if He has built this guard around Him and for nothing and no one will He allow it to come down. In that sense, He is supremely alone, atop some unscaleable peak way beyond the reach of ordinary mortals, or so it seems. In the case of previous avatars, this 'loneliness' if it can be so called, was to a far lesser degree. Both the Krishna and the Rama avatars were 'involved' – on the level of drama – in family and friends with all the attendant emotional interactions. Even in the incarnation of Shirdi Sai though the family factor was absent, He nevertheless allowed some very close personal bonds with a few chosen devotees who were very free and uninhibited in their approach to Him. (for e.g. Shama, Tatya, etc). This easy familiarity is difficult to envisage, in the case of our own Sathya Sai. It is not as if He is not a veritable stream of love for His devotees at all times. It is just that even maya cannot fully or comprehensively conceal the imposing grandeur of His Truth. It shines forth and overawes the intellect.

In those days, Puttaparthi was like the back of beyond – unknown and unsung. It was virtually inaccessible with not even a motorable road. One had to wade across the Chitravati river to reach its divine shore. In those early days, our young Swami would personally receive all the devotees arriving on the banks of the river after the arduous journey. What an enthralling sight! Swami's form standing on the sands of the Chitravati awaiting the arrival of the devotees.... There are other charming tales; of Swami's penchant for swimming in the river! Of driving a car Himself and at a speed which made His companion mutter nervously, 'Sai Ram, Sai Ram' all the way! So it was not as if He did not enjoy pranks. He used to trouble everyone, but sweetly, and the pranks endeared Him even more. Later on, the avatar had to put on a sober aspect, to suit the time and His mission, but which discerning devotee has not missed the irrepressible merriment that plays ever so subtly on His face, more often than not?

In those days, young Swami kept two pet dogs – Jack and Jill. And naturally, they never left the side of their Master – not even during the night. This led to the charming scenario of one sleeping at the foot of the bed and the other at the head. Why, if dogs sometimes exhibit qualities nobler than humans, they also sometimes come with unique karma! Sai's compassion for animals ever manifested in gestures of caring. There are some delightful photos of Swami with various pets like deer, parrot, dogs, etc. and the tender expression on Swami's face speaks for itself. His love for His pet elephant, Sai Gita, and her love for Him is legendary.

Of all things, melody captivated the heart of Sai the most. In those early days, many long and happy hours were spent in singing – sometimes late into the night. A handful of devotees would gather around their charming Sai, as bees around the lotus, and with animated faces and charged voices sing songs of devotion. Sai, with manjira in His hands, would keep taal. The ananda of the bhajans would melt the features of Swami into greater beauty and the devotees would stare and gaze at Him to their heart's content. Sitting on the banks of the Chitravati on moonlit nights, those fortunate devotees witnessed many lilas. From the sand, Baba would draw out golden idols of the devotees' choice – also, small containers full of divine amrut, from which He distributed all around.

Having sung, played laughed with Him, little did these devotees realize then the marvellous grace that allowed it all. The day would come when they would look back and wonder – was it a dream? Is this Sai, aloof and unapproachable surrounded by thousands, gliding by in darshan with not even a look, *their* Sai, the same one, they had sported with in carefree abandon? Many of the devotees who had the good fortune of close proximity to the avatar in those early years, have been distanced – physically – now. Even the few who continue by the Lord's will, to be near His form, do not and dare not have the same easy familiarity with Him as in those earlier days. They have their memories and as gold never loses its value or shine, they too hold their reminiscences close to their heart.

One moonlit night, which Swami decided, ought not to be wasted indoors, found the group on the banks of the Chitravati for a midnight picnic. A picnic with a difference! There was no food – as yet – only empty vessels. Stomachs were rumbling with hunger! Everybody wondered what Swami would do next. Eyes twinkling merrily, He asked them to line all the vessels, covered with lids, before Him. By now, the group knew they could expect anything from their special guru and friend. Sure enough, their unquestioning belief was rewarded. With a tap on each vessel, their Swami filled it with sumptuous varieties of hot piping food.

Of all people close to the avatar, the special one who was allowed the greatest liberty was probably the chosen mother, Easwaramma. Her simplicity and overpowering maternal instinct clouded over nearly always all the other evidence relating to her 'son' – the extraordinary one! Through all the lilas and chamatkars, He remained over and above everything else, her beloved little Sathyam whom she needed to protect, nurture and feed! It ached the fond mother's heart to see that Sathyam hardly ate at all. In fact, not only in His eating habits, but in every way, her Sathyam was so different from the other boys. How she wished, He could be like any other ordinary boy – for then, He would have been just her own.

It is a constant source of wonder to those around Him as to how little Swami eats and yet maintains superhuman levels of energy. It appears Swami eats even that small amount as a mere formality for the sake of His devotees. His preferred food is the humble ragi, which is high in nutrition, low on cost and requires an acquired taste! One old lady in the ashram once quipped, "Only *He* can have it, because He's God!" Observing His sparse intake of food, a devotee once ventured, "Swami, You must be drawing Your nourishment from the five elements." The devotee felt he was making a good point… Swami's reply threw Him off balance! He said, "No, the five elements draw their nourishment from Me!"

Swami once revealed to some close devotees an interesting story relating to the kalpavruksha tree in Puttaparthi. When he was a lad of thirteen, he retreated into a world of solitude for six months. He confined Himself in an underground tunnel below the kalpavruksha tree on a hill. He had just a few items with Him – a kamandalam (the vessel in which sages carry drinking water), a dandam (staff carried by ascetics) a small writing desk contraption, a pen, an ink bottle, and a copy of the *Bhagawad Gita*. Some pure hearted devotees with His permission went to that spot later, removed the rocks and pebbles, and found the tunnel there. They ventured into the sacred area and saw all those items Swami had spoken to them about. However, Swami said, "People with doubting minds will not even find the opening of the tunnel and will have to come back disappointed." How can one explain these things? Faith is of the essence and the Lord always responds in direct proportion to the intensity of feeling in a devotee's heart. He has just one beautiful need – the pure love of a devotee. He is not looking for laborious recitations of holy texts, or elaborate and rigorous rituals, penances or austere denials or even formal reverence. He is simply looking for spontaneity from a pure heart. All the rest of it, as prescribed by most religions, is just a sadhan or tool to get a person going towards this goal of love. What benefit can the perfect recitation of the *Bhagawad Gita* be to the Lord who has Himself composed it? What satisfaction can offerings of wealth give to the Lord who holds it all in His palm? And, what pleasure can the mortification of your body give to the One who is the ocean of all-compassion and love?

The lotus of the Lord's love can grow only in the lake of a pure heart – and once it blooms, its fragrance and luster outshines everything that you have ever known. In the case of divinity, it is the law of ever–increasing returns! This definitely applies to His darshan, the more you see Him, the more you wish to see Him. That is the specialty of the Lord – nitya nutanam (ever new).

In October 1953, Baba gave His first official discourse in the Prasanthi Nilayam mandir that came up. It was the first brilliant gem of many thousands that Baba would scatter to humanity in the years to come. For over fifty years now, Baba has been tirelessly at work on many fronts for the welfare of humanity. In His exemplary life, lies the biggest message – *My life is My message.*

Many were the miracles that took place but they were only the background to Baba's grandest mission – transformation of the human heart. How did Sai propose to do that? "*I have come to light the lamp of love in your hearts, to see that it shines day by day with added luster. I have not come to speak on behalf of any spiritual practice or Hindu philosophy. I have not come on any mission of publicity for any sect or creed or cause; nor have I come to collect followers for any doctrine. I have no plan to attract disciples or devotees into my fold or any fold. I have come to tell you of this universal Faith, this divine Consciousness, this path of Love, this duty of Love, this obligation of Love*"

It is an ongoing saga. A saga of love divine...

Message

Spring time is a celebration. A burst of colourful flowers on the treetops, the atmosphere pervaded with the fragrance of the spring blossoms, the koel singing away her enchanting melody in a sweet voice... Life too is a celebration...each look celebrates the manifestation of the divine, each breath celebrates the existence of the divine, each word bursts into a song for the divine. As you soak in the beauty of the spring season, look within; experience the divinity within you and then, you will be celebrating life eternally...

1

Something More To Our Lives

Remember, only four days deserve the honour of being called 'red letter days' or days which have to be recorded in letters of gold – the day on which bhaktas gather to sing the glory of the God, the day when the hungry are fed, the day when one meets a great sage and the day on which viveka dawns on the individual.

Sri Sathya Sai

There will never come a moment, so matchless, as the one in which Bhagawan Sri Sathya Sai Baba came into my life. Of course, as I understood later, He had always been there, only I had been ignorant of this divine reality, which is as much a part of my life, as anybody else's. The right moment has to be awaited – with shradha and saburi – for, when it comes there is no looking back. The discovery, that there is something more to our lives, which is everything that a heart and soul can ever desire, is unmatchable.

Up to the age of the eighteen I hardly knew who God was. This had partly to do with the fact that there were so many gods in my life! First and foremost, the most noble and loving parents, who looked after every need of mine as only gods can. As I look back today, childhood appears to be a gentle swirl of happy images in which broken toys and tears played their role but the overriding feeling was one of warm contentment.

My father nurtured in me a deep love for nature on the one side and good reading on the other, and the joys of these filled my canvas with the most attractive colours. That was the time I was caught up with the grand painting itself and had no time for the Supreme Artist behind it all. My mother nourished and pampered me as much with her sweet love as with her sweeter remonstrances, which imparted to me those important values without which life has little meaning. In fact, when I look back now I realize, just how much God pervaded my life; being the silent benefactor, doing everything and saying nothing! I could never have dreamt that this silent benefactor, this all do-gooder could have a face, a name, and a form. Very few things ever prepare human beings for a face-to-face encounter with the divine. So lost are we in the trappings of the material that we miss entirely the subtleties and possibilities of spirit. I think, of all discoveries, there can never be a greater one in a person's life than the realization that God exists. When that happens the heart exults in the fact that 'God's in His place and all's right with the world'. Hearing those first whispers of the divine is like a new birth. The second most stunning realization, for believers, is that the Supreme God can, from time to time, manifest on this earth in different forms, to deliver humanity. There are many especially in the West, who cannot stretch their reason to accept this. Yet, one of the greatest religions of the West, Christianity, is based on just that premise – the fact of a God-like man walking the earth. In Hindu belief, which has the advantage of drawing from the most unbelievably ancient and advanced body of religious and philosophical thought—the *Vedas*—God manifests periodically in every age as an avatar. '*Yada yada hi dharmasaya, glanir bhavati Bharata, abhyutanam adharmasaya, tadatmanam srujamyaham.*' (*Bhagawad Gita*)

So the real big moment in my life came, though without my realizing it of course, when my father walked into the house one day, with a large framed photo of Sri Sathya Sai Baba under his arm, and a book about this 'holy man.' (*The Man of Miracles* by Howard Murphet.) We were surprised. He had always prided himself on being a rational agnostic, who did not set store by religious rituals and holy men. Yet, here he was, keenly giving us a background to the photo and the book. The very fact that he, with his extraordinary intelligence, was giving fair attention to the stories and the photo was enough reason for all of us daughters to fall in line too. In this way, our first lessons in faith and surrender began at home itself, with my father! If he said something, it had to be so, because we felt he was just too wonderful and intelligent, to ever get it wrong.

Baba's photo was set up initially in my parents' bedroom. The three college going sisters read the book turn by turn. It found a responsive chord in each one's heart. The youngest and fourth sister was too small as yet to understand what was happening, but she knew it had something to do with that Person in the orange robe and dark curly hair called Baba. She quickly got schooled into doing a reverential '*jai*' to His photograph!

In the most natural and unobtrusive manner, one by one, the family members slipped into a devotional mode. This was a little surprising considering the lack of it earlier. In the sense, there had always been more of a spiritual rather than religious consciousness in our house, with greater accent on inner feeling than ritual. If anything, we were nature-mystics – in love with nature. Even my dear grandmother, though more overtly religious than any of us, was very flexible and liberated in her approach. She never carried her religiosity to rigid extremes, which is sometimes inconvenient to people around. However, she made one very important contribution to our religious background; she had a temple constructed to the family's deity, Radha-Krishna. Consequently, our days of childhood and growing up got inextricably woven in Radha-Krishna lore. Visits to the temple on festive occasions afforded a different kind of old-world enchantment. Janmashtami or Krishna's birthday was the one magical time of the year when this temple came alive for us and we took part in the ritual celebrations. Special sweet savories were prepared for Krishna as also other delectable food items to be offered to Him at the stroke of midnight. Till such time as these offerings could be made to the Lord, we all fasted. But, what a delicious fast! The idea was to avoid only certain regulars like rice, wheat, etc., but there was no embargo on other specialized 'fast items!' Thus, we cruised happily through the day to the midnight hour when there was legitimate feasting to celebrate the divine birth. However, right through childhood, apart from this annual burst of religious activity, the rest of the year was relatively free from it, with Jesus predominating more around Christmas because of our convent school upbringing. We celebrated Christmas with great enthusiasm as children and especially enjoyed the tradition of the Christmas tree, cake and gifts! The only other Hindu festival that brought the Gods out from the closet was Diwali. The whole house was lit up with diyas, my mother did Laxmi pujan and we children looked forward to the crackers.

With the arrival of Baba in the house, our latent spirituality started expressing itself. My father brought more Sai literature and the photos multiplied. Bhajan cassettes made their entry into the home. Devotional melody wafted in the air. As often happens in this stage in a person's spiritual journey, everything, coincidently conspired towards strengthening our faith. Just down our lane, we discovered a family who were devotees of Baba. They were keen on organizing bhajans and other activities in the neighbourhood. My father started attending these occasionally and slowly the whole family was quietly drawn along as in one common stream of devotion. This feeling for Baba came upon us like a gentle breeze, and without our realizing it stirred us in the deepest recesses of our souls.

We had heard of many miracles of Baba happening in devotees' houses, but they never seemed to happen to us, however hard we tried! Stories about vibhuti emanating from photos were legion, as also about fragrances like sandalwood etc. filling the air. We would sniff the air but it would always turn out to be a false alarm. Invariably, somebody had lit an agarbatti. On one occasion, we felt there was something stuck on Baba's photo and all of us called out to each other, in excitement, only to discover it was the ash of the agarbatti which had fallen on the glass! By now, we had got into the daily practice of doing a small puja everyday after bathing by lighting agarbattis and chanting a few prayers. Initially, this was done by all of us in front of the solitary photo in our parents' bedroom. By and by, a lovely mandir came up or just 'grew' into our house, in which, of course, Baba's photos easily outnumbered all other gods! The separate mandir provided a sacred space for each one of us to establish our own one to one spiritual connection. On Thursdays, garlands strung with fresh flowers from the garden were offered, as it is marked out as a special day for Baba's devotees. In this manner, we all cruised along in our newfound belief in Baba's divinity, which for some reason came very easily to all of us. There was no struggle of faith or questioning. Like a fish takes to water naturally, without analyzing or wondering how, we slipped into, what I can only call, the waters of His grace.

2

Signs And Wonders

The signs and wonders that I manifest can be called chamatkar *(miracles) which lead to* samskara *(good character) which urges one onto* paropkara *(doing good) resulting in* sakshatkar *(self realization).*

Sri Sathya Sai

Reading or hearing about the fantastic phenomena associated with Baba's divinity is only a prelude to experiencing it yourself. This of course, may happen in innumerable ways. When it happens, you are transported at Baba's direct entry into your life.

One morning, a flushed Mr. Kailash came to our house to tell us that vibhuti, amrut, roli, rice etc. were emanating from Baba's photos in his house, in thick cascades. They had collected quite a bit in jars already and the flow of grace had continued unabated. We were invited by him to come and witness it ourselves. We all rushed to his house, just down the lane. On entering the mandir, we saw all the framed photos and there were many of them, almost entirely covered over with thick clusters of vibhuti, turmeric and sindoor and some even had amrut flowing out in a stream. We had only heard of all this, but now we were seeing it with our own eyes. There was a divine fragrance hanging in the air and the whole vibration of the mandir was divinely charged. Bhajans were on and in complete awe and reverence we sat down crosslegged to absorb the experience. The vibhuti flow in their house, in amazing proportions, continued for two whole months. This incident was a big spur to the faith and devotion of existing devotees, and it also attracted a lot of new devotees. Our faith too became stronger and Baba started pervading our lives even more.

It was also around this time that He first appeared in our dreams. Apart from the guidance and instruction the dreams gave, the sheer delight of His darshan, stole our hearts.

At that time I was in my final year of B.A. in Lady Shri Ram College for Women in New Delhi. I was staying in the college hostel and one of the first things I did on my return was to put up a small picture of Baba on my hostel room wall. I even got into the habit of lighting an agarbatti everyday. My friends wondered 'what's with her?' I hardly knew myself, but it was all just happening as if on its own. My final year exams got over and I went back home to Kanpur.

One morning, I got an excited call from Delhi to inform me that I had scored a first division in English literature honours. In my previous two years, I had got an average second division. Not that I had prayed for a first division – marks were never considered very important in our family. However, I do remember how in the examination my pen just flowed. Everyone was amazed because English honours not being a very scoring subject, there were very few first divisions in the whole of Delhi University and I had got one! Well, I was sure, *that* photo on the wall had something to do with this. I joked with my friends about the positive fall-out of lighting an agarbatti before exams!

With my B.A. done, the question was, what next? I decided to sit back at home in Kanpur and think it over. That took me all of one year! Which I didn't mind at all, because having spent three years away in a Delhi hostel, I simply longed for home. Even the three years I had been in Delhi, the pull of home was such that on the slightest pretext (long weekend, university strike etc.) we would just hop on to a train, third class, and land up in Kanpur. I don't know what it was but the kind of inner peace I felt just being at home is difficult to describe. It was said that our house was actually built on the riverbed of the sacred Ganges, which flows through Kanpur. Maybe that contributed to the special vibrations of the place. Apart from that, my parent's unique personality did a lot towards lifting my childhood and growing up years out of the ordinary.

What my father primarily did was sharpen our inner senses for touching joy in small things. The sweet-pea in the garden; the rain-cloud in the sky; the poetic line; the aroma of brewing tea; the dew drop.... all became a matter of simple celebration. In fact, we named our house on the dew that falls from the heavens. We all wished to give the house a name as it just had a postal number. And the whole idea was to come up with something *really* original. It was my father who came up with the idea of 'Green Dew'. What could be more fresh or original than that? Our house has two huge lawns, which every morning get dewed over to look like carpets of green and so my father said, "It seems here, even the dew is green." That's how Green Dew came into being. Another matter that it took a whole while for the world to accept it, for we kept getting mail addressed to 'Honey Dew', 'Green View' etc! Anyhow, my paradise was my home and I wished to spend some more time there rather than go traipsing here and there. Sitting and sipping tea on the verandah with a good book, the garden in bloom, my parents around me, I needed nothing else. Kanpur being a small town, there was not much scope for 'doing anything,' and for the moment that was exactly what I wanted to do.

Shortly, everything in our lives was perceived as Baba's grace. I think, because of this conscious perceiving, in some way, everything in our lives did become Baba's grace! Often, Baba stresses the need to see and accept every life situation as a gift from God and to ever affirm the grace implicit in it. We are constantly drawing in our own universes with our thoughts and reactions and thinking positive, draws the bounty of the universe to us.

My grandmother, at this time, was a dear old lady of eighty-two years with a remarkably alert mind and a lovable disposition. Religious in her own way, she believed firmly in the power of the repeated chanting of the Name and I remember her lips moving with this japa, constantly. One night, my father had a dream in which he saw Baba come and take our grandmother away with him on a train. My father saw Baba standing at the rear end, in the guard's bogie, waving a green flag. Next morning, while happily sipping her morning cup of tea, my grandmother peacefully crossed over to the other side. Without any pain or fear she was gone with, and to, Baba on a new journey, as He had shown in the dream the previous night.

Shortly after this, my father experienced his first vibhuti miracle. All of us had to make a trip to Bombay leaving him alone for a few days. He felt pretty lost without the presence of his sweetly nagging wife and noisy children. To add to this, his chronic arthritis flared up, causing unbearable pain in his joints. A point came where he could hardly walk and had to hobble around. Our domestic help had to assist him in even taking a few steps. My father was extremely despondent as he felt that he would have to go in for surgery. One day, the pain in his knees got particularly excruciating. As my father had always been very active, he felt utterly distraught. He was sitting under the big photo of Baba in his bedroom. Something made him look up to the photo and say, "Baba, only You can help me now, if You wish." Just then, the postman knocked. In a perfectly timed visit, He delivered a letter. My father couldn't believe his eyes. The letter was from Puttaparthi! It was from an old friend of his now settled in Baba's Puttaparthi ashram. This friend, Mr. Narayanana, a wry old man was a brilliant scientist and an initial atheist who, after experiencing Baba's divinity left everything to go and live in His ashram. The funny thing was that my father hadn't heard from him in years. The letter contained photos of Baba and a packet of vibhuti. In his note, Mr. Narayanana wrote, "Bishun, I have no idea why I suddenly thought of you and felt compelled to send this vibhuti, atheist that you are! But remember, I too was a die-hard atheist and here I am. Don't pass over this chance. Put that scientific temper on hold and seek the experience. It is phenomenal...." The vibhuti was the special one Baba had materialized on Mahashivaratri that year. While churning an upturned silver pot above the idol of Shirdi Sai, streams of the *vibhuti* had poured from the empty pot by the circling motion of Baba's hand. My father realized that the arrival of the vibhuti was not by mere chance, but a direct answer to his prayer. Baba had responded to a devotee's need, as he always unfailingly does. My father immediately applied the vibhuti on his painful arthritic knees. What happened next happens to thousands of devotees, but the wonder of it is never reduced – like somebody running a hand over a magic slate, the pain just disappeared in a trice and completely! My father could hardly believe it! His heart welled up with love and gratitude for Baba. He stood up and walked around with a look of complete wonder on his face, like that of a child. Now he couldn't wait to communicate this miracle to us in Bombay. He phoned us and recounted the whole episode. The arthritis was completely cured by that single instance of application of vibhuti and never surfaced again in my father's life.

This incident gave a further impetus to our devotion. We now felt a strong desire to visit Puttaparthi. But before that happened, we were to make a trip to Shirdi to offer homage and seek blessings from Sai Baba's shrine in a remote village in Maharashtra. All Sathya Sai devotees believe Him to be the reincarnation of Shirdi Sai Baba and to a chosen few, this fact has been revealed in stunning ways. There is a Dixit family, which has had the rare privilege of drawing grace in an unbroken stream from both Shirdi Sai and Sathya Sai.

Shirdi Sai declared just before his samadhi in 1918, that he would come again after a period of eight years. Exactly eight years later, the year 1926 saw the advent of Sri Sathya Sai Baba in a small village in Andhra Pradesh, in south India. Thus, alongside pictures of Sathya Sai in our mandir, there were Shirdi Sai pictures too and we all developed a very loving relationship with Him also. However, all Shirdi Sai devotees do not necessarily believe Sathya Sai's connection with Shirdi Sai. And neither does Baba encourage the idea to convince them of the same. He states that He has not come on earth to create dependency on His form or even to His particular Name.

I never call upon people to worship Me, giving up the forms they already revere. I have come to establish dharma and so I do not and will not demand or require your homage. Give it to your Lord or Guru, whoever He is; I am the witness, come to set right the vision.

It is adhering to the divine principles behind the Name and Form, which is important. He further states that His mission is to reawaken mankind to the splendid truth of His own reality in which the Self stands revealed as the highest Guru. It is of no concern to Him by, and through which, Name and Form the goal of self realization is achieved, for, in any case, 'all is one' and as He unselfconsciously affirms, "all Names are Mine, all Forms are Mine..."

Shirdi Sai gave the impression of being a benign and compassionate God. His charter of eleven sayings proclaims in no uncertain terms His unbounded love for His devotees and His unfailing care of them. So, our first pilgrimage was to Shirdi. On one of our annual trips to Bombay, we broke journey at Manmad near Shirdi and went for darshan to the shrine. It was a spiritually rewarding experience and we felt blessed to have set foot on the sacred soil of Shirdi.

3

Playing The Game

Jagat *is the play, the pantomime, the sport...*

Sri Sathya Sai

"This is All India Radio.... We now take you to the Green Park Stadium, Kanpur, for a running commentary, on the first day's play of the cricket match between India and England....."

Cricket was one game that always held our family in thrall. As children, we were drawn into the orbit of this game, because of our parents' interest in it. During a Test series, cricket fever would be at a pitch. We would be tuned in to the commentary at all times. And yes, winning was everything! The swinging fortunes of our cricket team decided our moods and emotions. Fours and sixes hit by our batsmen would transport us to delight, and conversely, falling wickets would throw us into despair. Kanpur being a Test match center, the action would directly come to our doorstep for five glorious days. During that period, all roads would lead to the Green Park stadium and the whole town would buzz with cricket talk. It seemed that we had a deep bond with the game but we could never had guessed at that point, how deep and enduring it was going to be.

It was in my college hostel room, one morning in 1972 that I scanned the newspaper to see the names of the cricketers selected for the forthcoming tour of West Indies. There were some unheard of names and my eye fell on 'Sunil Gavaskar…' Humph! I thought and then articulated my feelings to my roommates. "*How* do they expect to win if they select these Gavaskar – Shevaskars in the team?" Well, the rest is history – both on and off the field. The same 'Gavaskar' went on to blaze a legendary trail, not only in his first epic tour of West Indies but also in his entire cricketing career, playing for India. The same Gavaskar went on to become my brother-in-law, getting married to my elder sister Pammi (Marshniel) in September 1974.

My sister's name Marshniel – unusual by any standards – needs a note of explanation 'Marshniel' is the name of a French rose – creeper. Around the time when my sister, was born, my father a rose – lover, who loved to plant exotic varieties, had just added this particular one to his collection. On the day my sister's name had to be registered in school (St. Mary's Convent High School), the first bud burst into splendid bloom. My father decided his first-born daughter would be called Marshniel. However, I must add, she is 'Pammi' to most of us – not nearly as original maybe, but easier to handle for most!

My sister met Sunil at a friendly match in Delhi and that meeting opened a new innings for both of them that would last a lifetime. When they announced their decision to get married, it came as a wonderful surprise to the whole family. Our little hometown acquired overnight celebrity status and Sunil was nicknamed affectionately, the son-in-law of Kanpur.

When my parents went to Bombay to meet Sunil's parents and 'fix the match', they were in for a very pleasant surprise that would put a divine seal on the whole connection. One of the first things my parents encountered in Sunil's house was a big-framed photograph of Bhagwan Sri Sathya Sai Baba – smiling, with His hand raised in blessing. They could hardly believe their eyes. After doing namaskar to the photo, the two families sat down to talk and the entire conversation centred around Baba! Everybody felt thoroughly pleased at the newfound Sai-connection.

The photo had a most interesting story behind it, which was recounted by Sunil's mother. One afternoon, on 5 March 1969, when Sunil's first ever Ranji Trophy match was on, she was given a vision of Sri Sathya Sai Baba on the wall of her kitchen. At that time, she knew nothing much about Baba and had never even seen a photo of His. The commentary was on, and she was praying to her family deity for Sunil to score a century. While doing her chores, she shut her eyes for a moment and made the prayer. Then she was startled, because on the wall facing her she saw this Baba in an orange robe with His hand raised in blessing. And Baba uttered these words in Marathi, "*Ghabru nako, tho century kartho bagh*" (do not worry, wait and watch, he will score a century). Her bafflement turned to amazement when Sunil did go on to score a century – 116 runs!

Sunil's mother was now extremely keen to get a photo of the divine Baba who had given her a vision in her house. She understood it was Sri Sathya Sai Baba. That same evening she went hunting for it in the Dadar market near her house. At that time, there were no pavement hawkers. Near *Manahar* Bakery, a man came, even as she stood there, and spread a white cloth on the pavement. He had not even spread out his wares. She was prompted to go and ask him whether he had Sathya Sai Baba's photos! She further specified that she wanted a *particular* photo with His hand raised in blessing. The man had a bag with him. He put his hand into the bag and picked out from the top a photo of Sri Sathya Sai Baba – with His hand raised in blessing! She realized that the manner in which she had got the photo was unusual and astounding. She gave that photo to Sunil after recounting the story to him. She got the one that was on the wall later, when the second Ranji Trophy match came up at Pune. On the morning of the match, she suddenly realized that she had no photo of Baba's at home. Leaving everything, she walked from Dadar to a photo frame shop that she knew of near Shivaji Bhavan. She asked the shopkeeper if he had Baba photos. He looked through his pile. There were one or two photos of Baba but not in the blessing posture. She didn't want those as she had a specific one in her mind. She walked away from the shop. Something made her turn back and ask the shopkeeper to have another look. He chided her, "Why are you bothering me in the morning, haven't I looked already," but she requested him to look again. He did so and found the exact photo that she had in mind. Even the shopkeeper looked dazed as he felt he had not seen that one before. She took the photo and hurried back home just in time before the start of the match. Sunil went on to score 164 runs in that match. That photo was later put up in Sunil's room and was the one my parents saw after entering their house.

With the same photo, my sister too had an experience in the early years of her marriage. This was in the incipient stages of her faith and devotion. Though she believed in Baba, she was not wholly sure as to who or what He really was – Guru, Holy man or God? She was staring at that framed photo one day. There was a flower tucked on top of the photo-frame. Her mother-in-law ritually placed it there every morning after her bath. Days, weeks and months, the flower was placed and my sister did not remember it ever getting dislodged from there. That day she spoke to Baba and asked Him to give a much longed for sign for strengthening her faith. She asked Him to make the flower fall there and then. Just as she finished saying this, the flower fell down with a soft thud. She gasped. He had given the sign. He had responded to the sincere call of her heart. She rushed to the photo and picking up the flower touched it to her forehead, and thanked Baba. It was a small but sure beginning.

Whenever Sunil batted out there in the middle for an India Test match, my sister made it a point to see Baba's photo which was kept in her wallet, for every delivery he faced. Also, by the 'expression' on Baba's face in the photo, she could make out how Sunil would fare, as in one photo she could see different expressions. The day she felt Baba was smiling, Sunil would do really well, but on days when she felt she saw a frown, Sunil invariably got out early! On such days, however hard she tried, to turn the photo this way and that, she could not 'force' it to smile!

One of the very first experiences Sunil had was during the Australia tour of 1977 when Bishen Singh Bedi was captain of the Indian cricket team. During the three-day match against Victoria, Sunil slipped on the ground while fielding and tore a muscle in the thigh. It turned out to be a severe injury. In those days, the Indian team did not have a physiotherapist travelling with them so Sunil's injury was shown to the home team's physiotherapist. After he was examined, Sunil was informed that it was a severely torn muscle and he would be out of the game for the next six weeks. This was a big blow as the next Test match was starting within a week's time. Sunil was in excruciating pain and unable to stand or put any pressure on the right leg. He phoned Pammi in India and informed her about this development. Pammi immediately told him, "Apply Baba's vibhuti". Sunil said that he had none with him. "I'll send you some right away. Apply it in the affected area, I'm sure it will work." The prospect of Sunil being fit enough to play for the next Test, which was four days away, seemed a total impossibility, so he was not picked for that particular match in the Test squad. In the meanwhile, Sushil Doshi, one of the Hindi commentators of All India Radio was leaving for Australia. Pammi arranged to send Baba's vibhuti through him. Sushil Doshi arrived two days prior to the Test match in Brisbane and handed over the vibhuti packet to Sunil. Sunil, who was still hobbling around with that painful leg immediately applied almost half of the vibhuti packet on the affected area hoping for a miracle. Pammi's words 'I'm sure it will work' came back to him. After the vibhuti application, Sunil tried to stand up and discovered to his amazement that he could do so with minimal pain. So he immediately rubbed some more on the affected area. He wondered if he was imagining that with each application he felt a little better. When the following morning a day prior to the match he could make it to the practice ground, the team manager expressed his surprise and told him that even if he was fifty per cent fit, he would want Sunil to play and would not announce the final eleven till a few minutes before the toss. The Test match morning dawned. Sunil still felt sore but was able to walk around. On reaching the ground everyone wanted to know how he felt. Sunil demonstrated by going on to the field for a light jog! They included him in the playing eleven (against medical advice) and Sunil went on to score his eleventh Test century in that match!

Another story Sunil loves recounting is from the early eighties. Sunil had come to Puttaparthi for Baba's blessings and it happened to be Bakr Id. Sunil was taken to the boys' hostel for the occasion and once there, Baba stumped Sunil by asking him to speak – on Bakri Id! Sunil didn't know a word on the subject and yet he had to obey the divine command. Baba smiled sweetly and blessed him and conspiratorially whispered, "Just go and stand there, I will do the rest." Sunil went to the podium and the words miraculously began to form in his mind on a subject he knew nothing about. He gave an extempore speech for ten to fifteen minutes on Bakr Id to the boys. To this day, he doesn't remember a word of what he spoke. But he remembers with a laugh, how everyone told him what a wonderful talk he gave!

It was also during this phase of their lives when Sunil was living constantly in and out of the kit-bag, playing for India, that they got a couple of chances to visit Baba in Bangalore and Madras. At one such meeting, in a personal interview, Baba materialized a navratan mala for my sister. He also materialized a silver vibhuti dibiya for Sunil filled with vibhuti, which He said would keep refilling by itself as it was used. And all this was just the beginning…

4

Anandam, Anandam

No one can come to Puttaparthi without Me calling him. I bring only those people here who are ready to see Me....

You may be seeing Me today for the first time but you are all old acquaintances for Me; I know you through and through. I know your past, present and future...

Sri Sathya Sai

Puttaparthi! Nobody had even heard of it. Yet, we were busy making plans to go to this nondescript remote village in south India, which was for us, a sacred destination.

The whole family was in Bombay on a vacation, in the month of July in 1976. My father got the sudden inspiration to visit Baba's ashram in Puttaparthi. What better time than now, he said, when we were half way there already? It would be our first ever trip. The idea caught on, and by and by, we became a group of nine members – my parents, three of us daughters, my aunt, her daughter and Sunil's mother and her daughter.

The journey to Puttaparthi by train was eventful. There was a different flavour right through. Disembarking at Guntakal station, with all our numerous pieces of luggage and parking ourselves in the waiting room there, was a new experience. There being no direct train to Puttaparthi, we had to break journey at Guntakal, spend the night in the waiting room and catch another train the next morning.

We couldn't understand a word of what anybody spoke in the south Indian dialects! What we did understand was that we would have to forego our cuppa chai for the 'coffee-coffee' everywhere! Also, we knew it would be *only* idli, dosa, sambar all the way. We didn't mind that of course. South Indian cuisine can be quite delectable. Overall, there was this subtle edge of excitement to everything – even the delays and inconveniences. We didn't really know where and what we were heading for. It was not any kind of a typical journey to any known place one had any idea about. If anything, it was *the* most adventurous journey of our lives, without our realizing it.

That night, which we spent in the waiting room, there was a heavy downpour. The heavens just opened up and the rain clattered on the roof of the waiting room with sufficient noise and force to keep me from sleeping. There was a brilliant son-et-lumière show of lighting and thunder accompanying the rain. This heightened the drama of the moment.

However, the next morning, when we boarded our train, the air was bright and clear, cleansed by the rain....

With a strange feeling, I made my first entry into the ashram compound. I couldn't believe it that somewhere in my close radius, Baba was actually present in His form. It was an exhilarating thought. I got a very clear feeling within, that Sai was aware we had come. I had seen so many pictures of Him, but as every devotee agrees, seeing Him actually is a totally different experience. The pictures don't come close to capturing His mystique. I couldn't wait for that moment of darshan now – that first precious glimpse.

The ashram in those days was a dream. Darshan was an altogether different experience being 'open air' and 'on' cool sands that felt good to walk on and sit on. Of course, on hot summer days (and Puttaparthi steams in summer) it was intense tapas – but one which devotees willingly underwent for the rich reward that followed of seeing Baba walk by in darshan on nimble toes, as if treading on air. It is said and speculated that He actually walks on air – a few inches above the ground and so the floating motion and the lotus softness of His feet.

But before that, there was a lot to learn about the ashram and its rules as one soon discovered. In that sense, our first trip was more like a divine picnic than a spiritual sojourn. We were unschooled in the ways of the ashram. I was like the majority of educated youngsters of that age, inclined towards a western mode of dressing. Being new in the ashram, we had no idea about the dress codes and other rules of discipline. That first evening, I had my first volatile encounter with the ubiquitous seva dal! Clad casually in my blue jeans and short pink top, I strolled out to get a taste of the place. I was immediately accosted by a seva dal lady, making angry gestures. She was vehemently drawing an imaginary pallav (scarf) around her shoulders again and again, trying to convey to me the need for ladies to cover the shoulders appropriately. It took me some time to register her complaint. As is the wont of most individuals at correction, I took immediate personal affront at her manner. Not only that, in my pride of intellectual reasoning, I questioned the wisdom of something so archaic and seemingly old-fashioned. The divine Guru – Baba – had not wasted any time! The teaching process had begun. Red in the face and arguing hotly in my own favour, I went back to the room muttering to myself, that one could worship God as well in a saree as in jeans and did such a triviality matter to Him? My father, with his cool intellect and deep insight explained to me that every place has its own environment and aura and one should respect and not offend it. Moreover, he added dress codes promoted discipline which is the hallmark of any good ashram. Luckily, I had caried some churidar kurtas along and those, coupled with sarees borrowed from my mother, saw me through my ten days of my stay in the ashram.

Those ten days flew by as if on wings. There was such an exotically different flavour to the whole experience of being in an ashram... the waking up at dawn, the early morning hush punctuated with the chirping of birds, the soft hurried footfalls of devotees hurrying to darshan, the tulsi vrindavans being watered by old inmates, the Vedic chanting of priests, the scents of the jasmine bowers interweaving into the fragrances of incense, the sonorous strains of bhajan singers on their nagarsankeertan round... the whole scene struck a very deep responsive chord in my heart.

And what to say about my first darshans? Can I put it down in a line or two? Not really. The impact of darshan was something that even I did not realize right away. That magic of darshan was something that would unfold itself, more and more for me, in the years to come.

However, one of the first things to realize was that Baba was not like anyone else. You could not miss that. A few days into darshan and you realise the fact that for all His divine attraction, He is essentially remote and unapproachable. No one, to my knowledge, has ever found Him anything but imposing, even intimidating. He exudes a natural power and authority. He commands awe, like no other.

In the ashram, my father met up with his scientist friend, Mr. Narayanana and personally thanked him for the vibhuti received in the letter, which had cured my father's arthritis. The two 'scientist' friends had a lot to talk about but it had nothing to do with science! The talk was only on Baba and Mr. Narayanana regaled my father with many astounding stories about Baba's divinity.

Of that first trip, three memories stand out more clearly than the others. The first one was a car darshan of Baba that I was lucky to get on the street outside the ashram. I happened to be there when a sudden flutter in the street announced that Baba's car was coming that way. Like everybody else, I too, got quickly into position on the edge of the road. Normally, there is always a big crowd. But that day, I found myself in a solitary spot, awaiting His car, His possible glance and benediction. Shortly, the car was seen approaching and the excitement of a bonus darshan mounting …I folded my palms and waited breathlessly on the pavement hoping Baba would be seated in the car on my side of the road. He was! And the window was rolled down. This was a great chance indeed. As the car passed by, I looked eagerly to catch a glimpse. By His grace I got much more than that – a direct powerful look, from up-close, eye to eye that communicated something deep in terms yet unknown to me. I felt dazed – and elated. I cherished that exchange and tucked it away in a corner of my being, to draw upon from in the years to come. Now as I look back, I feel that I am better able to decode the meaning of that look. It said – "patience – the time will come." The look also confirmed in my mind the feeling that Baba could see right inside me and knew everything about me.

The second and third memories are to do with our last day of that trip. My father had hoped that the family would be summoned for a direct audience, but when we were not, right into our last darshan, we were not unduly disappointed. Firstly, because we were so full up with the experience of darshan itself – the glorious chance of seeing Baba walk by twice a day. And secondly, the fact that we had no pressing need just then for an interview apart from the sweet wish to simply gain closer proximity to His form. However, the Lord never sends back any devotee with less than he needs, only in most cases, one is not able to immediately realize this. We limit the infinite capacities of the Lord by thinking that only when He looks at us directly does He take notice of us and only when He calls us for an interview, does he acknowledge our problems and us. Just the act of darshan in itself is an all-potent one and full of grace if one is open to receive it.

In the last darshan of that trip, my father had carried a huge tray stacked with a heap of vibhuti packets, photos, lockets and rings for blessings. The question was, would he get a chance to offer it to Baba? And given a chance, would Baba touch the tray and bless it? This strange suspense becomes a part and parcel of a devotee's life in darshan – will He, won't He...look, talk, give...? I think that when an avatar takes birth there is nothing more diverting to Him than His own unpredictability and inscrutability in the eyes of His devotees! It would be a tame and colourless enterprise if everything the avatar said or did was just so, where His moves were predictable and His ways easily understandable; Where He would give pat answers to each one's problems and provide instant solutions. That would in a way, defeat the whole purpose of His descent on earth. He comes primarily for aiding our spiritual growth to self-realization, which cannot take place without tremendous inner tuning and effort. That tuning is compelled only when the external guru, especially if He be the avatar Himself confounds a bit to encourage intensive self-inquiry.

My father sat in darshan on the men's side with that stacked tray, waiting... if Baba lightly touched and blessed the contents, he could carry it back as divine prasadam to many others waiting at home. A hush descended as Baba approached. All eyes were fixed on the orange robed form, slight yet majestic. It was as if the collective soul of the assembled gathering, arched towards Him, awaiting a response. A benign look here, a smile of blessing there, materialized vibhuti for someone else; many were the ways in which He provided succour, in that seemingly straightforward walk through the mandir. My father, lucky to be in the front held the tray aloft on his outstretched hands. However, devotees know being in the front or at the back makes no difference in Baba's scheme of things. You may be right in front but He may skim you like air, and conversely you may be sitting way back and He may single and draw you out as only He can. So, when Baba stopped by near my father and looked at him, it was a big moment. Baba pointedly looked at the stacked tray with a trace of amusement. My father told Him, "Baba, leaving today." Baba gave a gentle smile, stretched out His hand and blessed the tray, placing his full palm over it! And there was more. He then placed His hand on my father's shoulder and patting him lovingly said, "*Anandam, anandam.*" What a moment! My father had got darshan, sparshan and sambhashan, in one collective spurt of divine grace. We ladies on the other side had no idea about the divine interaction, though we were secretly hoping that 'something' might happen. It was only later when we all met after darshan that we were given the glorious details by my father. What a lovely send-off.

There was another surprise awaiting us. It happened just as we were leaving the ashram. There was that sudden stir in the streets that announces the arrival of Baba's car. He was coming that way! We quickly parked our cars on the side and getting out lined ourselves on the edge of the road for 'the car darshan'. Shortly, the car arrived. There were nine of us awaiting Baba, in a straight line, with smiles and folded palms. We were on the 'right' side of the road, for Baba was seated in the car on our side. Would He look at us? Bless us? Baba turned His head to look straight at us. And then, His face broke into the most beautiful smile, even as His hand raised itself in blessing in abhayhastha. In fact, even today I remember that moment as a frieze, because in that instant Baba was exactly like a very popular photo of His, which seemed to have come alive. He looked radiant when He smiled. We were thrilled.

Our first trip to Parthi had come to a happy conclusion. Feeling buoyant, we all returned to our respective worlds.

5

A Very Suitable Boy

"What you need to cross the sea, is the bark of bhakti. *Throw off all burdens, become light and you can trip across with one step on one crest and another on the next. God will take you through. You have no need to bother at all. For, when He does everything, who is concerned about what?"*

Sri Sathya Sai

After my return, I got involved in my college studies. I was at that age when parents start looking out anxiously for that 'suitable boy' – mostly elusive of course! I was in no hurry, but my parents worried about where my 'type of a boy' would come from. I had my own views on many subjects. One of them was that subjugation of any sort to a husband or interfering in-laws was totally out! However, one thing I did tell my parents was that my main precondition for a husband was that he should be a 'good person'.

I joined the law college in Bombay and had I but known it, it was to be the locale for meeting my future husband. The time had come for this 'good person' to walk into my life. The mysterious and intriguing ways in which destiny unfolds is something nobody can ever fully understand. Humans go through the motions of worry, effort and aspiration but ultimately the trump card always lies somewhere else; in some unseen hand...call it destiny, fate or the hand of God. Being introduced to the blue-eyed boy (literally) of Law College – Subodh Paranjape – I could never have dreamt that one day he would be my husband. He was extremely good-looking, with green eyes, and was every college girl's dream. Two years after our initial meeting in college, that unseen hand miraculously brought us together in matrimony. I clearly remember that full moon night when Subodh proposed to me! After a sumptuous meal at the Chinese restaurant, Chopsticks, we were driving back on Marine Drive with the Queen's necklace twinkling merrily. When Subodh proposed, I looked surprised. The evening had been no different to many similar ones that we had spent together. Except for the fact that after the meal while strolling on the lit promenade by the sea, I saw an old man dash across our path with a picture of Sai Baba. It was after that on the drive back that he proposed and I accepted. Intriguingly, Subodh told me later that he had not premeditated on popping the question that very night – it had just happened!

How intricate is the pattern of each one's life! Who can tell what, when, where? These are eternal mysteries best left unsolved, for isn't this what lends drama and momentousness to life?

Some imperative it was that made me wish to go to Parthi to seek Sai's blessings for our marriage; so strong was this sudden desire that I decided to fly down alone from my hometown Kanpur to Bangalore. As there was no direct flight from Kanpur I had to fly to Delhi and catch a connecting flight. My elder sister's sister-in-law Kavita, was wedded to cricketer Vishwanath and resided in Bangalore. They being devotees too, I hoped to request them to accompany me. This was in November 1980 just prior to Baba's sixtieth birthday celebrations and the World Conference.

On a cool cloudy day, Vishy, Kavita and I drove down to Parthi for a single darshan. It was after a gap of four years that I was going to Parthi again (November 1980), and my heart beat faster at the prospect.

What I remember of that one darshan is that I was seated in the third or fourth row on the cool sands of the mandir ground. And for some reason, when Baba came and walked by me, my heart almost jumped out in excitement. I don't recall whether He cast His glance directly on me or not, but when I realized that He was moving on, and my one solitary darshan was slipping away, I couldn't contain myself and I burst forth loudly with His name, "Baba, Baba, Baba....!" He, of course, didn't bat an eyelid but the sevadal near me did and how! She made it very clear that I had transgressed. At that time, I may have mildly resented her attitude but many years later I was to understand it much better. That was during the trip when I went to Parthi as a sevadal worker in the year 1992 and realized the difficulties and special challenges of the task, which changed my entire outlook on the issue.

But for the moment, Baba had walked by me and I had been unable to seek direct blessings from Him. Now what? I rationalized it in my mind that just getting His darshan was blessing enough. Yet, my heart longed for some direct contact. I was holding this letter regarding my forthcoming marriage in my hands and had hoped to offer it to Him. Walking out of darshan, with the letter in my hands, I was forlornly thinking that I would have to post it. We had to meet Vishy on the men's side on our way out. People were just filing out of the mandir. We met Vishy and were just about to turn and walk out when the most unbelievable thing happened – as can only happen in the experience of a Sai devotee! Suddenly there was so much excitement – Baba had come out on the verandah again and was beckoning to somebody. Where a moment ago people had been moving around, now everybody stood as if frozen – with folded palms facing the verandah. A sevadal came to tell us that Swami had asked for Vishwanath! My mind worked like lightning and I quickly handed the letter to Vishy, requesting him to offer it to Baba if he got a chance. Vishy took the letter and hurried to the verandah. Baba spoke to him and in the course of that conversation, Vishy mentioned the letter to Baba. Apparently, he told Him that it was Sunil's sister-in-law's wedding… Swami asked, "*Kab*?" (when?). Vishy answered, "In December, Swami." At that, Swami took the letter and said, "Abhi time hai..." (There is still time)

I was thrilled. Not for nothing is Baba known as the last minute God! When I had given up all hopes of His taking the letter, He had done it in His own inexplicable way! Kavita, Vishy and I drove back to Bangalore in the highest of spirits.

After my return to Bombay, I posted Baba my wedding card and prayed to Him to be present at the marriage ceremony. Devotees know that Swami (as Baba is fondly called) makes His presence felt in multifarious ways when the need is strong enough. On my wedding morning, 22 December 1980, I wondered what sign Baba would give me to indicate His presence. Well, at the exact moment of the ceremony, of the registered marriage and the exchange of garlands, the heavens suddenly opened with a soft shower of unseasonal rain! A funny thing happened here which amused Subodh and my family for years to come. The two garlands were lying on the table in front of us for the ceremony. When I was to garland Subodh, I picked up the garland but found it too heavy. So I raised it up just to check its length. Subodh and some others thought that in my confusion I was garlanding myself! Everybody had a great laugh. All my efforts to convince them otherwise were to no avail. Maybe, even the heavens smiled and so the rain! I was convinced in my heart that it was a shower of blessings directly from the Lord of Parthi. I told my husband that it was very shubha, but he only laughed, as he was unaware of my belief and also, was a very rational socialist.

At the wedding reception in Kanpur a few days later, a strange occurrence convinced me of the Lord's presence again. After the reception on the club lawns got over, it was discovered that a cobra had 'presided' over the proceedings from the top of the shamiana covering!

I felt happy that by the grace of God, I had found the 'good' man I had always sought as a life partner. However, there was one little problem. This good man, most humane, caring and generous and with a heart of gold, did not believe in rituals, *puja* or God! Well! Life is a challenge, says Baba, and here was one right away on the threshold of my marriage. I was very ritualistic in my habits of performing a daily puja, carrying pictures of Baba around everywhere, doing a namaskar whenever I passed a temple etc. and my husband was probably the other extreme. Maybe his bit of spiritual sadhana had been apportioned to me, as his better half! My husband, however, never objected to my spiritual-religious leanings as long as I didn't try to convert him. I told him he needn't fear on that count but that when the time came the Lord Himself would do it and then he wouldn't be able to do much about it. Subodh gave me a half amused, half skeptical look about that possibility, but I was confident that one day it would happen. I remembered the lines from Shirdi Sai Satcharita, where Baba says that let His man (devotee) be at any distance, a thousands miles away, he will be drawn to Him like a sparrow, with a thread tied to its feet...

6

Family Life

God is not an outsider, staying in some heaven or holy spot, far away from you. God is in you, God is in every word of yours, every deed and thought. Speak, do and think as befits Him. Do the duty He has allotted, to the best of your ability and to the satisfaction of your conscience. That is the most rewarding puja.

Sri Sathya Sai

I soon got immersed in my domestic obligations. In those early years of my marriage, I lived the life of a regular modern day housewife, and Baba's place then, was in a corner of my bedroom at an altar, where I did my daily puja. He was God, as He still is! But at that time He was entirely and only God – to be worshipped, revered and supplicated for blessings. It was mainly a formal relationship.

Fancying myself to be a writer of sorts, I took up a job with a monthly magazine as assistant editor. In spite of my intense love for writing, I did not enjoy my work. I discovered that it was blunting my desire to write, maybe because I was just not a nine-to-five person. I felt constrained in an office atmosphere. I found myself suddenly chained to a small desk and chair in an air-conditioned office where I had to sit willy-nilly. The only high for me in those days of imprisonment was when the tea boy entered the office with that tray of ambrosia – hot tea in chipped glasses. Tea is nothing if not a soul brew – the one constant in a changing world!

My work problem solved itself when I learnt I was pregnant. I quit my job as the doctor advised me to take it easy. Nine months later, on a Thursday, I gave birth to a baby girl. It was a moment of joy for both my husband and me, especially because we had both wanted a daughter and in fact, my husband had already thought of a name for her – Rubianca. I had been a little apprehensive about my first delivery but my faith in Baba helped a lot to tide over my fears. On one occasion, Baba had given my elder sister a navratana mala that He had materialized and I wore that round my neck during the delivery. It gave me confidence and strength. This mala had become a talisman for the whole family. In fact, six months later it would come to my father's help in a sudden health crisis.

The months immediately after my delivery were hectic, as they always are for new mothers. There really was no day or night, just one endless stream of nappies, milk bottles, baby food interspersed with bawls (loud ones due to colic) and gurgles. Now when I look back to those days and to the peculiar single-mindedness that characterizes them, I wonder how such a focus would work were it applied elsewhere. To the exclusion of all else, the mother gets absorbed and occupied with her child...and her love becomes the perfect metaphor for the highest love of all – God's. Maybe all human relationships are merely metaphors for that supreme love which is the source of it all.

Around this time, we got a chance to get a darshan of Baba in Dharmakshetra, his ashram in Bombay. Baba had come to Bombay on a visit and we sisters decided to rush there as much to get his darshan as to seek guidance about our father's health who was recovering by Baba's grace from a recent heart-attack. My daughter Rubianca was about nine months old and I decided to take her along for blessings. We got a special audience, outside Satyadeep, Baba's lotus shaped residence in the ashram. As we devotees waited in a single file for Baba to emerge from the house, my baby daughter (ever a hyper active child) started bawling at a high decibel. In the reverential atmosphere of silence that prevails just prior to darshan, her shrieks seemed all the more pronounced! Holding her in my arms I took her to the edge of the garden to show her some flowers in bloom on a bush, pacifying her all the while. Just then, Baba emerged. Thanks, maybe to the petulant little one in my arms who needed a distraction, I was standing at a conspicuous spot, away from the others. As soon as Baba came out, he cast a distinctive glance our way. Who knows what nature of blessing flowed in that one moment? The fact that He cast a brief direct look towards my daughter was enough. I knew the value of that look and how far it could go. I felt the security of His blessings for my small daughter. She must have also felt the peace and joy radiating from Swami's aura, for miraculously, she calmed down and I hurried back to join the others.

> *Never take lightly the transformation that is taking place as I walk among you. All that My eyes fall on will be transformed.... The blessings you receive will express themselves in due time.*

We sisters had primarily gone for Baba's darshan with an urgent question regarding our father's health...should he or should he not go in for a bypass heart surgery at his age? However, though Baba passed by very close to us and my sister loudly mouthed the question, He ignored it and did not give explicit permission. That put us in a bit of a quandary. He had not even said a direct 'no.' However, we analyzed it to the best of our ability and came to the conclusion that

Baba's demeanour of disregarding the question was a hint to us that the surgery should not be performed. After going inside, Baba sent some vibhuti packets as prasad. We sent the vibhuti to our father and that, coupled with the navratan mala – the family talisman – aided his recovery. As it turned out later, our analysis under pressure proved correct and Baba's guidance had been perfect. My father carried on wonderfully after his attack for sixteen very beautiful years...our loving thanks goes to the most wonderful Lord, our Baba whose grace permeates everything in our lives.

Two years later I had my second daughter, Tia, who looked like a Japanese doll! With two young children, I became totally absorbed in child rearing, ever a challenging and rewarding task. On one side was my faith and devotion to Baba, as yet a corner in my heart, and on the other, my day-to-day life. For almost ten years into my married life, I lived a rather typical urban lifestyle, of wining and dining out, occasional partying and holidays to exotic places. My husband being a lawyer, got vacations twice a year and invariably we would take off for a welcome break somewhere or the other. Yes, God – Baba – was there, but in the background. He occupied a small, albeit sacred, space in my life. However, in times of crisis, He would be drawn out and brought to center stage, to occupy a much larger space in my consciousness and conscious self. In those moments of trial, Baba shot up to the number one spot with ease! Puja became more intense and focused and the vibhuti packets carefully tucked away came out.

Baba's description of married life is very accurate and spot-on: first two legs, then four legs, then six and then eight legs!! So true! What a leap it is from being single to being married. Where you were earlier responsible only for yourself, you now had to be responsible for so many others. Of course, there are two sides to everything and whatever maybe the challenges of married life, the corresponding joys are many of companionship, intimacy, as also the unique joy of indirectly creating new life, by bringing your children into this world. However, if one thinks deeply on the issue of marriage, it is what constitutes the main bulk of what is called 'samsara.' For, it is marriage that generates all kinds of attachments that keep multiplying and the cycle never ends. One's children, then grandchildren, and so on, each adding to the net of maya that spreads itself more and more over you with each fresh attachment. The down side of all these attachments is the heavy gray cloud of worry that hangs over them. The concern for the welfare and safety of loved ones becomes a background fear to everyone's life. Baba's precious advice in the matter is to learn to love in a non-possessive way...all problems in life stem from our need to grasp and claim possession over people and things. The term 'mine' should be converted to 'God's.' We should understand that nothing really belongs to us, it was given to us in trust and so should we regard it. Also, Baba says, 'expand your heart' – from loving only your family members, you should move to loving more and more people in the world. And most of all, He says, fix your attachment to the Prime Mover, Prime Source, God Himself and if you do so, then all your attachments will find their true perspective and fall into place.

Ten years passed in this manner and it was only in January 1992, that the doors swung open again. Baba came to Bombay on a visit and after a long gap, I was to have His darshan. However, at that time I had no idea of the impact His forthcoming visit and darshan would have on me. I had no idea of *what* the simple act of darshan would come to mean to me.

7

God Is Love

"Love alone can give you, a vision of God".

Sri Sathya Sai

There is naught else; we tell it in brief to all the beings of the world; sorrow not, the thought of the Lord alone is enough. Learn the faultless glory of our Lord and know its best to live in its thought...

Nammalvar

Prior to Baba's Bombay visit, I had been attending bhajans and a study circle in my neighbourhood of late. This had recharged my devotion considerably. Going for bhajans and singing there became a singular spiritual high in those days. It was amazing how bhajans had the effect of making me feel sharply, that all-important connection with God. Truly, as the scriptures say, God is present wherever devotees gather in love to sing His Name. Of course, academicians would wryly say, "Isn't He present everywhere?" but one cannot explain to them the feeling of the non-tangible becoming tangible as a Presence. That is the wonder of devotion – how it can draw out God from His rarified heights and make Him a living and felt Presence.

The ground was being laid for the future. For, when I finally got darshan of Baba in Bombay it became a momentous experience. Something happened – a sunburst of realization, that Baba was Love Incarnate, walking the earth. Earlier too, I had believed Him to be God. But, that was on faith. Now, I *experienced* Him as God, a living embodiment of the highest love. I was in a state of subtle ecstasy and floated through those five days totally absorbed in His darshans. How can anybody describe that state? One can only say that nothing else compares to it. Also, having tasted it, one feels compelled to seek it ever after. The funniest was that in those five days, except on one occasion, I don't remember having got a single direct glance from Baba and neither very close darshans. Yet, the impact was tremendous. We devotees often tend to fall into the trap of wanting Baba to look directly at us. (I myself am in that trap!) Not realizing, that He is in fact always looking at us, and has proved this to us many times over, if we so need proof.

The only time I got a kind of direct interaction was at a special darshan at Ravindra Natya mandir, a cultural center in Bombay. I will never forget that darshan, not so much for the split-second look I got directly from Him, as for the effulgence of His divine form, radiating love. There was a special ambience about darshan that day. It was under the open sky on a cool morning, with a benign warm sun showering sunbeams all around. Baba walked through the aisle in His bright orange robe bathed in sunlight. His hair caught the sun's light and framed His face like a halo. Divine iridescence! His soft eyes rained love and benediction all around. He approached the spot where I was sitting. With every step He took, it was as if He was coming into my life anew. I awaited Him with an exceptional book of poems written by my aunt S. Rashmi which she had asked me to offer to Him. Being in the third row from the aisle, I had to lean forward and stretch my arm for Him to be able to reach the book...yet, it fell a little short. The eternal benefactor, Baba Himself arched forward and with His outstretched hand, took the book. I felt thrilled at Baba's cognizance of the book and me!

Further down, Baba lovingly ruffled a little child's hair and materialized vibhuti for him, endearing Himself even more to the gathering of devotees. A close friend's daughter, Simali, had carried her history textbook with the hope of getting it blessed. Her final exams were a month away and the first book that came out of her drawer, she brought to darshan! Baba came to her and blessed the book by placing his full palm over it. Later, her results stunned everybody including herself. She got 98 out of 100 in history.

As for me, I was in a divine daze having experienced first time for myself that Baba was and is truly the very embodiment of the highest love. After this experience of Baba's darshan in January 1992, I wrote an ecstatic letter to my parents in Kanpur, declaring how I had realized that Baba was Love Incarnate. For a few days, a spiritual haze overpowered everything else and I read numerous books on Baba, the most notable one being, Diana Baskin's *Divine Memories*. Like many others who read this book, I was fascinated by the author's experiences with the avatar, with her being literally His next-door neighbour at one point! In this manner, books on Baba by devotees become very valuable, for they all present a unique insight or facet of interaction with the divine. The wonder is that there are no two books, which are alike – highlighting the fact that each devotee's path is unique.

> *There is a road from each heart to the source of all joy, namely God. Each one will come in his own good time, at his own pace, through his own inner urge, along the path, God will reveal to him as his own.*

It was around this time, that I started taking training for becoming a Balvikas guru. We were lucky to have a very motivated and competent guru training us. She inspired us tremendously, and after three years of training under her I became a full-fledged Balvikas guru. Balvikas is a worldwide Sai movement whereby children from the age of six upwards are imparted value education and given a spiritual foundation with the aim of fostering the spark of divinity inherent in them. Devotion to Sai is the prime motivation for the thousands of Balvikas gurus round the world to take up this loving seva for children to offer it at the feet of Sai. The children respond with singular enthusiasm to these classes in spite of the moral instruction implicit. Inculcating discipline on all levels and respect for all religions is a key objective of these classes. The little shishyas love their Balvikas classes even though their gurus impart some tough recipes for happiness – right action (dharma), honesty (*satya*), universal love (*prema*) and peaceful non-violence (*shanti* and ahimsa).

I started classes for Group One with my neighbour and friend Shanti in my building. This was in the year 1995 in the month of June. Later, I also started another class with a devotee friend, Bhavna at her residence close by. My Friday evenings were for my rendezvous with the Balvikas children in Bhavna's house. The Balvikas syllabus is a brilliant combination of human values education and spiritual instruction from our scriptures, and in teaching the children, we too learnt so much! Conducting these classes gave us gurus a positive charge. Moreover, Bhavna's house was redolent with devout vibrations, with many Sai activities like singing bhajans and a study circle being conducted there on a regular basis. When the class got over after all the sloka-chanting, story-telling, bhajan-singing, spiritual games, and the children dispersed with smiles on their faces, Bhavna would serve us hot piping lemon grass tea and hot snacks. Normally, we would have refused these because serving eats is not encouraged in Sai gatherings. However, Bhavna is one person who gets utmost joy in cooking and feeding others. The blessing, "*annadatta sukhi bhava*" (blessings to the one who feeds) I'm sure has come to her very often in her life. The manner in which she served us made us feel that it was nothing if not holy prasad coming our way. In fact, surprisingly, even Baba Himself acknowledged this trait of hers in Puttaparthi! Apparently, Bhavna before her first trip to Puttaparthi regularly offered 'naivedya' of halwa and Gujarati bhajiyas to Baba in her temple. When she reached Parthi, she happened to stay with an old and dear devotee who often cooked food for Baba. This devotee asked Bhavna to cook a few items for Baba, during the period of her stay and incredibly, asked for the very things Bhavna used to offer as 'naivedya'. Baba would send some of the food back as prasad and one day it came with the message that the dish had been cooked very well.

In the three years leading from Baba's darshan at Ravindra Natya Mandir in January 1992 to this time, that is 1995, there would be a lot more happening. Many trips to Parthi and finally a tremendous event for the city of Bombay in May of 1995 – Sri Sathya Sai Baba's five day visit. But before that, we were to make more many trips to Parthi. The doors had finally swung open.

8

Bend The Body Mend The Mind

Consider seva as the best sadhana. *Seva is more beneficial for your spiritual development than days of* japam or dhyanam.

Sri Sathya Sai

When they have approached Him, He moves yet nearer. When loving aspirations come to His presence, He touches the one who has laboured for Him, with a joyous ecstasy.

Rig Veda

The first opportunity came in September 1992, about seven months after Baba's divine visit to Bombay in January. The chance to go to Parthi dropped from the heavens. The Bombay sevadal was to leave for a ten-day seva stint in Prasanthi and my younger sister Mashu had put in her name. However, as she was in England on a vacation she was unable to come back in time. That's when I got the inspiration to go, as her ticket was already booked. I checked with our sevadal coordinators of the feasibility of this 'switch' and they gave me the green signal.

But prior to that, Baba gave me the green signal by giving me a dream. *In the dream, Baba is sitting in His chair, and facing Him is a group of ladies sitting in neat rows on one side. I am sitting separate. I am alone on the other side. With His finger, Baba indicates to me to get up and join the group of ladies.* This decoded clearly in my mind as Baba directing me to join the sevadal troop.

This decision was rather momentous for me. I was generally considered by my family to be of a delicate constitution, a little vague in my approach to things and not very capable of taking care of myself. This, coupled with my hesitancy to travel all by myself added to it. However, I was quite firm on my decision, or rather I should say, the issue had been decided for me by Baba! In this time, I had another dream, which further confirmed the fact that I was meant to make that trip to Parthi. *In the dream, I saw a splendid edifice with beautiful colours, which seemed like a grand mandir. There was a huge decorative gate leading to this paradise- like- place. In the precincts of this mandir, Baba is walking around giving darshan and I am following Him around everywhere. As He walks, from behind I can see the lotus soles of His feet, which quite enchant me. I look beyond the gate to the outside and feel sorry for the people out there unable to partake of this joy, because I feel this place to be verily heaven on earth.* Seeing Baba in the dream like this, I felt it was His call. This dream of mine was further decoded a few years later when the Kalyan mandap was constructed in the Prasanthi mandir: the ornate structure that came up was very similar to the one I had seen in my dream.

From the moment the Udyan express chugged out of the station, with the Bombay sevadal group, the trip was a divine adventure for me. There was a gentle rain that morning, lending a further ambience to the moment. Having always been a lover of rain, the shower and the lovely cool weather appeared as auspicious signs to me. I felt a strange excitement, different from any I had experienced before. My neighbour from the building, Shanti was with me and though she was not as yet a full-fledged believer, she also felt the excitement. At that point, we were just getting to know each other. We were not aware then, that Baba had put us together for what was to develop into a very long and spiritually fruitful association over the coming years. Swami's ways are inscrutable and fascinating. For ten years we had been neighbours and there was nothing to suggest that we could ever have any strong common ground of interest. But then Swami can make anything happen. Suddenly, we were talking the same language – of course, this language comprised just three alphabets – SAI. All the time, everywhere, down the years it was and has been Sai, Sai, Sai... a constant satsang for which we are deeply grateful.

The train reached Dharmavaram at 4:00 am the next morning. Can I ever forget that moment? Setting foot on that station, in that quiet pre-dawn hour with a cool breeze rustling the leaves of the trees, deeply thrilled me. The ride to the ashram in a bumpy roadways bus in the early dawn, took us through a very singular terrain of rocky landscape with stark hills in the distance. Yet, to my eyes, it was probably one of the most beautiful sceneries I had encountered. The first rays of the rising sun were stealing over the horizon, in brilliant streaks of red and gold. *Bhajans* were being sung with gusto by all – to the Parthi Natha, Sai Vithalla, Sathya Sai Krishna, the Hridaya Niwasi...the atmosphere was infectious and everybody looked joyful. It was after twelve long years that I was touching the sacred soil of Parthi again. The last brief one-day visit had been in November 1980, for seeking blessings for my marriage. Consequently, I felt elated on reaching Parthi...everything, just everything for me on that trip was shot through and through with other-worldly magic.

Right through those ten days, I was in a perpetual state of inner delight, inspite of the physically challenging situations I had to face. There were three of us in a small bare room, which had no beds or furniture of any sort. I had carried a folding chattai with me and my nights in the ashram were spent on that 'hard bed.' Bone-tired at the end of each day after the seva routines, but charged with the energy of darshans, I nevertheless got the sweetest sleep. It became clear to me what Baba repeatedly stresses about the mind being the key factor in everything. External situations are not so important as the internal mind-set. All situations can be made subservient to the mind – the mastermind. Everything is only as we see it. A physically uncomfortable situation, which would have been galling to me otherwise, was transformed because of my mental state. It took on the colour of my mind. I would not have exchanged that 'discomfort' of the room for any luxury in the world. In short, everything proceeds from the mind outward and not the other way round. You may have the softest, most comfortable bed, but it is of no use if your mind is agitated. On the other hand, if your mind is at ease, it can give you the best sleep anywhere. Apart from this, my entire routine at the ashram was strenuous beyond imagination, especially by my standards. I had never had occasion till then to really 'bend my body' (work hard), something of which I was doing a lot in the ashram. No doubt with that, the process of mending the mind had also begun right away – and I suppose, is still on.

The duty I opted for in the ashram was 'discipline,' which entailed maintaining order and discipline in the devotee ranks before, during and after darshan. On the face of it, it appeared a relatively easy task but was in fact, quite challenging, requiring immense tact and tolerance. The keenness of all devotees to get a good place in darshan creates a volatile atmosphere sometimes, in which, tempers easily snap...and the villains of the piece very nearly always are the hapless sevadals! At such times, I had to maintain my cool and under all circumstances speak politely but firmly. "If you cannot always oblige, you can speak obligingly," Baba's dictum really had to be put into practice all the time. I was lucky to get duty inside the mandir for it gave me grand opportunities for close darshans. This was extraordinary grace really, for I would get a chance to be either in the first or second row almost every day. That was the time probably that I fell under the spell of darshan! It was just so deeply satisfying to be able to rest my eyes on that graceful orange form, exuding love and grace. Having been introduced to the charm of God in form, I was captivated. This experience of darshan is a constantly beautiful aspect of the life of a Sai devotee. It has the unique power of refreshing your mind, body and soul. And the real wonder is how the worries of the world just fall away in the moment of darshan.

However, there were times when I felt so tired, that I felt I would just drop down in sheer exhaustion or fall sick – but by His grace that never happened. Somehow, I managed to muster up the requisite stamina to fulfill my duties. I do believe that I got this extra energy from Baba and I realized the power of darshan.

> *Never underestimate what is being accomplished by the act of darshan. My energy goes from Me as I pass you. If you proceed to talk to others, immediately the precious energy is dissipated and returns to Me unused. Rest assured that whatever My eyes see becomes vitalized and transmuted. You are being charged day by day. These blessings you receive will express themselves in their perfect time. My walking among you is a gift...*

One day, while doing duty as a sevadal in the mandir, Swami came to a child in front of me, who was holding a tray of sweets. He smiled lovingly at the child, blessed his tray and picking up a bunch of sweets flung them into the crowd. Being on duty, my behaviour had to be circumspect and I could not reach out for the sweets falling all around. However, I hoped and longed for one as prasad. After Baba had moved on, I looked to see two sweets lodged in my saree pallav. That is the way He works. In another similar instance of sweets-throwing, a sweet came to hit me straight on the middle of my forehead. Sevadal or no sevadal, I knew I had my claim on *that* sweet and made sure to collect it and keep it!

Ten days flew by and though by the end of it, I was tired in every pore and muscle, I felt an acute pang of loss at the thought of leaving.

Our last darshan of the trip was especially stirring. We had relinquished our sevadal scarves and were now seated for our last darshan opposite the Poornachandra hall, where Baba would be going in shortly. I had a camera in my hand (in those days this was allowed) and wanted to click Baba's photo with my own hands. When He emerged from the mandir gate, I got my camera into position and decided to see through the lens as He approached, to get the best shot. In a moment, I saw a smiling, beaming vision of Baba in my camera's frame, with His head bent a little to the side, waving goodbye to all of us seated there. It was so sweet yet so startling that I removed my eye from the camera, to put it right back and click a most hurried and excited shot! He was actually waving to all of us knowing that our duty was over and we were leaving that night. It was a perfect seal to a divine trip. Something had happened on this trip, of that I was sure. A shift had taken place in me, of a deeply spiritual nature, which would manifest more and more in the future.

After my return, I was in a divine stupor for about ten days, which was compounded by my physical exhaustion. I was so sweetly acquiescing to everything Subodh said that he actually got worried! Where was his firebrand wife, he wondered? My small daughters, of course were most happy, getting away with a lot more than they normally would. When I finally snapped out of this beatific state and displayed an element of aggression, my husband actually smiled with relief and said, "Welcome back!" As for my daughters, they formed a most favourable impression in their minds of this place called Puttaparthi where their mother had come back from in such a good mood. That stood me in good stead in the years to come!

9

The Moon In My Palm

You have got Me and it is your duty now to develop this relationship..

Sri Sathya Sai

Oh, how amiable are The dwellings, Lord of Hosts! My soul has a desire and longing to enter the courts of the Lord! My heart rejoices in the living God.

(Psalm 84)

After my return from the sevadal trip, I felt a major shift... Sai was now deeply embedded in my consciousness and just like a photograph being developed in a studio, His image was slowly emerging more and more clearer in my heart and in my being. I had always looked back on my growing up years in my home in Kanpur with awe and wondered how the rest of life could ever match up? But then, I hadn't reckoned with spiritual joy... As the days went by, it became evident to me that now my foremost wish was to connect to Sai – my spiritual center – in whatever way I could. And this produced a sense of deep wellbeing that surpassed everything I had ever known.

I also started getting many more dreams of Swami around this time, which became a very cherished connection with Him. Swami's dreams are a continuing source of wonder. Very often these dreams give telling glimpses of the future – in clear or coded ways. Sometimes non-devotees, people who have never seen or heard of Him, get a dream of His which often changes their course of life towards Puttaparthi! In the interview room, Baba Himself sometimes describes a particular dream in minute detail to the stunned recipient and even gives its meaning. In fact, so fascinating is this topic of dreams and there is so much material on it from around the world, there is enough for a separate volume.

Out of all the connections that devotees have with Him, I personally feel that the dream connection is the most reliable and fool proof. If one can understand the coded ways in which messages and hints are conveyed then the dream guidance is the most pat, most accurate. In fact, I would rate it higher than even direct communication with Baba because, on the form level oftentimes Baba creates confusion. The scriptures say that the Lord is kolhahul-priya – that He loves to create confusion. But, on the dream level, I feel, this trait is most restrained!

Apart from dreams, Sai gives actual 'visitations' to devotees in every corner of the world. He is also known to have been actually – physically present – in two places at the same time. Of course, reading all this can never convince one. Even I would have been extremely skeptical, like anybody else, if my own experiences of Baba's divinity were not backing the evidence. It is impossible to apply logic or any known rules to Him or His actions. His reality is so vast and incomprehensible, it cannot be encompassed or held by our intellect. The only way is to 'let go' the imperative to want to understand – and this of course, is where faith comes in.

My Swami dreams not only gave darshan, but also amazing hints to the future. Some scenarios in these dreams translated exactly many years later, making me reflect deeply on the preordained nature of things. The period from the present to my next trip in November 1993 was rich in dreams, which I started recording faithfully in a diary. In lean periods, when the connection felt weak, I would take refuge in this dream-sanctuary of mine. Getting a dream of Swami was and will always remain a highlight of my spiritual life.

A year passed and the desire to go to Prasanthi intensified. In this regard, I must say I was fortunate as my husband willingly took up the extra responsibilities of looking after our children while I was away. In fact, I am grateful for his wonderful support, for without it, I would never have been able to find my spiritual space, the way I did. In a lighter vein, he would joke about how my trips provided him and the kids the much-needed break from my lecturing and nagging.

It is said in the *Shirdi Sai Sacharita* that when you have an intense longing for the Lord's darshan, He himself arranges everything suitably for the right time. So it was that in November of 1993 a programme to go to Parthi materialized. Mashu (Tunisha being her real name, Mashu, the pet-name given by my grandmother as a take-off on Marshniel), who had missed the sevadal trip of the previous year, was very keen on a trip and so was I. Both of us got together and planned a trip – though, 'plotted' would be a better way to describe it. It was all hush-hush and very secretive as we were not sure how the rest of the family would take to the idea of the two of us just taking off like that. Sure enough, when our plans were revealed everybody was a little startled. There was a lot of concern about where we would stay, how we would travel alone to the south and how we'd get from Dharmavaram to Parthi and so on. We were in too blithe a mood to get affected by the general fret. "He, (Baba) will take care of everything," became our most oft repeated mantra in that period. And the mantra worked! He did take special care of everything, especially because I think, it was our first trip on our own. When we reached the ashram after the train journey and bus ride from Dharmavaram, we looked like two rag dolls, and just a little lost. The ashram was very crowded when we reached and we didn't know where to start. A little apprehensive, we made our way to the accommodation office. A sweet miracle right away! We were allotted a room immediately. I had, on an impulse, dashed off a letter to the accommodation office prior to leaving, requesting them to allot a room for the given period. And they had! The relief we felt when the keys were handed over to us! It was not easy to get room accommodation in the ashram and we had got it in a trice. It was of course only Baba's grace...the room to our eyes was more luxurious than any in a five-star hotel in the world. It had two small beds and a table – what more could we ask for?

The next morning we were up bright and early. We had to catch the token lines and hope for a good number. The thousands of devotees who are present in the ashram for darshan, line up in rows everyday (ladies on one side, men on the other as seating is separate for men and women in the mandir), to pick up a token number which decides the sequence in which the rows will enter for seating.

It was, and always is, a matter of great excitement for devotees, as to what token one gets. Getting number one is like getting the moon. The moon once landed in my palm! Being first in the line, I had to pick up the token and it was number one. I stared in disbelief, and then could not stop grinning happily, something which happens to everyone who picks this prized token. It was a pleasure to walk in first into the mandir for seating and I quickly rushed to the coveted corner spot for darshan. Mashu was next to me and both of us were very pleased as we took our places in the first row. The darshan music started and with quickened heartbeats we focused our gaze on the gate from where Baba would appear. Soon, Baba walked down the aisle, and the next thing we knew, He was standing in front of us, actually looking in our direction. I was holding a book by Baba and a pen hoping to have Him sign it. Baba looked at me, then at the pen placed on the book and said, "Wait, wait, wait." With His hand, he made the gesture of wait as He spoke. I felt happy that He had spoken to me and Mashu and I exchanged a smile. Even half a look from Baba is considered worth its weight in gold and He had actually spoken to us.

Baba walked His full round and went into the mandir. Many people got up and left their places, for taking their round of tea and snacks in the canteen. We stuck to our special places, as it was our norm to sit right through to bhajan time.

Finally, the evening bhajan started. Bhajan is always a very stirring experience in the mandir. The students sing soulfully, creating a very special vibration. That evening, the bhajans felt especially enchanting. Seated in our corner spot, we were assured of a close darshan again of Baba as He walked out. Shortly after the arati, Baba emerged from the temple. Slowly, He approached and turned the far corner, before coming down the aisle to where we were seated. It was a treat to be so placed and see Him walk the whole straight distance, in that gliding motion, robe gently trailing. Would He, would He not, was the question – as it always is – whenever He passes close by. The crucial moment came, the one possible golden chance... He was at the corner and in a moment He would be gone. We focused our gaze unblinkingly at Him. He was speaking to a lady, just across the aisle from us. He looked so close and immediate. But, to think that Baba is close and immediate just because you have proximity to Him is fanciful thinking! Devotees realize that soon enough, for it takes days, months, years and sometimes a lifetime to draw close to Him.

But there also come along moments sometimes, when amazing grace simply pours. Sitting there in darshan that day, one such moment was round the corner. I was gazing at Baba's back as He talked to the lady across, when He suddenly did a sharp about-turn – to face us directly. What followed was incredible – With his head bent a little to the side, He looked straight at us and gave a dazzling smile. It was a smile of recognition and welcome. His eyes were pools of light and His face was radiant. It was an exquisite moment. Was it real? If so, it was the sweetest ambush in history. Even before we could grasp what had happened, He had turned and walked away. Mashu and I looked at each other, both of us exchanging that silent, wonderstruck look, which said, "Did you see *that*?"

After that epic darshan, we had another one of an unusual nature. It happened one evening when the skies just opened up, most unexpectedly, on devotees seated for darshan. The beauty of it was that most of the devotees remained seated inspite of the rain. It was an experience of a lifetime to be sitting there in the pouring rain awaiting darshan, with Shiv Shambho bhajans resounding in the air. It became a powerfully charged atmosphere with the pelting rain making its own music and the bhajans vocalizing the collective devotion of all assembled there. The harder it rained, the louder the devotees clapped to the bhajans, with the devotional fervor reaching a crescendo. Then, just as suddenly as it had started, the rain stopped. The evening now shone bright with that peculiar white light, of rain-washed evenings. A breathless hush descended, with one question hanging tremulously in the air. Would Swami walk back on the rain-wet darshan ground or would He call for the car? This 'suspense', by and by becomes a way of life for devotees in things both big and small. The idea is to cultivate poise through the state of suspension till regular training and practice elevates it to equipoise in all things and situations.

For a moment, it seemed as if the car was being called, but then just as soon, it appeared that Swami would walk back. There was a shuffle of excitement and everybody adjusted their sitting postures to await Swami's appearance on the verandah. We were all drenched to the skin but nobody seemed to mind, judging from the expression on everyone's faces. The ground was soaking wet reflecting pools of light and the dusk-hour was lending a peculiar magic to the whole evening. In such a setting, Swami in His effulgent robe suddenly appeared…all eyes were riveted now on Him, as with perfect ease He stepped off the verandah, holding His robe delicately above His ankles. As He walked across, the resplendent hue of His robe glimmered in the wet ground.

There was a perfect hush. Being in the first row, we got a unique darshan. Swami came looking straight in our direction. A little closer, and I realized that He was looking directly at me with a piercing gaze. He kept walking with that gaze fixed on me. I was transfixed. Who knows what work was accomplished by that laser beam? We can never know, but we can enjoy the experience and draw illimitable grace. We have to drop understanding, even the imperative to understanding and dive into pure experience – disengage the mind and engage the heart.

What a marvelous feeling it was sitting soaked to the skin in the open air, but never having felt better, or more truly aligned with the best there is. Many times I have wondered as to how and why the mere sight (***darshan***) of a Being can confer so much soul satisfaction… There are no easy answers. Even the Vedas could not explain it and declared '*neti neti*' (not this, not this.) Baba had given my sister and me consecutively the same deep penetrating look and because of that both of us were on a high. Once back in Bombay, though swept into my day-to-day activities, I found my mind going back to Parthi again and again.…

10

The Dance Of the Fairies

"God... moves the dew to drop, the lotus to bloom, the butterfly to flit and the sun to rise. That is all the power, all the wisdom, all the love, all the miracle that ever was, is, and will be."

Sri Sathya Sai

The first half of 1994 turned out to be a very trying one. One pressing problem after another dogged us. A very distressing episode regarding Subodh's health in December 1993 really shook me up. It eventually turned out to be a false alarm but it threw me completely out of gear. It had happened while driving back from Pune to Bombay. Subodh was at the wheel, I was beside him and our two small daughters, were in the backseat. Subodh's father was unwell and he was tense about his health. The acute tension triggered a kind of chest pain in Subodh while he was driving. Luckily, we knew somebody at Lonavala and I told Subodh that we should immediately go there. I rubbed vibhuti on him and made him wear the navratan mala, which happened to be with me and I prayed intensely to Baba. Our kind acquaintances in Lonavala took us to a doctor's clinic where some tests and check ups were done post haste. As these were being done, I paced feverishly outside in the compound, repeatedly taking Baba's name and praying intensely. Those were indeed agonizing moments. The reports came and miraculously they were clear! What a blessed relief! I sent a silent prayer of thanks to Baba. It was never clear what happened that day but I am sure that whatever it was, Baba's grace saw us through and saved the day.

All this took its toll and I felt worn out. That's when Subodh told Pammi and Sunil one day, "If you all are planning a trip abroad, just convince Shammi to go along too…" He felt I needed that break. That's how the idea took shape and a trip to England got planned with Veenu (the sister just younger to me and settled in Mumbai) and Mashu too joining in. This was in September 1994.

A good friend of ours was married and living in a town called Stord in Norway. She had often told us to plan a visit there. One thinks of Italy, France, Switzerland, Austria, Spain, when one thinks of Europe. But, Norway? It was the country with fjords, yes, but whoever would think of going there? It was just a geographical location and too remote for me to even desire it. 'It is a pristine country', our friend insisted, and that if we were nature lovers, it was just the place for us. With our friend warmly inviting us to be her guests it was a wonderful opportunity, we all agreed. The soul of adventure is doing the undone. Trying a new path, new way, or new destination. We got our visas done pronto, all set to sail. Literally! For, we took the steamer *Colourline* from Newcastle Port, England, to Norway.

But our first halt was London. We have always loved London and feel quite at home there. We have lovely friends, the Vadgamas in Barnett, London, who take the greatest care of us. London is full of charm. The parks, the olde-world pubs, the tree-lined streets, the florists booths bursting with flowers, the quaint shops and perfumeries, the cobblestoned Shakespearean by-lanes and even the London Underground! There is a lot to do. However, the first thing to do, even in London, was to listen to Baba's bhajans in the morning! I would wake up early, tip-toe to the kitchen to fix my first cup of morning tea and then sink into the drawing room sofas to savour the tea and bhajans. Later, the music and the mood would shift to Capital Radio through the day, to evening jazz or violin or folk music.

We had heard about the Hard Rock chain of cafes and how it's one time owner, Isaac Tigrit, was a great devotee of Baba. Apparently, every Hard Rock café outlet, round the world, had a picture of Swami. One day while returning from Oxford street in a bus, I started thinking about Hard Rock café. We had decided earlier that we would locate one and go there. The bus wound its way through the streets of London and about five to ten minutes after thinking about Hard Rock café, I saw it staring at me from across the road. Emblazoned in red, its name winked at me, somewhere near Hyde Park Corner.

We followed up this discovery by going to the café the coming Thursday. When we reached the place, we saw 'Love all, Serve all' (Baba's saying) in big letters at the entrance. That was exciting for us. We saw a long queue, which we joined. Someone came up and told everyone that since it was lunchtime, only full lunch orders would be taken and I told him we had come only for dessert! Very sweetly, he ushered us in. I told him we wished to see the place. Inside, it was the usual 'hard rock' scene of funky music, décor and strobe lights. We were, however, looking for something else! It was a large crowded place and we glanced around. There, in the middle of it all, we saw Him – a big framed picture of Baba with His hands behind His back, the sunlight on His face, benignly watching over the place... And the funniest part was He looked entirely in place. If at all, everything else looked out of place! We had two delicious desserts and the affable person who served them, informed us that Isaac Tigrit had sold the place for sixty-nine million something and that he was starting a whole new chain of restaurants. When we mentioned Baba's photo, he said, "Oh, He'll always be there, He's

Isaac's guru, you see...." We saw and very clearly. We too knew that He would always be there, everywhere! Mission successful, we got back, on quite a high.

One day we visited the famous bookstore, Dillons. There was a particular book by Andre Gide, *Fruits of the Earth*, which we had been trying to get for a while. His other classic, *Strait is the Gate*, one of my all time favourites (the others being *Portrait of a Lady* by Henry James and *A Passage to India* by E.M. Forster), was also on the list. Besides, we knew there was an amazing spiritual section where we could pick up titles not easily available elsewhere. When we reached Dillons, we were surprised to see quite a crowd. We were informed that the famous author, John Irving of *The World According to Garp* fame, was there for a book signing session. I had read this book in my college days and had loved it. I couldn't imagine a male writer being so sensitive and deeply understanding of womens' issues. Having been something of a feminist before my marriage and before Swami came into my life, I responded very positively to the book and its off-beat humour. And here was its author! We went up to buy his latest book and have it signed by him. There were a lot of women vying to talk to him and get his autograph. This was not surprising as he was extremely good looking! When my turn came to get my copy signed, I asked him something I had often wondered about. It was related to what Swami often says regarding unity in 'thought, word and deed'. How easy was that? So I asked him whether he was able to put into practice the amazing sensitivity he portrayed for women in his books? He was nonplussed but only for a moment. He fielded the question with humour. Laughing, he said that no, he was an absolute ogre! The real question went a-begging.... A question of course that applies to each and every one of us. Before leaving the bookstore, we checked out the spiritual section. We saw some some books on Baba there! We picked up one by Phyllis Crystal titled *Cutting the Ties that Bind*.

One morning in London, I got up feeling slightly disturbed. Everything was perfect and yet not. There was so much to see and do (and buy!). I was losing myself. I could feel a distance with my Swami connection. I had prayed to Baba to be in the center of everything but I realized for that one has to make a constant effort. He is the center of everything. It is for us to be aware and realize that all the time. The departmental stores in London boggled me. There was a silent frenzy in people to buy all kinds of things. Can one buy bliss in a store? Could any one or even all of those attractive things in the stores put together give me what I was looking for? That was it. It depended on what you were looking for. And, unknowingly now, I was looking for the bliss I had once experienced in an empty room in Prasanthi Nilayam.

I was reading a book by Joy Thomas, on Baba at that time. I chanced upon the very quote of Baba that I needed. It gave me succor. It said, "*the pure mind reflects the reality clearly – God – that is the basis of Self as well as the objective world. God is immanent in every particle of the universe. The clear vision can experience him everywhere at all times, and that vision confers immeasurable bliss.*"

Onwards to Norway. We took a coach to Newcastle from where we had to catch our steamer Colourline. Being on deck the luxury liner, watching the waves, was another experience altogether. It was an overnight journey and we made the most of it. The temperatures on the upper-deck were freezing. There was a sharp cold wind slicing the air. But we stood there determinedly, holding the railings, facing the awesome expanse of sea. It was so invigorating. With only the small price of red noses to pay for it!

Dinner in the lavish lounge was an exotic affair. After a sumptuous Italian meal, topped with the most delicious tiramisu, and an evening of entertaining programmes, we made our way to our cabins. Even that thought excited us – sleeping in a cabin with portholes! What a sight it was through the portholes at night! An endless expanse of inky black sea rolling over with a periodic swell of rising waves, beating against the ship. This would create gallons and gallons of white gushing foam, spewing out from every side. Awesome, or scary depending on how many nautical bones you had in your body! "Sai Ram", I muttered to myself. What could one do without Him? The weather was a little windy that night and so it was not an entirely smooth ride. The steamer would lurch every now and then. Luckily, we didn't get sea-sick. Saying our night prayers with a little extra fervour, we finally slept. Outside, the dark sea tossed and turned. So did we – with the rocking motion, the whole night.

And then – daybreak. The clear light of a fresh new day. How different everything looked. The sun poured down light and warmth on the expanse of ocean. The waves, so menacing last night, now looked jaunty. The scene was transformed into a friendly picture postcard. I realized then, more than ever, the bounteous grace of the sun in our lives. Not only in its life-giving properties but also in it's ability to dispel the gloom of imaginary fears. Our seers and ancients in their wisdom extolled the sun and gave it an exalted place in their worship. Powerful mantras from the Vedas in praise of the glory of the sun were ritually chanted. The West is now waking-up to the wisdom of the East. The *gayatri mantra*, dedicated to the sun, is a universal prayer from the *Rig Veda*, which has stimulated tremendous interest in countries like USA and Russia. Scientific experiments in western countries have demonstrated and proved the incredible power of this mantra.

Our friends, Neeta and Pradip received us. They were perfectly wonderful hosts. Putting their other schedules on the backburner, they catered to our tourist instincts. What a country! Every bend and turn in the road made us gasp at the splendorous show of nature. Confronted with such magnificent natural beauty, the mind simply goes quiet. What can it say? The heart takes over and in simple language, it tells you – God exists....

Every day was a treat. We were spellbound by the natural beauty of Norway and its warm friendly people. After a hectic wonderful week, we were now down to our last day in Norway. We were to go for lunch that day to Helga's (a Norwegian) home, a close friend of Neeta and Pradip. Every moment in Norway had been a delight, as much for the bewitching show of nature as for the lovely people we kept meeting. The houses in Norway must be the most picturesque in the world. This is because Norwegians have a custom of dressing up their windows in the most charming ways. Driving from one place to another, we would get a feast of different window decorations of colourful flower baskets, candles, lace frills, etc. not seen anywhere else in the world.

Helga's house was an experience in itself! The garden, the shimmering lake and the hills beyond! As we sat down for lunch in the warm interiors, Helga lit a candle – another Norwegian custom. In the course of the meal Mashu asked her about the Aurora Borealis – the Northern Lights. We had heard stories of how people made special expeditions to specific points in the ocean, off the northern coast of Norway and spent days watching the sky, to 'catch' the lights. It is a grand natural spectacle called 'the dance of the fairies', where beams of translucent light shoot up in a semi-circle, into the night-sky. One could see them from Norway, but only from specific points in the extreme north and at specific times during the winter. Helga told us that the lights were a very rare phenomenon and though many tried, only a few, the most persistent or lucky, got to see it. Hearing about the lights made us start hoping. If only! Pammi ventured, "Maybe we'll get to see them...!" Everybody laughed "Well, maybe, one day..."

"For that maybe you'll have to make another trip in winter!" said Neeta. "This is only September when it is unlikely that anybody can see them from anywhere."

The conversation then turned to our desire to see a snowfall – not just fallen snow (like on Mount Titlis) but falling snow – the snowflakes floating down from above. It should not be such a difficult dream to realize in a place like Norway. "Yes," Neeta said, "anywhere but Stord in Norway! It is a coastal town and so rarely if ever experiences snowfall. In fact, the only thing we rue about this place is that we don't get to see a white Christmas – for that we have to go up north."

That evening, our last of the trip, we met a doctor from Oslo in Neeta's house who mentioned the Aurora Borealis again. He told us how he had made five expeditions up north and camped at Buda in the bitter cold of January to catch the lights. And he got to see them just once! When we expressed our hope to see them some time, he kind of scoffed!

That evening, me chatted quite late into the might. A little while later, we said our goodnights and retired to our rooms. Veenu and me were in one room and Mashu and Pammi in the one opposite to ours. I had set up an altar for Swami in our room. I decided to do my japa before turning in. I was chanting with the japa mala in my hands when something happened! Such excitement! I heard Neeta shouting out our names from her bedroom window above. She was calling out excitedly to all of us to come to her room at once. Veenu rushed out and along with Pammi and Mashu went to check what was happening. "Come up," Neeta shouted, "the Northern Lights......!!"

Had I heard correctly? Well, it took all of my spiritual resources that day to finish my round of *japa*. I could feel (and hear) the high excitement all around but had to keep sitting with my eyes shut. Pammi came rushing in to call me and saw me in my meditative mudra. I kept chanting the Name (very fast I must say) but my mind, at that moment, was more on His creation than the Creator! It was such a funny sight – my lips just couldn't help breaking into a smile. Surely, He too must have smiled, if not laughed outright.

I completed the japa and ran upstairs. All of them were huddled at the window, which had been opened to get a clearer view. I rushed to join them. It was freezing. The cold night air rushed in and froze our noses and cheeks. We bent forward to look out. It was unbelievable. It was the dancing fairies – the Northern Lights – in the distant night sky. We were speechless. Could it really be? Was somebody flashing a gigantic green torch light? It soon became clear very that what we all were seeing huddled together that cold Norwegian night was Aurora Borealis. Neeta and Pradip were even more stunned than we were. Never had they in all their years in Norway seen the lights from Stord. And never had they dreamt that they would see them one day from their bedroom window.

Pammi was ecstatic and was sure that it was Swami! Her intense wish had been granted by and through His grace. Mashu and Veenu looked dreamy-eyed. That very afternoon Mashu had enquired about the Aurora Borealis at Helga's and now she had seen them! We watched the lights till they dimmed and then slowly faded away. Pradip said in a dazed voice, "Is this real, can such a thing happen?" Pammi breezily answered, "Anything can happen if He wills it. NOW, look out for the snow…..!" They laughed, so did we – and, so did He!

Our faces continued to glow as we got into our warm beds. We felt wide awake. Pammi commanded, "Don't draw the curtains, you never know…"

We wondered if we would ever get sleep that night. Our brains were on over drive. However, we did sleep for a couple of hours or so.

I still do not know what it was that woke me up in the middle of the night. Snowflakes falling from the heavens above in the silent night have never known to make any noise, have they? All I know is that I was suddenly awake. There was this huge sloping sky-window facing me. It was pitch dark outside but something was happening. The dark awning of the night-sky pinned with sparkling stars was rolling over, or so it seemed. It was such an unusual startling sight. I rushed to the window. It took a whole minute for it to register. When it did, all I could say was, "My God!" Millions, yes millions, of tiny white snowflakes were falling gently slantingly from the skies above over the whole countryside. Exquisite, beyond words. It was like a Rumi poem! "*With one silent laugh, You tilted the night and the garden ran with stars*". I stood transfixed. But only for a moment. I had to wake up the others. I called out to Veenu, "Get up." I then sailed into Pammi's and Mashu's room, "Hey folks, are you all sleeping or what?" Pammi divined something right away and got up at once. She saw my face and intuitively picked 'it' up. She gasped, "No!" I said, "Yes! Come fast." It was the repeat of the earlier scene with all of us crowding the large windows in my room now. We were ecstatic – Pammi most of all. Hadn't she told us already! Of course, it was Swami again!

We somehow managed to get some sleep after all that excitement. There were no further interruptions. (I mean, anything could have happened – the midnight sun, for instance?) In the morning, we awoke to a white expanse of snow-laden countryside. The trees looked extremely pretty just like Christmas cards! Neeta and Pradip could not quite believe what was happening. We stood, all of us on their balcony taking photographs in an exuberant mood. The sky was ablaze with the most incredible colours. We captured the show on video. Pradip looked bemused. He had only one thing to say, "You're not witches, are you?"

It had really been an extraordinary experience. Seeing the Northern Lights and then the snowfall from a small coastal village in Norway, where such phenomena rarely happened. Pammi's faith had not been belied. Her wish had been honoured by the universe, maybe because of its intensity. We stomped onto the soft snow in their yard. The snow was soft and crumbly. And how could we forget Swami? We made a big OM on the snow and wrote Sai Ram in big bold letters (all our friends and acquaintances, whether they like it or not, have no option when it comes to Swami. We do not leave Him out of anything. Whether they understand or not, they have to smile and go along). Incidentally, Neeta our hostess shares her birthday with Swami – 23rd November. When we heard this, we felt even more affection for her.

We were supposed to leave later the same day by boat from Haugersund. There was some concern about the road because of the snowfall. Miraculously, a bright sun took care of all that. By the time we had to leave to board the steamer, the snow had sufficiently melted. In fact, it was amazing, for later in the day, one could hardly imagine that the place had experienced a snowfall. What was even more mind boggling was that the snow had fallen in Stord not only in the warm month of September but over a small area and we were in the middle of it. It was as if nature had gone out on a limb especially for us. Out of all the Swami stories one has collected over the years, Pammi to this day gets the greatest delight in recounting the Norway one!

11

Spiritual Capers

Those who aspire to become true bhaktas *should search only for bases on which to build their* ananda... *All the available time should be used for holy purposes. You have nothing to do with the good and bad in others. Instead use your time in discarding the bad and developing the good in you.*

Sri Sathya Sai

In the year following our November 1993 visit to Parthi, we created opportunities to go to Parthi. We must have made four to five trips that year. At that time, it was basically Mashu and I who made the trips. How can I ever forget those divine capers to Parthi/Bangalore/Kodai, at the drop of a hat? It was like a secret life, rich, mystical and exhilarating. Pammi and Veenu were not as yet regulars on the trips front. They were to come in later after 1995.

At the end of every trip, I would come back to Bombay more determined than ever to do the necessary sadhana for attaining the goal. At that time, to my simple mind, the goal only translated to one thing – greater proximity to the Form. In little little ways, I started bringing about changes in my daily life, patterns of behaviour, ètc. My one overpowering desire was to please Swami by trying to follow what He has been repeating down the years. It was not easy, but every bit of effort was a beginning. I believed without a doubt the omnipresence, omnipotence, and omniscience of Sri Sathya Sai Baba. It's only when you believe in that fully can you begin to get conscious about your thoughts, words, and deeds. I got into the habit of doing self-audit. Every time I lost my temper, had a negative thought, judged others, etc. or slipped up in any way, I quietly acknowledged to myself that I had made a mistake. Swami says the first step is this awareness. Unless we first recognize and then accept our follies, we can never move on to correcting them.

I inculcated more sadhana into my life. This trains our spiritual mind and cleanses us. However, Swami often emphasizes that sadhana is just a means and not the end. It is to be given only that much of importance. It will have no value, however rigorously you do it, if correspondingly your mind is not getting purer, if your words are not getting sweeter and your actions nobler. The whole purpose of sadhana or any spirituality is ultimately to make you a better person, more divine.

It was with great joy that I attended bhajans regularly in devotees' houses. There were other activities too like study circle groups, as also the Balvikas training classes that I had joined. Likhita japa was another sadhana that I took up. Swami has often emphasized the importance of awaking in Brahmuhuratam, in the early hours of morning (3.00 a.m. to 6.00 a.m.) I opted for the outer limit, and set the alarm for 5.30 a.m everyday! Swami says the vibrations in the mornings are purer and because of the soothing silence and lack of disturbance at that time, meditation becomes more fruitful. In those early days, when I was just discovering the joy of spirit, it was no struggle to get up in those cool silent dawns for meditation. Some strange energy would get me awake at the right time and I would be just propelled out of bed. Who needed sleep when you had a rendezvous with spirit? I would sit in front of my mandir on my prayer mat and chant the twenty-one Omkars. At dawn, the Prasanthi mandir reverberates with the sonorous chant of the Omkars. Swami often says that we should make our homes and hearts into Prasanthi Nilayam. I guess this was my small way of making a beginning. The Omkars set the tone for inner quietude and help to clear the debris. A subtle fine-tuning takes place, making it easier to catch those all-important waves from deep within. However, technically I have never been one to meditate. So after the chanting and saying of my prayers (the *Gayatri mantra*) I would 'wind up' the meditation and try not to slip back into my cosy bed. I got into the habit then, of hearing Baba's bhajans that early hour and it is something I do right to this day. My day has to start (though not necessarily at 5.30 a.m. always) with tea and bhajans in that beautiful early morning solitude. No doorbells, no phone bells, no kitchen clatter, no traffic noise, no sounds – except for early morning birds. I would feel very tuned to Swami and often feel His presence in the particular fragrances associated with Him. Even in chilly Kanpur winters, I would awaken early, and with my teeth chattering, in my socks, gloves and shawl, pad to the study or *chhota kamra* (a cute 12'x12' area lined with books on every subject under the sun and now our spiritual watering hole too) to put on my Sai bhajans. Those sweet dawns. That delight. Nothing, just nothing can be said about it.

Siddhivinayak is a very popular Ganesha shrine in Mumbai. It is a living testimony to faith. Not only does man have to prove himself to God and pass His tests, but even God has to prove Himself to man and pass his tests! It is as mutual a give and take as in any other relationship. The beloved deity in the Siddhivinayak shrine has apparently proved Himself to devotees in numerous ways and incessantly. Why else do the number of devotees thronging the shrine keep swelling? Tuesdays, marked out as a special day for the community of the faithful, sees serpentine queues. Thousands of devotees come there, each with a different prayer. Lord Ganesha presides there benignly taking care of all. My sisters and I too, decided to go there with our prayers. Mostly, before a trip to see Swami and after it, we would go to the shrine and pay our respects. I even had a dream which communicated to me that this particular shrine is a most potent one and that even devas frequent it occasionally, from the side entrance!

All our prayers and sadhana must have melted the heart of the gods, for many divine trips to Prasanthi, Brindavan and even to Kody materialized. The secret plans for trips to Parthi created a high in us. We were a like group of three or four who would just take off – either it was somebody's birthday in the group, some festival or just the 'call' as we liked to say. As my youngest sister Mashu was unmarried, she had no problems on the domestic front, but one or two of us had to employ extra tact – and sometimes tactics – on those recurrent take offs. Luckily, our husbands were understanding and indulgent and this was purely Baba's grace.

In our group of devotees in Worli, it was in Mrs. Supriya Damani's house that I first started attending my Sai bhajans. A lovely devotee of Swami's, she often accompanied us on our trips. On one of those trips with her, we happened to be in Parthi on July 27 which was Mrs. Damani's birthday. However, on the morning of the 27th, Mrs. Damani woke up feeling feverish. She had a severe cold and headache and couldn't make it to darshan. That was very disappointing, both for her as well as for us. We kept thinking of her during morning darshan. However, miraculously she recovered well enough to come for darshan in the evening. That cheered us and we hoped that she would have a significant look or something from Swami to mark out her special day.

We got the fourth or fifth row, which was not bad at all. There was every chance of getting a clear darshan from our spot. And if Swami chose to look our way, then it would be fantastic. The music started and Swami in his graceful majestic way came into the mandir. He slowly approached us but then walked by giving only a very cursory general glance. Mrs. Damani was happy with that. For her, to have been able to come for darshan that evening and see Swami was blessing enough.

When Swami walked into the interview room, many people got up for tea and snacks. We decided, as was our norm, to stay on. This way, we got a chance to shift forward into better places and also get an occasional glimpse of Swami if He decided to walk out on the verandah after the interviews. That was the time when getting a close darshan of Swami's was the very summit of our expectations.

It must have been our lucky day, for all the three of us got first row seats (in the side block) near the pillar. That brought a big collective smile on our faces, and we revelled in the divine treat.

The evening bhajans started. This can be quite a sublime experience. The mandir reverberates with devotional fervour expressed through the bhajans. With the evening shadows lengthening, the whole mandir gets bathed in a soft light. A sweet serenity descends over one and everything else is forgotten.

In such a scenario, we awaited Swami's appearance after the evening arati. Some suspense is always linked to Swami's movements! At this point, we were wondering whether Swami would walk down the aisle on the far end or cut across the wide open mandir ground diagonally on His return. If he did the latter, we (and especially Mrs. Damani) in the first row would get a fabulously close darshan, with a chance maybe of a look. I felt sure in my heart that Swami would not let the day go by without some slight acknowledgement to Mrs. Damani. Many come to Swami on the days of their personal celebrations like birthdays and anniversaries, etc. for blessings. And it never ceases to amaze me how most of the time Swami responds. He always knows. What day of celebration it is for whom. And in one way or the other, He manages to impart something special to the devotee on that day. This, I suppose, is purely for the devotee's satisfaction. For Swami, all days are alike and He teaches us the same thing. But He goes along with us in such moments out of sheer love and compassion.

Arati over, Swami came out. He started walking down the aisle, the far end. We were disappointed thinking we had lost our chance. But as devotees learn, Swami is always up to something! He kept walking, making it seem as if He was going to walk through that aisle. Here, from our first row seats, we looked at Him ardently. Suddenly, just when He was about to enter the aisle, with all the devotees seated facing that way, He suddenly swiveled, did a graceful about turn and started walking down our line! All the devotees adjusted their positions immediately and like sunflowers turned around. Swami laughed at His little joke and so did the devotees. We were thrilled. In fact, because of His little drama, we would get a better and even closer darshan than if He had walked diagonally straight from the verandah. Now, He was walking parallel to our line, just inches away. We folded our hands in namaskar, with Mrs. Damani in between us and awaited Him. For a minute, we lost sight of Him as He was behind the pillar. And then, were our eyes playing a trick on us? He emerged from behind the pillar and looking at us, said, "*Kya samachar*?" (what news?) Of course, we felt it couldn't be us He's talking to! So we just kept smiling into the air. He repeated louder, looking directly at us, "*Kya samachar*?" He then added, "*Kidhar se ayya hai*?" (where have you come from?). Now I was sure. Seeing that the other two were quite spaced out, I spoke up, "Swami, Bombay." He repeated, "Bombay", stretching the word. I then ventured, "Swami, her birthday..." indicating Mrs. Damani. But even before I said it, Swami had started materializing vibhuti. With a most gentle smile, He extended His hand and poured the vibhuti into Mrs. Damani's palm. It was a beautiful moment. Mrs. Damani was beside herself with joy and so were we. After darshan, several ladies came up to her and told her how special the interaction had looked. One lady even said that she had seen a beam of light emanate from Swami's eyes towards Mrs. Damani. For days after that, whenever we met each other, it was only "*Kya samachar*?" to each other!

12

The First Interview

You will learn everything worth knowing in my classroom. I will expose you to all states of being, so that you may learn to rest in Me in all of them.

Sri Sathya Sai

That was the time my dream consciousness was flooded by many of Baba's singular dreams. The elation at His presence in my dream and the disappointment at His not, were two emotions strung out from day to day! Even Mashu had numerous dreams and every morning we would greet each other with an animated querying look, which asked the one big question related to having seen Him in a dream or not. And if either of us had been graced, we would immediately repair to a secluded corner with our teacups and bright faces to recount our dreams.

Around this time, I started, uncannily, seeing dreams related to cricket matches. Surprisingly, my brother-in-law, Sunil Gavaskar featured in most of them. I presumed that the recurrent scenario of a cricket match was maybe meant to be a symbol for how life itself should be lived. Little did I guess that there was to be a far more direct and literal translation of those dreams in the near future. This underlined two interesting facts; firstly, that Swami's dreams are not ordinary dreams but have a deep significance and secondly, how it seems as if everything in life is pre-ordained, even the small details.

One morning I saw a dream in which in a large stadium, a cricket match was in progress. My brother-in-law, Sunil was at the crease and a large spotlight was on him. The funny part was that Baba too was in the dream and the stadium appeared to be in Puttaparthi. We, the family members, had special seating for the match in the devotee stands. This was in April 1995. This dream was to be decoded in a very direct manner two years from then. I had another dream in which Sunil figured: This *dream showed that Baba has come to His Bombay ashram, Dharmakshetra and all of us get special front row seating in darshan.* This dream was to be dramatically decoded very shortly.

Exactly a month later, Sri Sathya Sai Baba came on a divine visit to Bombay in May 1995. That was also the year my brother-in-law, Sunil was designated sheriff of Bombay and in that capacity he was invited for a welcome address to Swami at Dharmakshetra and present Him a commemorative bat.

The 10th of May saw Swami arrive in Bombay on a five day visit. The ashram ground was packed with eager devotees patiently awaiting His arrival. It is amazing to see devotees sit for hours sometimes, just to get a momentary glimpse. That itself, speaks for the power of darshan. Nobody really complains – everybody is driven to acquire that one look. When Baba finally did appear briefly that day, all tiredness was forgotten and everybody was refreshed by the darshan. There was mangal arati after that and the trip of '95 got underway. A lot was to follow in the coming days – most of it thrilling and full of grace.

There was darshan at Dharmakshetra twice a day and large crowds thronged the venue for the same. Early morning there was nagarsankirtan, which was crowned by a divine early morning darshan on the balcony in front of Swami's residence. Many were blessed to witness His divine aura in that pure surcharged atmosphere of dawn. A lady acquaintance of mine who did not really believe in Baba and was there merely out of curiosity, was stunned into belief when she saw instead of Baba, her *Ishtadevta*, Dattaraya's vision in His place. Many have had similar experiences where they have seen, in place of Swami's form, a vision of their own chosen beloved deity. *Shirdi Sai Satcharita* is replete with instances like this, where 'doubters' have been converted instantly!

Getting a special audience with Baba is always the sharpest desire in most devotees. Normally, this is very difficult to come by and there is no predicting how Baba may receive you – if at all. On 12th May, we got a chance of a special audience outside Satyadeep. My parents too got this great opportunity. Satyadeep, Baba's residence in the ashram, is a very charming place. There is a lane winding up in a sharp hilly swerve to this lovely tree-filled area, in the middle of which is a lotus-shaped structure. The entire upward curving lane is lined with trees and flowering bushes to make it all very picturesque. It was with some reverence and awe and a host of other emotions that we drove up the incline and then made our way to the waiting line of devotees sitting silently there, in three rows of chairs. We took our places. Shortly, Baba appeared. What a moment it is when He walks through a door and is suddenly visible, to longing eyes. Everybody sat up and folded their palms in reverence. My parents were seated in the second row and I was behind them. I got the feeling that He gave a knowing look in my father's direction right away. He approached closer, and conversed in a merry manner with the group beside us. Then he made a diagonal cut and broke into the row where my father was seated. He moved directly towards him smiling charmingly and saying, "*Bahut khush, bahut khush*," (very happy, very happy). This was a splendid moment for my father. He stood in front of my father's chair with His one elbow resting on the backrest of the chair in front. My father took the opportunity and bent down and lovingly clasped Baba's legs in a sweeping-scale padnamaskar. Baba conversed with someone on the right, then turned back to my father, took his proffered letter and lovingly patted his cheek. My father was overwhelmed by this gesture. My mother seated next to him was overcome with emotion too. Baba then walked out of the aisle, into the front. Somebody asked for padnamaskar and Baba granted it. Meanwhile, seeing our chance, we – Pammi, Mashu and my sister-in-law, Snehal – also lined up on one side for an 'attempted' padnamaskar. Swami, however, had moved onto the other side. We followed gracefully. I walked to where He was standing and softly intoned, "Swami, may we touch Your feet?"

"Yes, yes," He said in soft tones, and one by one, we all went and took His padnamaskar. The moment was replete with solemnity and beauty. Snehal, Subodh's sister, was with me and got a padnamaskar too. This was significant because it was her first ever darshan of Baba. When nice things happen to nice people you always feel good inside. Snehal, is many things – a strong personality, a brilliant lawyer to boot, but over and above everything, a wonderful human being.

There was a slight drama behind the scenes. Veenu and her husband Shrikant had got held up in traffic and couldn't make it for this darshan in time. Veenu was miserable, to put it mildly. But Baba always has something lined up! He made up for it in the most glorious way. The following day, Veenu had the most incredible 'special audience'. A few people were lined up on both sides as Baba approached. Veenu awaited Him breathlessly, being part of that group. Baba came to her tapped her on the head lightly and said, "I have blessed you...." As He was walking by, she said under her breath with feeling, "love you, Swami..." Swami walked on. But after the space of three or four people, He turned and looked at Veenu and said emphatically, "I love you too!" Somebody handed him two roses. He took them and turning back to Veenu extended His hand and said, "You keep that!" Wondrous is the only word for it! Veenu was euphoric.

This was a very important moment for Veenu. Though she had tremendous feeling for Swami, it had been kept a little in check up to this point. In fact, till now, it had been only Mashu and me who had been running to Parthi and chanting Swami's name all the time. It was only with this visit of Swami's to Bombay that Veenu and Pammi too joined the Parthi bandwagon!

A few years ago, Veenu had had an unusual encounter with Swami at Satyadeep itself. It had appeared as if Swami had rebuffed her strongly. She had been pained by that seeming rebuff but had realized later its deeper import. Before going for that darshan, she had put a question to Baba mentally on a very urgent personal matter. When Baba appeared outside and somebody in the group wished to click snaps, Baba agreed. However, when Veenu who was in the same group, started entering the frame of the snap, Baba very loudly and sternly said three times, "No, no, no..." It was a rude shock to her. She stayed apart while the snap was clicked. She was feeling the pain of that rejection when she called me in Kanpur to recount the episode. It was then while talking that we realized that the 'no, no, no' was Baba's answer to her, about the personal question she had put Him! And it was a perfect answer as time revealed. The stern tone was employed to underline that in no way should Veenu even consider the said matter. Baba's ways are unfathomable, but we can be sure that they are always for our good. Interestingly, when that roll of photos was developed later, all the other photos were fine, except the one clicked with Swami – that was a blank!

The highlight of that whole trip for us was undoubtedly 14th May. That was the day the function was organized at Dharmakshetra, where my brother-in-law was to felicitate Swami and present Him a bat! That opened a door for the family to get special seating for darshan, a scenario which I had seen in a couple of dreams a few months back. After years of yearning for closeness to the Form, this was indeed a boon.

The prior night, excitement ran high in the family at the prospect of Swami sending two cars the following day, one for Sunil and one for the family! We felt exuberant. The next day saw us reach Dharmakshetra bright and early. We were taken up right to the front (the dream!) and Sunil was led to the stage to sit next to Swami. Sunil has a very calm temperament and nicknamed 'yogi' by all of us, took it in his equable stride. But to us sisters nothing is 'just nice', but always, 'too wonderful', 'too good' or 'too exciting'! Consequently, we could hardly contain ourselves and this showed on our faces. This made Sunil cast amused glances at us every now and then from the stage. And even Swami cast His benign eye over us many a time, with a divine smile playing around His lips.

Shortly, Sunil gave his welcome address in his capacity as sheriff of Bombay. The best part was when he presented Swami with a commemorative cricket bat, with the hope that some day one of Swami's students would break some cricketing record with it! We didn't know it then but that offering of a cricket bat was to be the beginning of a very exciting chapter for us, the events of which would, however, unfold only after another two years. For the moment, however, the entire gathering savoured the unusual and charming scenario of seeing Swami receiving and holding a cricket bat. The presentation was followed with a discourse by Swami which He concluded with the bhajan, '*Hari bhajan bina sukha shanti nahin*'. His face reflected the pure ananda of His divine nature as He sang. The devotees ecstatically sang along. How many, in the history of time, can claim the rare privilege of such a sankirtan? – Singing not only *to* the Lord, but also *with* the Lord. His ananda communicated itself to the devotees.

"The beaming joy on the faces of this vast multitude is the food I live on. Your ananda *is my 'ahara' (nourishment). I do not feel like talking to you at all for I desire only to communicate to you My joy*

and to get into communion with your joy. This mutual fulfillment is the essential thing; talking and listening are subsidiary."

One has to always keep this awareness sharp, that this is no ordinary guru, not even a Satguru, but something far, far more – the unnamable, indefinable THAT! It is not easy, for the powerful maya, envelops all in a thick fog of unknowing.

Soon after the bhajan and arati, Swami smilingly concluded the darshan by walking off stage. We sighed, and felt a kind of loss, for one can never have enough of Him. As we stood there, there was a recognizable flutter. We saw somebody come running towards us urgently asking for Mrs. Gavaskar (Sunil was backstage, after his speech). Pammi rushed in. Now, Mashu, who has an amazing aesthetic sense, had made a beautiful album on Swami. She had spent days over it, pasting His choicest photographs and painting gorgeous designs around them. It was sheer delight for a Sai devotee to go through the album because the turn of each page presented a unique frame. She had carried the album to darshan that day in the hope of getting it blessed by Sai. She quickly handed it over to Pammi, who took it along with her. Apparently, just outside Satyadeep, Swami met them. Pammi put forward the album saying, "Swami, sister has made.." Swami took the album and leafed through every page. Mashu's deepest wish at that moment was that Swami may sign in it. Swami took a pen and did sign – on two pages! On one page, He gave a handwritten message, 'do good, be good, see good, that is the way to God'. On the other page, He signed 'with blessings Sri Sathya Sai'. Mashu had always hoped that if ever He signed anything for her, He should sign His name, Sri Sathya Sai.... Her wish was fulfilled without her knowing it. Pammi told Swami that the sisters too were there. Swami said, "*Malum, bulao, bulao, unko bhi bulao,*" (I know, call them too).

Thus, even as we stood there with the darshan crowds dispersing, there was an urgent second message. "Swami has called you *all*..." Magic words. How can one describe the scene that followed? It was as if there was a current passing through us, the way we ran up the stairs, faces alight. My friend, Shanti was in our group too but she was not sure if she too was supposed to join us. Seeing her hesitation, my mother told her emphatically to come along. That cleared her doubt and she rushed in with us. We were then driven up the curving incline to Satyadeep. We couldn't quite believe this. Frankly, I was breathless with excitement. It was to be our first ever interview. Even as I walked in, I suddenly remembered a recent dream. In it *I see myself standing outside the interview room. To my right is a group of people who have been called in. Baba comes towards us and indicates to the group to go in. I stand separate from them to their left. I query Baba, "Even I?" and He smiles sweetly and indicates, "Yes". I walk in with the others into this bare room, which has different sized* dhurries *(rugs) spread out on the floor. As we enter, Baba tells me, "We won't talk, we will just sit around and take in the atmosphere..." The general impression was that we had finally gained entry into that hallowed spot known as the interview room! This dream was just about to decode.*

I will never forget that moment when I suddenly found myself in a smallish room, which had Baba sitting there awaiting us. My first glimpse of Him inside was dramatic. He was sitting behind an intricate wooden screen and on entering I caught the brilliant flashes of his orange robe through it. I will always remember that. It was a larger than life image. We walked around the screen, to come right in front of Baba. Sunil, very decorously introduced us to Him! "I know, I know," He said, giving an appraising glance to us. Then, with a twinkle in His eye, He said, "My gang...my gang has come." We sat down around Baba's feet trying hard to digest the reality of being so close to His divine form.

Baba spoke with my parents, addressing them individually, making the moment especially memorable. After twenty years of devotion, my parents experienced their first direct physical contact with Baba. As such, we were all quiet and gazing at Him completely mesmerized. It is not easy to say anything at all once you are in His august and overpowering presence. The first thing to realize is that one does feel different in His presence. For one, there is a very powerful current, which seems to draw every bit of you into it. Though Baba is quite like a divine host inside, even the skeptics will have to concede the essential difference that one feels in His presence in that enclosed interview room, that sets Him apart from any other human form. For this reason, one can never be entirely relaxed when in the immediate divine presence, because of the divine aura, which is almost tangible. One is always taut and very alert inside, hanging on to His every word. However, this experience is mostly confined to the interview room or when one is otherwise in proximity to the form. It may or may not be felt in the act of darshan when Baba walks through the crowds on His daily rounds. This is not to take away from the unique beauty and power of darshan itself. In fact, there are many, and I count myself one of them, who feel that the plain splendour of Swami's darshan as He walks by, cannot be matched by anything else. Also, an individual does not have to be *near* the Form to benefit from His energy or aura.

Many are the miracles that have happened to people sitting in remote areas of the mandir during darshan. Miracles of transformation and otherwise have taken place in every corner of the world even to people who have never set eyes on Swami's physical form. So, it is important to remember not to limit Him and His power to just the Form.

But for the moment, we were in that little room, fortunate to be experiencing the proximity and wanting to make the most of it.

Swami spoke to almost every member of my family – except me. I don't even remember Him giving me a look. I just sat there, and soaked in the atmosphere! (just like He had told me in the dream!) That was good because frankly I felt dazed at the sudden proximity to Him and was unable to sort out my own reactions and feelings just then. It was like when you wait and wait for something to happen, when it finally does, you don't know what to feel. Yet, the momentousness of it all did not escape me.

He spoke to my mother asking after her health. Looking at us, He said about her, "very noble mother". He also enquired from my father about his health. He turned to Mashu and asked her, "What do you read, bangaru?" (a term of affection used by Baba meaning 'gold'). Mashu is an avid reader and her reading tastes range from P G Wodehouse to Aurobindo. She was so thrilled that Swami was addressing her that she beamed and said, "Swami, *apko* ......" (I read Your books).

Nana Chudasama and his daughter were also in the interview room with us. Swami spoke about the excessive wealth of people in Bombay and how it should be used for humanitarian purposes. He specifically mentioned the need for more charitable hospitals of the highest standard to come up, to serve the needy. Speaking about money Swami said it was like a shoe; if the shoe was too large or too small, it would be uncomfortable. In other words, having too little or too much money, both were not desirable.

After that there was some more interaction with Sunil and Pammi. Looking at Sunil, Swami smiled and showing his white handkerchief said that Sunil was, "pure, spotless, like handkerchief....". The family felt delighted at that compliment for Sunil. Right from the beginning, Swami exhibited the greatest affection for my brother-in-law. And down the years, He was to give Sunil many many more lovely compliments.

After that, Shanti asked for padnamaskar. He said "yes, yes." After blessing some photographs she was holding of her family, Swami swivelled around. Very patiently He allowed each one of us to take His padnamaskar. This was in May 1995 and it was all just beginning.

13

"I Will Give You Nice Dishes"

"Proximity to the Lord, gives true happiness..."

Sri Sathya Sai

Swami's seventieth birthday and the world conference was just a month away when I had an intriguing dream. In the dream, this scenario takes place: *I see Swami chuck a paper plane into the air at the cricket stadium in my hometown Kanpur. After that, I see Swami riding in a resplendent chariot down the streets of Parthi under a brilliant sun. The roads are lined with devotees and I too am one of the crowd.* This dream was to be decoded very shortly on Swami's seventieth birthday – every bit of it, even the chucking of the paper plane. When I had the dream, I knew that the chariot meant Swami's birthday, but I was bemused to see myself in the devotee ranks. At that point, there was no chance of my making it for His birthday celebrations. Mashu and me had just returned from a trip to Parthi and it would seem inappropriate to rush off again. Secondly, the problem of getting train bookings at such a short notice, as also accommodation in Parthi at the time of His birthday did not appear feasible. The desire, however, was strong.

Then, a phone call from one of our Sai friends changed the picture. She had an extra air ticket to Parthi for the birthday and she asked us to avail of it. Mashu having no other obligations at the moment, was more than happy to respond to the 'call.' I couldn't dare tell my husband of my wish to join them. For, maybe nothing less than a personal invitation from Swami would have coaxed him into accepting just then. Well, in a way, that's exactly what happened. My sister was all set to go and I was feeling just a little wistful. Then, one night, I heard His voice in my dream, softly saying, "you also come...I will give you nice, nice dishes to eat..." That did it! It was as good an invitation as any one could get from the divine avatar! I spoke to my husband, and surprisingly, he didn't demur at all. Immediately, I booked myself on the direct flight on the 22nd, lucky to get a seat a day prior to the birthday. This had me walking on air and I remained air-borne till I finally touched down at the airport in Puttaparthi! Taking a flight to Parthi felt wonderful and exchanging warm Sai Rams with co-passengers even more so. As we came in to land, fleecy white clouds in a very blue sky and the low hills circling the airport provided a very picturesque setting. Could anything be better than this, I thought dreamily? Could there be happier landings – than in the abode of highest peace?

Prasanthi Nilayam is called the 'abode of the highest peace,' and one's first taste of the place does give that. However, by and by, the road becomes tougher...the 'peace' is always there, but it is no longer offered on a platter, you have to work for it. That, in fact, is the bottom line of the spiritual path. The initial phase is always easy and the first brush with spirit is always heady. It is like stumbling upon the most unbelievable treasure in your own backyard! You are beside yourself with the discovery, and for a while all is well with you and the world. This is called the spiritual honeymoon period, when the spirit "woos" the human soul and no demands are made. This is the time for thrills – the chills come only later. Anyhow, I had landed in Prasanthi and there was nothing more to think beyond that moment.

That evening, I called my husband and then Pammi to inform them of our safe arrival and to say 'wish you were here.' Well, a wish in Parthi sometimes takes on the force of prayer. What my sister then conveyed to me had me exclaiming in the telephone booth, in a high-pitch, "What?" Had I heard right? "You're coming for Swami's birthday…? (which was the next day.)

"How?"

"HE is sending a chartered plane…"

"WHAT?"

"Sunil has been invited to be master of ceremonies along with Alvin Kallicharan (the West Indian cricketer) for the evening function. So we'll be there tomorrow afternoon. Be there to receive Swami's guests, at the airport," she said in her breeziest tone. We were *zapped* – that's the only word to describe our feelings.

That night, we could hardly sleep. In any case, it was not very practical to sleep, because we had to leave our rooms at 3:00 am in the morning, to get good places at the Vidyagiri Stadium. By His grace, we did get very good places, considering the teeming crowds. In fact, our places were to prove especially lucky, as we realized later.

It was a beautiful morning. And it was not fanciful thinking, for the devotees to think that nature itself was out on a limb, celebrating this special day. There was an ethereal quality to the dawn that day – to the gorgeous tints of gold and red in the eastern sky, to the green hills serenely witnessing the show, to the elegant flocks of white birds, in perfect alignment, gliding across the sky. The wait was long, as it always is, but worth every moment. None from the gathering could have rued the bodily discomfort for the reward of darshan that day.

Brilliant fireworks lit up the morning sky to herald Baba's arrival. He gladdened every eye with that first glimpse from the chariot, as it made its way through the stadium. As resplendent in a white robe as any other, Baba waved and blessed the multitudes – raising both His hands in blessing to the right and left of the moving chariot, to cover all. The atmosphere was sharp with expectation. Later, there was a speech by the chief guest – the then President of India, Shankar Dayal Sharma and some others before Baba gave His divine discourse.

After the morning programme and arati, there was a surprise in store for us. There was to be a special tree planting ceremony, as a symbol for world unity and peace by Baba and the spot for that was just next to where we were seated. The steps leading up there were next to us and when Baba walked up the steps, we were afforded the most unbelievably close darshan on that most impossible of all days. I even imagined Baba give me a quick direct look on His way back to the car. I was thrilled – for whether He looked at me or not, I had got the most fabulous chance to see Him from close, on that very special day.

A lot more was to happen that would have us spinning with excitement. First, we had to go to the Puttaparthi airport to receive Sunil and my sisters arriving in the afternoon. They were coming as Swami's guests in a chartered plane, so it really felt very special. When the small light aircraft became visible in the blue skies of Parthi, I suddenly recalled my dream – the one in which I see Baba chucking a paper plane into the air. This was it! This was the decodation! I marvelled at the way the whole dream had tied up – the paper plane (charter flight) the cricket stadium (Sunil) and the chariot (birthday time.) That dreams of Baba are a stupendous connection and provide an amazing method of information and instruction was again driven home to me. A car had been sent by Swami for Sunil and after exchanging animated 'Sai Rams' with each other, we all headed for the ashram. As Swami's guests, they were driven to the elegant guesthouse and we all wondered whether all this was really happening! Veenu, being part of the entourage, still chuckles about how she bumped into none other than the then president of India on walking out of her room! (At that time, Shanti Bhavan had yet not been constructed and so Sunil and Alvin Kallicharan were put up in the same guesthouse). Even my friend Shanti became part of our group. How this happened was that Subodh, who had not been able to come because of work commitments, offered that extra seat on the plane to her and she was only too thrilled to take up the offer.

A stunning thing happened with Veenu. She was booked to go to Tirupati by train with her husband, immediately after her return from Parthi. In her mind, in jest she told Swami that He had brought her to Parthi by plane but He was sending her to Tirupati by train! That evening, there was a knock on their door in Swami's VIP guest house. It was a doctor from President Shankar Dayal Sharma's entourage. And what he said made Veenu's jaw drop in disbelief. Very courteously, he conveyed the message that the presidential party was going onwards to Tirupati after the birthday celebration in a private aircraft – and that there was one extra seat if anybody wished to avail of it! Such are the kind of sweet things that can happen to Baba's devotees! For the record, Veenu did not avail of the offer as her husband was waiting in Bombay to go with her in the train.

In the guest house, delicious savories were laid out on a dining table and we were all invited to partake of this divine repast, for it was nothing if not divine prasadam. We partook it with a feeling of immense gratitude and humility. With a start, I recalled the words I had heard in my sleep and which had drawn me to Parthi for the birthday celebrations – "I will give you nice, nice dishes to eat..." I felt a warm glow in the region of my heart.

Before we knew it, it was time for the evening function at Vidyagiri Stadium for which Sunil along with Kallicharan was to preside as master of ceremonies. Two cars were sent for us and we were taken to the stadium. Sunil was taken to the stage. We ladies were seated below at a close distance. The stage was set – literally – for the evening's drama to unfold. The colours of the evening were perfect. The lovely flower decorations and lights twinkling all over created a wonderful mood of celebration. When Baba finally came, with expectation at a pitch, all eyes were focused on His slowly moving car and when he alighted, everybody savored the moment of darshan. The programme got underway and Sunil compered the show competently after takings Swami's blessings. There is a lovely photograph, very dear to Sunil, commemorating that moment, when he bent to take Swami's padnamaskar and Swami smiled most lovingly at him and blessed him.

There followed musical performances by renowned artists from the south and also from internationally acclaimed jazz singer from the UK, Dana Gillispi. The specialty of the whole evening was Swami sitting on a beautiful jhula gently swinging watching the proceedings from there. It was a sight for the Gods, especially the manner in which Swami kept His lotus feet tucked together, (as one does on a swing) slightly raised, to accommodate the swinging motion. Every time the jhula swung forward, the devotees in the audience got a divine darshan of the lotus soft soles of Swami's feet! Those marvellous lotus feet that by themselves proclaim divinity. However, total faith is never so easy to come by, however strong maybe the indications of divinity. The ever-powerful maya – being the upadhi of the Lord Himself – forms the very basis of this creation and cannot be easily dispelled. The scriptures tell us that we have to break through it and that can only be so for only a few realized souls at a given time. If we all saw through maya, all at once that very moment, our world as we perceive it, would vanish...and that would not do. The world is a stage, which has been set up by God Himself and is meant to be there for the drama of life to be played out. So, though an avatar displays many signs that indicate His divinity, and in the course of his earthly sojourn, He does marvellous things unendingly, all this massive evidence falters in the face of the powerful maya, when it exerts itself. That is why devotees pray ardently to Lord Ram, that He who is in control of this maya, should protect the devotee from her 'tricks.'

The birthday programme concluded with the musical sisters from the south singing a melodious lori to the Lord, and it was a fitting finale to the grand show. I was on a high, having being able to watch the proceedings in that unique setting under a starlit sky – and most importantly, at a close distance from the stage where Swami was seated.

The cherry on the pudding was getting a small piece of the birthday cake graciously given to me in darshan the next morning by an unknown person sitting next to me. It was a very tiny piece – small in size, big in grace, and I further divided it into as many crumbs as I could to pass it around! Shortly, Swami came by and stopping near us, spoke to my sisters. I found myself looking at His feet, placed just before me, as He stood there talking to the others. I looked up at Him and seeking permission, lightly touched His lotus feet, with devotion. Swami smiled gently and uttered softly the magic word, 'bangaru'. I was ecstatic and that feeling did not diminish all the way back to Bombay.

I tried to hold on as much as I could to that special feeling even in the midst of my worldly activities. What exactly is this feeling? At best, it can be described as being supremely at one with your deepest self, which makes you feel happily in tune with the entire universe. But, this has to be experienced and not read about… For, just as there is no outer limit to divine love, there is no complete definition for it. The only thing one can do, if one is sincere enough, is to pray for it – Oh God, let me know Thee and Thy love…

14

Transformation Of The Heart

A house cluttered with lumber will be dark and without free movement of fresh air. The human body too is a house. Do not allow it to be cluttered with superfluous curios, trinkets or trash.

Sri Sathya Sai

Swami's brand of spirituality is not easy to follow. It is a spirituality, not of words but of action and transformation. Transformation not of the world, but of yourself. It is wonderful to sit in a hall and listen to learned dissertations on the *Gita* and other spiritual texts as it creates a frisson in the mind of the listener. There is a feeling of mental stimulation. The intellectual discussions become an exciting word play – an opiate for the mind. However, in that intoxication sometimes, the main focus may be lost. *"Everything that is not 'you' is an object; it is luggage for the journey; the less of it the more comfortable the journey."*

Swami's spirituality is not couched in sophisticated abstract language. It is in simple words about simple truths. Swami says the highest truths are always the simplest. The spirituality He advocates covers even the small important details that make life more sacred and meaningful. His words like, 'help ever, hurt never', 'love all, serve all', 'start the day with love, fill the day with love, end the day with love' seem so simple but are actually so difficult to follow in our day to day lives. But the beauty is that when one starts on this journey, one thing leads to another and rung by rung the pilgrim ascends higher and higher. *Above all, try to win grace by reforming your habits, reducing your desires and refining your higher nature. One step makes the next one easier. That is the excellence of the spiritual journey. At each step, your strength and confidence increase and you get bigger and bigger installments of grace.*

Knowledge of esoteric religious subjects is one thing but practice of even small spiritual truths is another matter altogether. It is very difficult to change even one small bad habit of ours. Swami tells us that all change has to start with ourselves. *"Sow a seed of good thought, reap a fruit of good action, sow a seed of good action, reap a fruit of good habit, sow a seed of good habit, reap a fruit of good character, sow a seed of good character, reap a fruit of good fortune."* He says that changing our bad habits into good ones, transforms our character piece by piece till the whole picture changes. He emphasizes that there is no point in knowing the *Bhagawad Gita* or any religious text by heart, if one cannot apply even one stanza to one's life. What can God gain by your knowing a spiritual text by heart? He is not interested in your ability to memorize! So, what does He want? *Not, this holding a garland in the hand and indulging in paltry conservations in holy places. I do not want nor do I appreciate anyone bringing flowers and fruits in my presence. Bring Me the fragrant flower of a pure heart and the fruit of a sadhana mellowed mind: that is what I like most, not these things available outside yourselves for so much of cash, without any effort that elevates the mind.*

Thus, just knowing the scriptures is not enough and does not a jnani make. There is a story of a Muslim pir Luqman, reciting a religious text loudly and with intense feeling. A learned Muslim priest accosts him and asks him a little sarcastically whether he understood what he was reciting. Luqman, with a blissful expression answered that he had no need to understand it – for his God perfectly understood it! And it was for Him that he was reciting! Thus, intellectual stimulation can become a block. The idea is not to activate the mind but to still it. That is why Swami says, "die-mind" – is the real diamond for a spiritual seeker!

Another point Swami repeatedly emphasizes is the need for building self-confidence. In his inimitable way, He says, "Self-confidence leads to self-satisfaction which leads to self-sacrifice that leads to self-realization."

Self-esteem remains one of the most important values. This has nothing to do with external achievements, which are rated by the world. There is a very fine line between self-esteem and false pride. False pride or vanity is pegged on external praise. Self-esteem is entirely an inner experience, a knowing, a one to one between you and yourself. Nobody, but nobody, can give you self worth. It proceeds from within and it comes from a deep-seated inner communion with the spirit which subtly communicates to you the precious value of self – *your* self. It commands you to acknowledge your own worth. This attitude can come only from believing God's word that He made us in His own image. That we are all sparks of the divine. This does not mean one is perfect or flawless. Of course not. But imperfections and flaws are part of His divine design. The idea is to polish them and reassert the innate purity that is our true nature. The whole play of life is just that – a battle between the apparent 'good' and 'bad' – the kurukshetra of the Bhagavad Gita is only a metaphor for this basic duel of life. In this ongoing battle, we humans ever so often, lose again and again – till we win. Losing is only a step to success. One must never lose the spirit. The *atma* within is ever untarnished and pure. One should have the feeling that King Porus from our history lessons had, when he lost in battle to the mighty Alexander. The Greek monarch asked Porus as to how he should treat him in defeat. Porus squarely answered, head held high, "Treat me, as one king should treat another…."

I *love* that story. It is one of my favourites from history lessons in school. We may often feel vanquished but must never forget that we are all Porus' or kings in spirit. Keeping that in mind, we should think, speak and act. We should live up to our divine heritage.

15

Happiness Is Union With God

"There is only one Hero and that is God. However, zero by the side of one becomes ten, which has value. You may be a zero but you acquire value when you turn to God."

Sri Sathya Sai

You and I have spoken all these words, but as for the way we have to go, words are no preparation.

Jelaluddin Rumi

In October 1996, Sunil expressed his desire to visit Parthi for Swami's blessings. We sisters were not to be left behind. Luckily, we managed to arrange things on the home front so that we could all make it. My husband and his family, remained ever supportive and understanding of my frequent trips. It was only on the odd occasion when it appeared I was overdoing it that he would express mild reservation on the issue. But strangely, he could never get himself really upset – no doubt because his heart too was melting towards Baba.

Landing in Parthi, we had no idea of what an epic trip it was going to be. At that time, we sisters had not been initiated into wearing sarees and we normally wore plain churidar-kurtas in muted colours to darshan. So it was, that we trooped into darshan in our churidar-kurtas and awaited Baba's arrival. In darshan, a Sai devotee friend told us how Swami preferred lady devotees to wear sarees. "When you go to a temple on a festival occasion, how do you dress?" she asked us. She continued, "Every day here is a festival, and we have the living God giving darshan in this temple..." Swami says, "*In the shelter of the Lord, transform every moment into a sacred celebration.*" We got the message. (From the next trip onwards we started wearing our best sarees).

Swami came by, looked at my elder sister and then walked on. After finishing the men's round He walked on to the verandah. A minute later, we saw that Sunil was standing on the edge of the verandah, looking towards the ladies section. Now, that is always a big moment. For, when a male member of a family looks searchingly from the verandah towards the ladies section, it is usually a signal for the ladies of the family to get up and make their way to the interview room. We were so nonplussed by this sudden development that we just kept sitting for a moment or two, wondering what to do. The helpful sevadals then told us urgently, "get up, go" and only then did we realize what was happening. We jumped up and in an excited flurry made our way to the verandah.

The feeling of 'that walk' is quite beyond compare. It is something you may have waited for, for years and years – for whatever reason. Reasons can be plenty – pressing personal problems for one – considering if there is anybody who can ease them, it is Him. However, there can be other reasons too. Like the simple one of just wanting to get the experience of Baba's divine proximity.... And at that stage of my life, I fell into that category. Apart from the desire of seeing Him from close quarters and being in His immediate aura, there was no other thought. I suppose this is what the scriptures describe as the pull of spirit. This attraction to spirit is the basic nature of every human soul. When the time is right, it just manifests.

So there we were, walking with quickened steps to the verandah. Quite like a dream! Swami, as is His wont, was waiting there on one side like the perfect Host of hosts. Very graciously, we were ushered into the interview room.

There was a large Russian group inside and we were right at the back of the small room. Everybody's face reflected joy – Swami's most of all. He looked completely radiant. Sitting down on His chair in the corner, He called Sunil to His side. He patted him lightly and checked whether he was wearing something around his neck or not. He waved His hand and materialized a navratan mala for him. This was the second such mala, Swami having given one earlier in Sunil's cricketing days. Swami then spoke a bit to the whole assembly of people in general terms. He took in the other groups one by one into the inner room, while the rest of us waited in the hushed atmosphere outside. Shortly, Swami emerged through the door, pushing the curtain aside.

It was our turn to go inside. His fond affection for Sunil was evident right from the beginning. Though we sisters sat in a semi-circle around him, with Sunil on the far side, it was to him that He gave most of His attention! When the talk of diamonds came up in some context, He pointed to Sunil and said, "He is my diamond…!" Sunil, in his yogic way remained equipoised by the sweet compliment; it was we sisters who got bowled over by it. Understatement has never been our forte, and our collective expression to things can sometimes be a bit overpowering.

After a few personal questions pertaining to the family, Swami materialised a beautiful gold chain with a heart-shaped pendant of 'OM' for Mashu. We felt delighted at His loving gesture. Mashu's face reflected absolute joy. He opened the clasp of the chain and helped her put it on. This made it even more special!

Pammi then requested Swami to pay a visit sometime to our home in Kanpur. At this, with a straight face, Swami said, "Kanpur? Why I have come there very often," (*bahut ayaa hai..*). We presumed His statement to mean that He travels in spirit all the time. But then, He placed His little finger on His nose, spanned His palm across His cheek to touch His ear with His thumb, and said, "See, easy!" (ear is 'kaan' in Hindi and nose is 'naak' – so He showed how easily one could cover the distance between Nagpur and Kanpur!). There was a spontaneous burst of laughter at Swami's little joke. Swami then materialized a ring for Pammi, which, however, was a story to have a sequel later in the day. He put the ring on her index finger.

All the while, I had been sitting quietly on one side of Swami's chair not having uttered a word. There was a break in the conversation and I heard my voice. The words just came out – "Swami, I want to make you happy…" I had not pre-meditated on saying this. It took everyone, including me, by surprise. Maybe, Swami's teaching, *the joy that you cause in the heart of God is the only worthwhile achievement,* had really found its place in my heart. There was a pause, and then Swami looked at me and said simply, "Be happy…." He then gave some precious gems on the subject of happiness – how it was not outside us anywhere, but within our hearts and in our own minds – *Dil mein, man mein, ghar mein nahin* – not in the material *samsar*. He concluded His little talk on happiness, by saying, "Happiness is union with God…" He also said that it was important to, "be happy always".

Swami then made affectionate enquiries about our parents in Kanpur. He referred to them as "your sweet parents", which really thrilled us, that He should remember them so lovingly. When towards the end of the interview my sister sought blessings for the whole family, He said, "yes, yes" but also added that the ideal prayer would be to seek blessings for the whole world – *Loka samastha sukhino bhavantu*……. For all were basically one large family. He told Sunil and Pammi that He would come to their house in Bombay. He also mentioned something about how He would perform Sunil's sixtieth year *shashtipoorti* ceremony for them which is equivalent to a spiritual remarriage.

Once in the outer room again, Swami went into a little ante-room and came out with a couple of His robes. He graciously gave one to the Russian group who had requested it for their center in Russia. With the second one He played a little game. The four of us were standing at the back and He glanced over us, as if debating whom to give it to! We looked eagerly at Him and He mischievously played dodge-ball, pretending to throw it to one but flinging it to another! It came flying across to Veenu (third in the line). She was ecstatic! He looked at the rest of us and made that crestfallen expression, '*ayyo pappum*' and went right back to the ante-room. He came out with a fresh pile of neatly ironed soft orange robes for the rest of us. We were delighted, with the robes as also the manner in which He had given them to us. Getting His robe from His very own hands was the stuff dreams were made of and in this case, literally so, because a couple or so years back I had dreamt of it. *In that dream I am actually wearing an orange robe like Swami's and He looks at me appreciatively saying, "Ah...." with a pleased smile. I look at Him in the dream and say, "It's mine", to which He responds softly, "I know". I then say, "It's very soft...."*

Holding on to the robes and the vibhuti packets, with bright faces we streamed out of the interview room. Back in the room, we expressed our excitement by going over the events. We didn't tire of recreating the whole scenario over and over and dwelling upon the nuances. Pammi felt just a trifle disturbed that the ring Swami gave her was for the index finger. She kept fiddling with it and mentioning how she was not used to wearing a ring on that finger. She tried putting it on her ring finger but it did not fit.

That evening, we sat in darshan, still beaming with joy. We couldn't believe it when Swami came and then called us for another interview! It never rains but pours, they say, and by the end of it we were drenched in Swami's grace.

Second time around, there were far fewer people in the interview room. We all got to sit close to Swami's chair. That little room, as soon as you enter it, hits you with its divine vibrations. The atmosphere is concentrated. You feel different. It is the kind of feeling you get in the garbha-graha or innermost sanctum of any holy place. Even non-believers have to concede that there is something undeniably different in the immediate presence of Swami in that room. If you say He is a guru/swami/sage/holy man/God-man/saint, none of these descriptions really fit the bill. He defies categorization. In his own words, He is unknowable, indescribable and beyond measure. *Do not try to measure Me; you will only fail. Try rather to discover your own measure. Then you will better succeed in discovering My measure.*

I was lucky to be sitting close to Swami's chair just by His side. I never expected, however, that Swami would address me. He did. Turning His head towards me, He asked softly, "What is devotion?" A moment to savour. I looked steadily into His dark deep eyes and said, in as even a tone I could, "Swami, devotion is love for God......" Swami smiled with satisfaction and said emphatically, "Yes..." It appeared I had got it right.

It was a simple enough reply, which even a child could have given, but it becomes different when the reference point of anything is Him. Simple questions, simple answers, a look, all acquire deep significance in relation with Him. Words like, 'wait wait', 'very happy', 'I will see', 'when did you come', 'where are you from' would appear innocuous to the lay person, uninitiated in Swami's ways of communication with His devotees. Swami's often says that He does not waste even a single word and even that spoken in jest, has a significant import. Each and every word and gesture of Swami counts. Swami says so much, in so little and we say so little in so much! For instance, 'wait wait' can mean a day, a month or a span of many years. 'Where have you come from?' can pertain to geographical location or have a deeper spiritual connotation relating to the supreme source from where we have all come. 'I will see', could mean a private audience with Him or just that He will look into the matter – at His pace and in His time. This is a key understanding devotees have to reach by and by. His time scale is different to ours and His words have significance and weight far beyond our human understanding. We have to pay attention to every word of His, for it is worth its weight in gold. That is why, I had every reason to feel elated at Swami's 'Yes', to my answer on devotion.

Swami then spoke at length on the subject of devotion and how it was different from all other kinds of worldly love or attachment. This relationship with God is the only permanent one, being the eternal relationship between atma and paramatma. Everything in the world is transient, and our highest endeavour should be to attach ourselves to the one unchanging reality – God. Love for family members, though desirable, qualifies as attachment and only love for God qualifies as true love, which alone gives supreme bliss. Swami further elaborated, "Devotion is a deep ocean...."

I kept nodding my head to His words but it would be a long journey to reaching their fullest realization in my life. At one point, in the course of His talk on devotion, He suddenly turned to me and asked me, "How is husband?" He then went on, "Worldly life is transient, like passing clouds...... Joy, sorrow, everything will pass by, yes?" He looked at me questioningly and repeated that "Yes?", as if seeking my response. Vehemently I nodded my head and said, "Yes", at which He imitated the tone of my 'yes', mimicking my voice and made a classic statement. To this day, my Sai friends tease me about that one! Swami said with a twinkle in His eye, "*Haan, bolne mein hero, karne mein zero.....*" (a hero in speaking, a zero in doing). There was a burst of laughter in the interview room and mine was the loudest. I loved His pulling me up like that! And it was so true.

All my life my biggest problem has been my positive ease with just 'being' rather than 'doing'. I have grown up spending hours on my verandah watching the passage of raindrops from the sky and their dalliance with the leaves in the garden before falling to the ground below. A Chinese philosopher, Lin Yutang wrote a famous book called *The Importance of Doing Nothing*, and I loved the title, though I never got down to reading the book. I suppose I didn't need to. The distilled essence of my life's philosophy was in the title of that book. In stillness, in quiet, in solitude, I experienced the greatest ease and sense of well-being. This was before Swami came consciously into my life. After He came, it was His smaran that replaced all previous states of well-being and euphoria. It dawned on me that the Creator is infinitely more beautiful than His creation and that in seeking Him all is sought and all is gained. However, Swami, the divine teacher, gave a new turn to my understanding. In simple words, He made me see that action has to be undertaken and one can't afford to be poetic about laziness!

With relation to the talk on devotion, Swami said of me, "Devotion hai, but sometimes mind wavers, monkey mind." He told me to dedicate all my actions to God, "Whatever you do, do for God...."

Talking on the subject of worry, Swami said, "What is the shape of worry? Worry has no shape. No eyes, no legs, no hands. Worry does not catch us. We go and catch worry." He also spoke of the alternating experience of pleasure and pain in life, how they were two sides of the same coin. "What is awareness?" He asked, showing us His handkerchief. He first showed just the corner of the hanky and then the whole of it. He then said, "Total picture is awareness." I decoded that to mean that the bit of the hanky is our humanness, our body senses, etc., which we take to be our full reality. However, that is only partial awareness, the total picture is that we are divine.

"Which is bigger, the number one or the number nine?" He answered it Himself saying, "one is bigger, because it is one plus one plus one and so on which makes the number nine or any number however big. Without the one there cannot be more – all comes from the One."

He suddenly turned to Pammi and asked her for the ring He had given her in the morning. Pammi froze! Was He taking it back because she had complained? She took off the ring reluctantly. Even as she did so, Swami said, "I know, I know….. *kaun se finger mein pehna diya*… (which finger has He put it on?) whole day complaining…" Devotees just love it, when He reveals His omniscience in these small things. We beamed at His all-knowingness. Swami took the ring, then blew on it. He then put it on her ring finger – the perfect fit!

When our turn came to go into the inner room, Swami came and stood before us and indicating the door with a sweep of His hands said a little mischievously, "*Chaliye ji*" to us. We all laughed because of the manner in which He said it. Swami looked at Sunil and the others present and said with an amused smile – "Ladies, hysteria……"

Inside, some personal advice was sought and Swami guided us on those matters. Veenu mentioned her small children – son, Shiv and daughter, Shaina and expressed some worry over the naughtiness of her sharp-witted little daughter. Swami joked, "No, no, but then she is just like you! And the mental age is the same also no?!" How we laughed at that.

It had been a wonderful day. After years sometimes, comes along a day like this and it remains with you forever. We left the interview room and couldn't stop talking. Two interviews in a single day – our first in Parthi – after a period of twenty years. It had been in 1976 that we had made our first trip to Parthi in a group of nine family members.

16

Chitchora

Whenever, and wherever, you put yourself in touch with God, that is the state of meditation.

Sri Sathya Sai

As much as you may want, time does not stop still when you are in proximity to the Form. Very soon you are out in the world again and the realities of day to day life descend. Then, the real spiritual effort starts, the idea being to spiritualise your daily life and cultivate equipoise in the face of the trials and tribulations of life. It is only the evolved souls who can 'let go' of worldly worries. Problems of all kinds are ever attached to life, and if one problem is solved the next one is not far behind. So what is the trick? Only one. Problems won't change or stop coming but we can change our approach to them and stop receiving them in the way we do. *"Give each problem the attention it deserves but do not allow it to overpower you. Anxiety will not solve any problem. Coolness comes from detachment. Above all, believe in God, and the efficacy of prayer.* We show lack of trust in God by worrying. Swami says,

"When you worry about your problem, why should I?" True surrender is placing your worries at His feet for God never lets His devotee down. However, His wisdom decides how and in what manner He will help – not always as you may want it.

The subtle 'in-swing' in my lifestyle started manifesting more now. Our pattern of eating out practically every weekend started changing and being at home became a soothing alternative to outings. Even earlier, before Baba came into my life, socializing had been a kind of compulsory drill, with my heart never in it. Now, I took every opportunity for *satsang* and spending more and 'more time' with Baba. Now, nothing gave me as much joy.

I told Subodh that Swami had enquired after him. He tried not to show it but I knew that in his own way, he was secretly thrilled at Swami mentioning him. Who wouldn't be? I had always wanted my husband to turn to Swami and discover His love. Swami was sowing the seed and it would germinate at the right time. My daughters had less of an option, as far as Swami was concerned! They just grew up with Him in the house! However, it was never thrust on them – as much as they wanted, in the time that they did. It can sometimes work quite in the opposite way if something, even if it is good, is forcibly thrust on you. Feelings cannot be forced, they must sprout spontaneously if they are to have lasting substance. The climate for this can be created, and then it just happens on its own – the way we see it happening on such a large and wondrous scale, with Balvikas children round the world.

One of the first things I did was to enroll my children in Balvikas. Luckily, along with my neighbour and friend Shanti, we started a class in our building itself. This channel of Balvikas is a most magical one for children to enable them to discover their divinity and connection to God, and I feel most grateful and thankful for it. Children grow to love God spontaneously, not just because their parents or any other senior member of their household wants them to do so. They develop their own personal relationship with a loving God. Swami says, "*Rules engender rigidity and force. They do not bloom out of love or spread love. There is always a way of doing a thing without the strain of a rule. Find that way.*" Loving instruction is the hallmark of *Balvikas* teaching. 'You can take a horse to the water but you cannot make it drink', holds true in this as in any other matter. Also, if it has to happen, it will, and if it doesn't, nothing will make it...

There are so many cases where, in a family, only one or two members are believers and the rest skeptical or noncommittal. It is not anybody's fault I think, just the play of karma as also the readiness of the particular person for spiritual experience. Also, in this case, there is a further angle – of recognizing and accepting Sri Sathya Sai Baba as the avatar and not a mere 'guru'. Once that is done, the challenges only multiply! Marvellous stories, miracles galore apart, the all pervasive and powerful maya never lets go. A small disappointment, a failure, a loss, and one's belief gets shaky, and this, even though there is loads of evidence standing stock-piled all the while, proving the avatar's divinity. Initially, there is always a mistaken notion that He will solve all our problems with a magic wand and that if only we can muster the appropriate faith and reverence, our lives will become entirely problem-free. Of course, it is not like that. He is here not to take away the problems, but only to guide us to tackling them in the best way possible. Welcome everything, Baba says, and say yes to both happiness and sorrow because both are a composite part of our human experience and one cannot be felt without the other. The spiritual goal is to go beyond both these transitory states and reach that plane of equipoise and balance where there is sameness of reaction to both. This can come only from true awareness. Baba says, "Passing clouds...neither exult nor lament, see it all for the dream that it is."

The children joining Balvikas pleased my husband as he felt that it would bring more discipline into their lives. He readily accepted that the work Baba was doing was on an epic scale and that nobody could fault that. When the children sang a bhajan or recited Sanskrit shlokas, he looked happy and proud.

In this way, slowly but surely, Baba's influence became more and more pervasive and persuasive in our house. Our scriptures have given the name –chitchora (stealer of hearts) to God not for nothing! It is done with such subtle divine stealth, that before one realises) it has happened and then there is no looking back. In fact, in the case of my husband, it was really a case of chitchora. There is a heart-stirring rendition of the bhajan, '*Chitchora, Yashodha ke baal*', by a female singer in the Madhuram series of audio cassettes, which I once picked up in Parthi. My husband fell in love with this bhajan. He was so captivated by the words and the pure soulful singing that he would hear this bhajan over and again. Even I loved it as I felt it had the power to move us deeply. Both Subodh and I also loved country music. There was a particular number by country singer, Randy Travis, 'Forever and Forever, Amen,' that was 'our song' and we never tired of hearing it. Now, however, even that slipped to second place with 'Chitchora' stealing its way to the top! This bhajan touched my husband in his innermost core and subsequently drew him closer and closer to Baba.

17

"Why Do We Love You So Much?"

God has the quality of attraction and attracts to Himself whatever is good. Iron alone attracts the magnet because of its relationship with the magnet. The magnet can be compared to Paramatma *(Supreme Soul) and iron can be compared to the individual soul.*

Sri Sathya Sai

In 1996, we were unable to attend Swami's birthday celebrations. However, prior to that, in the month of October, Veenu and I managed a seven day trip.

That was truly Veenu's trip! For the week that we were there, Swami spoke or interacted with her almost in every darshan. This went on day after day, darshan after darshan. In one, Veenu even asked Swami, "Swami, why do we love You so much? At that Swami turned and in an imperious right royal tone said, "It is My nature..."

At another time, when Veenu asked Him for padnamaskar, with a mischievous tone He asked, "*Kai ko*?" (why so?). Veenu answered that because she was His devotee. At that Swami asked her even more mischievously, "Those sitting at the back –are they not devotees?"

During this whole week of amazing interaction, between Swami and Veenu, I was the silent spectator! For me it was wonderful just to have Swami stop by each day. It gave me all the opportunity to get the darshans I so loved. Then, one day, towards the end of the trip, in His usual way Swami stopped by the spot where we were seated. Veenu was in the first row and I was behind her. Swami stood just before us – and then He looked at me direct and said softly, "Good girl...." I looked up at Him with my usual smile. He repeated this "good girl" again. I smiled broader. Swami was looking straight into my eyes while speaking. And, He went on speaking! Again and again, He repeated, 'Good girl'. Incredibly, He said this about nine times, each time in a different intonation and tone! Finally He said it to Veenu, indicating towards me. So Veenu smiled and looked up at Him. He asked her with a note of insistence, "Is she a good girl?" At that Veenu said, "Yes Swami, she is a good girl..." All this naturally took a while and everybody seated there got a prolonged darshan. When Swami finally moved on, down the line a couple of foreigner ladies who were witness to the interaction, expressed their wonder at it. They said they had rarely seen a darshan like that one before! Interestingly, I had seen this scenario in a dream prior to the trip. *In the dream, Swami stops by in darshan and looks into my eyes and then speaks to me. It is a long significant exchange. When he moves on, a foreigner lady tells me, "We saw the look He gave you..."*

On the second last day of that trip, Swami came to where we were seated and asked, "*Kabhi jata*?" (when are you leaving). Veenu very spontaneously, gave an unconventional reply. She spoke our heart! She said, "Swami, *man nahin karta (jane ko)*...." (one doesn't feel like leaving). Swami did not let that pass. He too gave an unexpected and unusual reply. With his one hand pressing down in the air, He gestured the signal of 'keep sitting'. Then in clear tones, He said, "*pratishtith raha, pratishtith raha*...." He said this twice, both times making the gesture with His hand. After that He walked on. Veenu was a bit confounded by that and so was I. What exactly did He mean? And what did '*pratishtith*' mean? After darshan, we discussed it and were told that it meant, 'stay fixed', or something to that effect. We were also told that we ought to take permission before leaving since it appeared Swami had said 'to stay'.

Next morning, Veenu wrote a letter to Swami asking for permission to leave. She felt a little disturbed with the previous day's interaction. Swami must have understood the turmoil in our minds, for He came straight and took the letter. He also gave the permission by Himself saying, "*jaata hai*?" (leaving are you?) and then added for good measure, "good bye...."

To this day, we have not fully understood that interaction. Maybe it was a lesson to weigh our words when we speak to Swami (this applies to thoughts too). We may speak or think lightly, but Swami takes every word of His devotees seriously.

Veenu has had some other amazing experiences. Once during a whole trip, Swami ignored her completely. Every darshan, she kept hoping that He would look towards her. On the last day of the trip, with not a single look having come her way, she mentally told Swami that at least that day He should come straight to her – "like a magnet", she thought. Well, Swami came in for darshan but ignored her again. Feeling dejected, she was sitting near the mandir after darshan, when a Sai friend approached her. Enthusiastic 'Sai Rams' were exchanged. The friend had a small plastic bag in her hands, from which she took out something and gave it to Veenu. It was a photo of Swami, but a very special kind. In this context, very, very special. Handing it, she said, "This photo of Swami's is actually a magnet....!" Veenu's expression had to be seen to be believed! "What?" she said, her face lighting up with joy. She could hardly believe it. She thanked her friend effusively. Through the instrument of her friend, Swami *had* come to her – 'like a magnet'!

Another time, after Swami gave us an interview in the morning, He stopped by, near where Veenu was seated. A lady from behind, who was a resident of the ashram, asked Swami loudly for prasad. Swami did not respond immediately, but after crossing one or two ladies, He looked at Veenu and told her enigmatically, "*Tum usko do*...", ("you give her") indicating the lady who had asked for prasad. After darshan, Veenu immediately sought out that lady and gave a packet of vibhuti from the interview room as prasad, as directed by Swami.

Veenu's two small children, Shiv and Shaina have also been drawn into Swami's stream of love. For every trip and every birthday of Swami's they make it a point to sit for hours, making cards for Swami, which they send along with their mother. The cards are a blaze of attractive colours and cutest poems on Swami, which touch the heart! Every time, to this day, Swami has made it a point to take these cards, sometimes in the most unexpected ways. Once, in the interview room, He opened the cards in front of us and with a pleased expression read them from top to bottom!

How keen is Swami's gaze and how aware He is, of who is in darshan and who is not, was made more than clear to us one day, on another trip with Mashu. Mashu, who was feeling a bit exhausted, decided to miss one darshan and rest it out. Swami came towards Pammi and asked her right away, "Where is sister?" Pammi stuttered something as an excuse, "Swami, not well – in room". At that Swami made a 'hmmph' sound suggesting 'tell me another!' Phew! Immediately after Swami walked into the interview room, Pammi made a dash to the room and told Mashu how Swami had missed her in darshan and enquired after her. That gave Mashu all the energy she needed! She was up in a trice, all exhaustion forgotten, and she got ready to make it back for the bhajan darshan. After bhajans and arati, when Swami walked back, Mashu was back in her spot! On His way out, Swami gave a dramatic acknowledgement, by giving Mashu an unbelievable look. He stopped at the corner, before turning left to Poornachandra, and directed a very pointed and amused look to Mashu, who was looking anything but sick! In fact, she was now glowing like a bulb!

Another time, Veenu's close friend, Shailaja was called for an interview in Prasanthi. Veenu was, at that time, sitting outside in darshan. At one point in the interview, Shailaja closed her eyes and made a silent prayer for Veenu. At that, Swami looked at her and said, "Yes, your friend, sitting outside…" Shailaja couldn't believe it! She said, "Yes, yes, Swami, Veenu…." Later, when Shailaja recounted the story, Veenu was understandably ecstatic hearing about it!

Baba once materialized a gold chain and pendant with his visage for Veenu, which is her cherished talisman till today.

In February 1997, my parents came to Bombay on a visit. It had been over twenty years since they had set foot on the soil of Parthi. As there was a direct flight now to Parthi from Bombay, it was an ideal opportunity to make a trip with them. On 23rd February, my parents, Sunil and us daughters, flew down to Parthi.

The flight takes just over an hour. On a beautiful day with cloud clusters sailing in the blue sky, we touched down at Parthi.

By Baba's grace, that trip with our parents, went off very smoothly and everything was taken care of. Accommodation, food, etc. We had felt a trifle keyed-up on their count because of their age and health factor. But we needn't have worried. The divine Host had thought of everything!

How much – we learnt, when Baba called us in for an interview. It felt very special – to be able to walk in *along with* our parents…

Inside, Baba right away turned his attention to my father. He asked him his name. My father answered, "B.L. Mehrotra". Baba repeated the surname and then told us how He had once stayed for one and a half months with General Malhotra in Kashmir.

Taking the cue, we invited Him to grace the house of this Mehrotra too! This invitation hung in the air and we looked at Him eagerly. In the expectant silence, a voice rose from the back corner of the interview room – yours truly! – asking Him, whether He would come?

It must have been something in my tone or expression or just the hint of innocent precociousness of the question, which made

Swami actually laugh out. His eyes sparkled. With His one hand He indicated towards me as if to say, 'look at what she's saying – as if it's so easy...!' The word He actually spoke was just, "Easy..." But it indicated that whole meaning.

A little later on being asked about what He thought of the devotees' love for Him, He declared, "I don't think....I am Love". Earlier, we had asked Him to sing a bhajan and He had demurred saying, He didn't have the throat for it! Now, He burst into the bhajan, *'Love is my form, bliss is my food...'* in the softest, most dulcet tones imaginable.

My parents asked some personal questions. He gave guidance and directions on these. To one gentleman Baba spoke of the preyas and shreyas factor. The gist of His talk was how creature comforts of airconditioned lifestyles was nothing compared to real atma ananda. He spoke for a while on atma ananda and said, "You have it – you are actually the embodiment of it, of love and peace."

At the end of the interview, Baba blessed my parents. When He asked my father about his health, he answered, "Baba, good...." At that, Baba rejoindered, "Not good, not bad". He patted my father's cheek lovingly. When my father bent to take padnamaskar, Baba patted his back many times, saying, "*bahut khush, bahut khush*" (very happy, very happy). He *did* look very happy. He said to my father, "*Santosh, santosh*". After that, we clicked several photos. Baba posed, smiling radiantly into the camera!

We, as a family, felt extremely grateful for the love He showered on our parents on that trip.

18

Into The Magic Circle

In the golden city of the heart, dwells the Lord of love, without parts, without stain. Know Him as the radiant light of lights. He is the light reflected by all. He shining, everything shines after Him.

Sri Sathya Sai

On all trips, the first darshan always holds the greatest charm. This is because after a lapse of time (days, months) one gets the chance to behold the divine form again. Of all first darshans, there's one I will never forget. It was on Ladies Day, in the year 1997 during the birthday celebrations.

The Ladies Day – 19th November of every year (incidentally, the birth anniversary of India's late prime minister, Indira Gandhi) – was ordained by Baba, to underline that greatness has no gender. On this day, lady devotees enjoy certain privileges in the mandir, normally reserved for men. They get to sit on the hallowed front verandah, normally a male preserve. Swami's discourse on that day has a lady translator. Even the chanting of the vedic mantras, normally a very tight male preserve, is also done by venerable female devotees. No action of Baba's is without a deep meaning. In this gesture of Ladies Day is implicit the important message that ultimately, all are one – and that male and female are merely roles in the cosmic drama, the soul being gender-free.

That year saw us reach Parthi on 19th November. It was late evening when we walked a little breathlessly into the mandir for our first darshan that day. The mandir was magnificently lit and the devotees splendidly attired for the occasion already seated for darshan. There was a rustle of silk all around to which even we contributed, having discarded the churidar-kurtas for kanjivaram or temple sarees! There was enchantment in the air. We were led up to the front near the hallowed verandah. There was a golden pool of light created by the ladies seated there. This was because they were wearing resplendent red and gold sarees gifted by Swami. The brilliant lights falling on their saree pallavs created a reddish-golden glow all around them. It felt magical.

On the occasion of His birthday every year, Swami gives sarees to ladies who are fortunate to be doing His work in some capacity or the other. Every year, Swami Himself selects the sarees giving us a fine example of His attention to every detail. Of all the lovely sarees Swami has given down the years, I never found a saree more gorgeous or riveting than that particular one. Never having been much of a saree person, till then, that saree nevertheless caught my eye. Maybe seeing a whole bevy of ladies wearing it together created special effects!

There was an expectant hush that signals Swami's presence in the vicinity. Myriad lights twinkled all over and elegant flower arrangements adorned every nook and corner. My heart beat faster as we settled down to await Him. Suddenly, Swami appeared, coming out from the interview room. It was my first darshan after a long gap. His appearance lit up the surroundings as nothing else can. Looking at Him, I wondered if there was anything else to seek? Yes, there was – to see His radiant smile again – not necessarily at me, but to anybody. The wish must have come straight from my heart, for shortly I got an incredible smile darshan. It was after the santoor recital by Pandit Shiv Kumar Sharma, for which were present also, our late Vice President Krishen Kumar and his aged mother (over ninety years old). Swami came right up to his mother who was seated on a chair very close to me. She wanted to do namaskar to Swami, but because of her age was unable to bend easily. Swami himself bent over and solicitously assisted her. While doing so, He gave her the most extraordinarily radiant smile. I watched rapt, because it seemed that Swami's whole face was bathed in pure light. How quickly my wish had been granted!

The birthday dawned bright and beautiful. Festival days in Parthi are always charged, but the birthday is especially so. The faces of devotees are brighter, their step quicker and their hearts more hopeful. That day, after being seated we were unable to do our normal japa and meditation in darshan as we couldn't help but watch the grand spectacle all around. The path from Poornachandra into the mandir was carpeted with flowers and we wondered what colour robe Swami would wear. On the birthday, there is always that little suspense before He appears, about the colour of His robe. Swami often wears a different coloured robe to His usual orange one.

The moment finally came and the boys started playing the band. Swami emerged in a yellow robe – *pitambar dhari* Sai Krishna – and everybody arched forward to catch that first glimpse. Swami walked, rather glided through the darshan crowd with a gentle smile on His face and a benedictory glance. There was the usual gala birthday cake awaiting Him on the verandah, made by the Italian group every year. Swami lit the candle and cut the cake to the joy of the assembled devotees. What a special 'birthday party'!

Later on in the day, we were delighted to receive five small pieces of the birthday cake as prasad brought for us specially by our dear friend, K Subramaniam, who stays in the ashram. Naturally, we felt

Swami had sent it for us! In the ashram, devotees take every act to come directly from Swami because they know that things happen here for a reason. It is so everywhere, out in the world too, but in the concentrated atmosphere of the ashram and in the proximity of Baba, the awareness is brought into sharp focus. Later in the day, something was to happen which would emphasise this further. Veenu, while going for dinner, was met by Mr. Chiranjeevi Rao in the foyer of Shanti Bhavan. Very courteously, he handed her two sarees, saying they were from Swami. He also added, "One is for Mrs. Gavaskar, and the other for you." This was no chance occurrence – it was all to Swami's plan – who has to get what, when, where.....

It was thrilling for the family to receive the sarees from Swami, those lovely red and gold ones which I had admired earlier. Next morning saw the two of them proudly wear them. If the two other sisters felt just a little left out, they needn't have, because just a year later they were to be similarly blessed by Swami. It really is His drama the whole way. He scripts the plot, He gives the turns and twists, as and when. We have to just go along with the Master Director's plans.

19

Cricketing Tales From Fairland

The universe is the field where God sports.

Sri Sathya Sai

A cricket match? At Prasanthi?

The game of cricket is deified in India and has many votaries. In India, people are not just fond of cricket, they are devoted to it. And cricket is a metaphor for life itself. One of the popular sayings attached to cricket is – its glorious uncertainty. But if there is anything that is even more gloriously uncertain than cricket, it is what Baba will do next. He says, "Love My uncertainty…" One had better! Because, one can never say with Swami. Things keep happening here in Parthi, in so many new ways….

Prasanthi Nilayam had been buzzing for a while now with Swami's plans to host an international cricket match, 'The Unity Cup'. Finally, a date for the match was set and announced. The match was to be played at the Vidyagiri stadium. Predictably, there was a lot of excitement at this unusual precedent being set in the spiritual abode of Puttaparthi.

Swami made Sunil, in his capacity as a national cricketer of repute, one of the important instruments for organizing this event. There was a lot of liaison work, co-ordination of dates, etc. to be done with many international cricketers. Sunil and Pammi, with Baba's blessings, threw themselves into the task, putting everything else aside. They felt honoured with the chance to do something for Him.

Round the clock activities started to get the stage – in this case, the field –ready for the event. To get a cricket pitch and ground ready at short notice requires tremendous planning and expertise. But as we have seen down the years, anything – be it a super specialty hospital, or a water project – can be got ready, with Swami's blessings. Swami, known for His eye to detail, oversaw the preparations minutely, through every stage. He would drive down often, after darshan to the Vidyagiri stadium. He showed, by example, the need for personal attention to any task. He also inspired and recharged, with darshan, the numerous people working hard on the job.

It was in connection with this cricket event that Swami gave us the delightful opportunity to be instruments for bringing out a souvenir. A month ago.Mashu had had a dream, which predicted this entire event of the souvenir! That was the time she felt that she was going through a phase where things were just not working out. She did not want to take any step without the 'concurrence' of Swami. When Pammi told her over the phone in Kanpur about how she should get cracking on ideas for the souvenir, she demurred. She said she would only do it after checking it out with Him. That night, Swami gave her the dream. *In the dream, Baba is talking to her informally like a friend. He tells her, "I think I am ready for a media presentation". At that Mashu says, "You mean something like an album." "No," says Swami. "I was thinking more in the nature of a book". "Oh," Mashu responds. Swami continues, "the title will be,* Tales from Fairland...'. *you will be working on it with two others. When you come here, I will introduce you to them.*" That decided the matter for her and she happily got down to the task given to us by Swami.

Tales from Fairland. The title, I thought was very enchanting. It could have come only from Him. However, though we all loved the title, we felt a bit doubtful about it passing muster. "Fairland?" We could imagine the raised eyebrows, "What – land?" Maybe if we could make the title clearer, we could get around the problem. In the introductory write-up for the book, we explained briefly the context of 'Fairland'. We said how India was the 'Fairland', where noble virtues had always reigned. For all our worrying, when the time came the title passed muster without any problem – how could it not? Had it not been given by Swami Himself? It was our mistake to have doubted, that it would not. Not only the title, but the souvenir itself, by His grace, turned out very well. After all the snags and delays, it was like a fairy-tale ending. Before that, there had been a lot of hard work, over a period of three hectic months. Morning to night, we were immersed in layouts, colour schemes, artworks, writing, editing, etc., etc. All the articles in the souvenir were planned and written by us. Subodh also wished to make a contribution. He did and that made me very happy. He wrote an interesting piece, in his own original style, called *The Sporting Spirit*, which showed the connection between our day-to-day life and sport.

After the main work of writing, editing, etc. was over, we had to decide on a suitable cover. Our main challenge throughout, in preparing this souvenir, was to show the link between sport and spirit. We had managed that in words but the problem was how to depict it attractively on the cover? We prayed to Swami to guide us and put a lot of thought to it. Finally, a brilliant idea just surfaced. We decided to have a cutwork cover! There was a cutout 'window' on the main cover revealing the green vista of the freshly prepared Vidyagiri stadium behind. The effect was dramatic. We felt very pleased. However, it meant nothing till Swami saw it and gave a – however slight – nod of approval.

In the first week of December, we spent a week in Bangalore, in connection with the Unity Cup souvenir. We were totally immersed in the work of getting the designs, layouts, etc. ready on the computer. Our day would be spent in front of the computer screen in the office of Mr. Rajaram (Shri Kasturi's son) and we were most excited at the way the souvenir was taking shape. Luckily, Pammi's sister-in-law, Kavita Vishwanath resides in Bangalore and we were able to make their lovely home our base. Kavita, the perfect hostess, served us delicious soft fluffy idlis and hot sambar and other varieties of south Indian fare for breakfast everyday. On those cool crisp winter mornings, this gave us the needed pep to take on the day!

We had spent five to six days in Bangalore and our work on the souvenir was almost done, when we got news that Pammi and Sunil had decided to make a short trip to Parthi. Our instinctive reaction was to join them there right away, but we wondered if we could do it, without a direct sign or message from Swami. We were tempted for a moment, for isn't Swami always happy to see his devotees?? However, our conscience did not allow that, and we sought a clear signal from Swami.

It has become a custom with us to take these signs from Swami before trips and other important events. There have even been times when we have cancelled our trips, for not getting the requisite sign. These signs and signals from Swami become a way of life for His devotees – with each one working out his/her individual equation of seeking and getting them. It is very fascinating to see the countless ways in which Swami guides and helps, those seeking guidance, in both big and small ways. The accuracy and promptness from Swami, through a sign, depends I think on the perceived urgency of the problem and the sincerity with which the help is sought. Whenever I have sought a sign half-heartedly, I have never got it – only when I have sought it in a focused and urgent way, has it come my way.

We wanted to go to Parthi, but wouldn't do so, without a clear indication. That night, we went to bed wondering whether we would get that green signal from Swami. If so, how?

For the souvenir, we had worked on a page of quotes on bhakti yoga from devotees of yore. One of my favourite quotes was Sant Jnaneshwar's, on the joy of getting a vision of the Lord. It went like this – *This golden day, the cloud of nectar is showering.. O, I saw Hari! O, I saw Hari! Murare is pervading me through and through* .... Well, that very night, with us awaiting the longed-for sign, I got a beautiful dream of Swami. *In it, I clearly saw us three sisters in Puttaparthi having a darshan of Swami and He clearly happy to see us there.* The funny part was that in the dream I did not see Veenu who was not with us on that trip, but in Kanpur, with my parents.

That was it! I awoke with a smile and waking up my sister told her about the sign and sang out loud, *this golden day, the cloud of nectar is showering.. O, I saw Hari! O, I saw Hari*! And that was it – we made arrangements immediately to head to Parthi.

On 8 December 1997, we drove down to Parthi. The air was very crisp and cool that December morning. It was exhilarating, this sudden turn of events. Without any prior planning or pre-meditation, we were heading to Prasanthi. What could be better? We sang bhajans enthusiastically most of the way. For the rest, we just beamed at each other or at the scenery outside the window.

Pammi was awaiting us in Prasanthi. We made it just in time for the afternoon darshan. We had just two darshans in all, this one and the following morning before our return. But it felt like the world's bounty. If grace is sweet, unexpected grace is sweeter. We hurried to the mandir and waited for Swami to appear. Shortly, darshan music started and Swami glided into view. Everyday, He does this, twice a day and has done so for years and years, and yet the moment is always new, electrifying and totally riveting.

Slowly, He approached and came to where we were seated. I thought He would pass by as He normally does, without any significant reaction. Unbelievably, I saw Him turn and give me a most direct look and smile. Then, He looked at each of us in turn, and with that same happy smile, said in a soft pleased voice, "Happy, very happy." *We* felt happy – at His reception, because it is never that easy to come by such a warm welcome, in the very first darshan – at least not at this stage, when we were many trips old. When you are new, yes, Swami is all sweetness, but once you are wisened over many trips and learning experiences, then it all changes! In a way, it seems that the closer you get, the farther you are! In other words, the more ground you cover, the less headway you seem to be making. However, the key word here is 'seem' – because it only appears that one's progress is stuck, it is not really so. It is an uphill climb, so the zest is greatest when you start at the base, but it flags on and off, at intervals. The idea is to keep going, and never let go of the *eka lakshya* – the one supreme goal. That day, in darshan, when Swami cast His benign eye on me, in that happy fashion, I felt an inch closer to my goal.

We were still celebrating 'the look' and that 'very happy' when the next day, on our second and last darshan of the short trip, Swami called us in for an interview.

Inside the interview room, the three of us were right at the back. There were quite a few other people present. Swami walked in, gave the three of us a look, and said, "Hooon..." Standing next to us He materialized vibhuti for all the ladies. He gave it to us and then to all the others. As He gave me the vibhuti, I felt His finger lightly touch my palm. Swami sat down in His chair and looked around.

Amongst us in the room was an ardent Italian devotee of Swami's from Rome, one Chinese lady and some others. Swami spoke to Sunil for a while and then introduced the Italian devotee, calling her vedam. (Apparently she had mastered Sanskrit and learnt various portions of the Vedas). As a proud parent would do, Swami asked her to recite something from the Vedas. Very promptly and with touching devotion – as a child would, who has been asked to recite a nursery rhyme – she recited some verses. She started off on a high note and Swami asked her to chant on a lower one. She did so and it was an incredible sight, in terms of the childlike and complete devotion she manifested, looking doe ey'd at Swami and referring to Him as 'Mother'. To everything He told her, she devotedly responded, 'yes mother, yes mother'. The Chinese woman sought curative vibhuti from Swami for her ailments. She just said, "vibhuti, vibhuti" to Swami at which Swami joked that there was plenty there, pointing to the plastic basket on the window-sill, full of vibhuti packets! She clarified that she wanted materialized vibhuti by Him and that too in a box (dibiya). Swami imitated her tone and then materialized a small container full of vibhuti for her. Sunil told us later, that though He has seen Swami materializing many bracelets, rings, etc., seeing this materialization really made his jaw drop!

After this, Swami took everybody in family groups into the inner room. He said to Sunil, "You last". When our turn came it was exactly 7.30 a.m, the time He had mentioned to Sunil, He would call us, the previous evening. When we entered the inner room, Swami was still outside. Without thinking, I went and placed myself at the left corner of His chair on one side. I sat down while the others were still standing. Swami came in and immediately told me to get up – and sit at another spot. It was in the manner of a ticking-off to suggest that I should not have placed myself without His direction. However, I now found myself right in front of His chair, facing Him.

He turned to Sunil and asked, "*Kya samachar*?" He spoke to both Sunil and Pammi at length about the forthcoming Unity Cup match. He wanted to know what to gift the players. Sunil humbly said to Him, "Swami, your blessings", to which He said, "blessings, yes, but…" implying that He meant something like a memento. He asked Pammi about the birthday sarees. Had she got them? He then said with a sweet conspiratorial smile, "*Match ki bhi sarees rakhi hain*," (the match sarees are also kept). Swami called Pammi '*grihalaxmi*' and many other similar auspicious-sounding names. He reiterated that after twelve years he would do their re-marriage ceremony when Sunil would be sixty years old.

Pammi broached the topic of the souvenir. Swami asked Pammi, knowingly, "You haven't written?" It was more of a statement than a question (the writing work had been done primarily by the other three sisters). Pammi replied with a twinkle in her eye, "Swami, I supervised!" At this He imitated her tone, and repeated the word, 'supervised!'. We asked for a message for the souvenir. He agreed. Earlier when Sunil had asked him outside for a small message for the souvenir, He had said emphatically, "Why, small message? – big message." This was one of the numerous lilas of the Lord, for we never did get the message – or rather we did not get it as a printed one! He must have given it on some other level!

At one point I told Him in some context, how He was the one who could make everybody happy. Swami simply said, "Be happy". I looked at Him devotedly then and said without any pre-meditation, "Swami, you look so beautiful when you smile." If that was not enough, I further added, "Swami, you should smile…" You could have knocked everyone down with a feather. The Lord was simply amused. He made a gesture to indicate, – crazy, isn't she? He said with a smile, "Sister, loose… all sisters, loose". We laughed. It felt so like a compliment. He then added in a heart-warming way, with a lovely smile, "but, good hearts…". Crazy, but good was the verdict on the sisters.

There was some talk about Subodh. I asked Swami a personal question pertaining to Subodh. Swami, often made it a point to ask after him.

After a while, Swami said, "How are parents?" He said that they were getting old and so we should take care of them and spend more time with them. He also very sweetly asked after Veenu who was in Kanpur, with our parents. "And how is other sister?" He asked. We were delighted that Swami remembered her. He smiled and said, "I have not forgotten". Swami gave us padanamaskar after that and concluded the interview.

20

"What Do You Want?"

Whatever you do, do with a divine feeling. Do everything for the pleasure of the Lord...

When you demand a thing, you must be prepared to pay the price, the price equal to its value.

Sri Sathya Sai

When the first copy of the souvenir came into our hands, we stared at it blankly. After working on it day and night, we were too saturated to get a perspective on it now. We needed someone else's view on it. In the printing, the colour separation was not nearly as perfect as we had visualized and hoped for. We felt a little anxious. Would Swami like it? Since the idea was only to please Him, His reaction was the most important. Praise from elsewhere, would mean nothing, without a pleased nod from Him. Devotees hang upon that slight approving glance from Him. If He does not waste a word, He does not waste a single look or gesture too. However, you have to be very alert and tuned-in to catch all His indications, for they are fleeting and quick. His students are adept in this matter! They watch His every move and catch His barest of glances, to promptly understand its meaning. What is required, is an unblinking focus. There are times when Swami, by the slightest flick of His head or just a raised eyebrow, calls a devotee for an interview. It would not do to miss that chance!

The eve of the match brought a surprise. A divine gift came from Swami – gorgeous yellow kanjivaram silk sarees, for each of us. We felt so blessed. A gift from Swami does not really have any material significance – it is a divine prasad that becomes a potent symbol of blessings, in the mind of the recipient. However, Swami's gifts are many and varied. It is not as if those who do not get any material gifts from Him are any less blessed. Swami has a thousand hands and a thousand ways of giving. What He gives in silence and on the inner level is sometimes far more than what can be given on the material plane. His gifting of material talismans may also be just a divine strategy to make us watch ourselves and scrutinize our reactions, on either getting them or not getting them. In fact, even His giving too much attention or not at all, on the form level, can be just another opportunity He gives for watching ourselves. Are we feeling smug, if we are getting too much attention, are we feeling deflated or jealous, if we are not? We have to do self-audit all the time. Also, we can be sure that soon enough, wherever one is, He will swing us the other way! He has no one favourite – all are His favourites. He only has different times and ways of showing it. Swami says, that all are one and alike to Him. The difference is only in the recipient, not in the Giver. It depends on the openness and readiness of the person to receive grace. *"God's grace is like the shower of rain or like the sunlight. You have to do some* sadhana *to acquire it. The sadhana, of keeping a pot upright to receive the rain, or the sadhana of opening the door of your heart, so that the sun may illumine it".*

Sunil presented the souvenir to Swami during the cricket match. When it was handed to Him on stage, we were close enough to see

Swami's minutest reactions. If we had been praying for a positive response, here it was. It was a beautiful day alright. As we wrote in the souvenir – "Green earth and blue sky make for a perfect cricket setting. In this case, made that much more perfect by a touch of flaming orange!" The atmosphere was festive... the scenic stadium ringed by hills in the distance, fleecy clouds in the sky, and star cricketers wielding the willow out there in the middle. As for the spectators, they had a double treat. The cricket, and a rewarding divine glimpse of Baba, every now and then. What a unique darshan – Swami, at a cricket match. We were seated near the stage, to the left and had a good clear view of Him.

Swami unwrapped the souvenir, and immediately conveyed His appreciation of the 'cut-out' cover. He turned to Sunil standing beside Him and said, '*Bahut achha*' ("very nice"). He turned the pages one by one, stopping to look at each one. He appeared to be *very* pleased with the contents. The most charming thing was how He would cast His glance at us from the stage every now and then, and tell us from there, '*bahut achha*..' We felt quite beside ourselves with joy. And we could not have dreamed that there was even more to come.

The Indian team won (players like Sachin Tendulkar, Rahul Dravid comprised the Indian team and Javed Miandad, Shahid Afridi, Salim Malik, Zaheer Abbas, Clive Lloyd were in the competing team). For the awards presentation ceremony, Swami walked across the emerald green pitch to the dais. Everybody looked happy and pleased, Swami most of all.

The star cricketers from all over the world were full of praise for the whole event. They marvelled at the wonderful cricket pitch prepared in such a short time. They were also impressed by the other arrangements. Swami's meticulous supervision and the motivated work of the devotees, lucky to have been chosen as His instruments, made it – the Sri Sathya Sai Unity Cup 1998 – a splendid event.

The next day, 31st December, in darshan, Swami called us in! We sat around Swami's chair and I had a bunch of our souvenirs on my lap. We hoped to offer Him one and maybe even get His signature. After materializing vibhuti for all the ladies, Swami settled down in His chair. Right away, He turned His attention to us and the souvenir. He looked at me holding the souvenirs and asked for one. I took the whole bundle and passed it across. In a soft tone, He said, "Only one". I gave Him one copy. He took it and asked, "Who all did the book?" Looking at us sisters, He said, "You three?" Then with a pleased smile, He stated, "*Bahut demand hai*" ("great demand for it") (about the book). Looking at the copy in His lap, He said appreciatively, "*Achha* get-up *hai*" (looks good"). Saying which, He started showing the cover to a lady near Him. I looked at Him keenly and asked, "Swami, *achha laga*?" (did you like it) at which He teased me, by laughing and saying, "*Tumne jo keeya, nahin achha laga*," (not, what you did!") He than said sweetly, "*bahut achha laga*...." (... very good....)

After talking to the others, He suddenly looked at me and asked, softly, "What do you want?" I was totally unprepared for this question. However, it's amazing when I think back to that moment how spontaneously I answered it. I don't even recall it forming as a thought in my mind. Looking directly at Swami, I said, "I want to always love you..." Well. It did seem I had perfected the art of saying the unexpected to Swami in the interview room. In this matter, I kept surprising even my own self, so what to say of the others? My sisters had that kind of stunned smile on their faces which seemed to suggest, rather beg of Swami, 'please, just bear with her...' Swami only smiled. He knew that what I said came straight from my heart. It was not a casual or light -hearted statement. Far from it... Looking pleased, with a graceful motion of His hand, He materialised three rings simultaneously. He indicated to us to extend our hands and slipped the rings one by one on our fingers. When my turn came, I extended both my hands, my fingers splayed and Swami scanned them left to right, slipping the ring (a gold one with His picture) on to the ring finger of my right hand.

Swami took our family inside and we settled down at His feet. He materialized a beautiful ruby necklace for Pammi and a chunky gold bracelet for Sunil. He put it on Sunil's wrist but could not negotiate the clasp! (this is a frequent *lila* of Swami – struggling with the clasp of the trinkets He materializes!) Even as He was trying to do so, very sweetly He muttered under His breath, "I can make all these things, but I can't do all this!" He mentioned His satisfaction over the Unity Cup. He told Sunil and Pammi, "*Bahut kaam kiya*," (you all did a lot of work), looking appreciatively at them. He appeared to be very pleased about the whole event. He spoke to them a bit about their son, Rohan, and praised him for always speaking sweetly and obligingly.

After that, He turned to me and said, "How's he?" Not expecting such a direct query, I just looked at Him. After a moment, I said, "Husband?" Swami indicated, "Yes." He then said about Subodh, "Good man." He also revealed that Subodh had been "with Shirdi" (meaning, he had been with Shirdi Baba). but added, for some reason, "but don't tell him." He asked after our daughters. After some personal family talk, He praised us sisters for working on the souvenir with a lot of unity.

There was a break in the conversation and I heard myself ask, "Swami, when you don't come in our dreams, does it mean you are angry?" His answer made us all laugh. He exclaimed, "Dreams! Where is the chance when you yourself are here every month!" He continued more seriously, "Why dreams? when the Reality is right here." A big message for each of us to seize the moment.

Do it now! Aspire now, adore now, act now, achieve now.

21

Master The Mind

Your attitude is the cause of your suffering or happiness. With whatever feeling you see the object, the same is reflected back.... When you see the world you see it in the colour of the glasses you are wearing.

Sri Sathya Sai

Swami Himself says that He repeats His teachings to us over and over, so that they really sink in. One day I sat and pondered over some of His key teachings. One that came to mind, was the one on the mind itself.

Master the mind, Swami says and be a mastermind. He further says, 'remove desires and no mind is left'. I realized in a flash how deeply significant this teaching was. I had heard it many times over but always in so many words that only created an academic appreciation in me. Sitting and brooding over things, I suddenly realized that it was only my mind playing tricks on me. What was the unclear discontent in me about? If at this very moment I could identify my desire and attain it, what then? Would not the desire be behind me and I seeking a new one? Life is essentially a journey to, a process, more than a destination. *The karma is more delightful than the consequence.* Destinations reached, goals realized, mean the end of the journey. What after that? More discontent and further goals. Life is more a reaching than a getting – and it is perfect like that. Because realized goals are put very quickly behind us to create new longings. If at the moment, I had to identify my immediate discontent, the pattern of my desire would run somewhat like, "Oh, if I could only be in Parthi in Swami's presence..." if that was to be realized, it would lead to, "Oh, if only I get a good place in darshan". The next desire running on the heels of this would be, "Hope Swami looks at me". Next, "Will He talk to me?" and of course, the next one, about wanting an interview. And after you get the interview, the desire for the next and the next... and so on. And the strangest thing is, however many times these small desires of ours are fulfilled, they never give lasting satisfaction. Passing elation, yes, but it dissolves all too soon. Better to have one big goal, a worthy one, the *ek lakshya* (one supreme focus) and put all your energies into moving towards that. All these small desires that we hanker after for fulfillment, deplete our energy for the big goal – the really worthy one of divine self-realisation. Here is where the 'master the mind' comes in; when you recognize the mind's constant tricks on you – swinging you from here to there, mood to mood, desire to desire, then you take the first step towards breaking its stranglehold on you. Also, when you master your mind, you can 'switch on' the desired state of mind or mood at your pleasure. Because it is all in the mind – the sorrow, the joy, the depression, the elation. Once you understand that, you can create your own moods, your own well-being... because then, as Swami says, you are the master dictating to your mind and it has to obey your commands.

We can describe this in another way, like when we desire a piece of jewellery, there is nothing in that metal or stone that can actually give or transmit happiness – put that beautiful ring in an empty room and what joy can it bestow to anybody? It is the mind of man that attaches value to it and so *imagines* itself to be happy when it gets it. Swami tells the story of a couple who were proceeding through a thick jungle, on a pilgrimage to an inaccessible shrine. The husband saw a precious stone on the jungle path shining brilliantly with the sun's rays upon it. He hastily threw some sand over it to cover it so that his wife may not be tempted to pick it up and get distracted from her quest. The wife saw the gesture and chided the husband for still retaining in his mind distinction between sand and diamond! For her, both were the same. Thus, it is not the object, however beautiful, but the mind that creates the feelings. If we master this mind, we can order it to create the feelings of our choice, even without getting the external object! This can be done by replacing outer goals with inner ones. This must be the meaning of *self*-fulfillment. Not only that, the joy we get this way is continuous and does not fade or cloy! Swami says, *"One has only to know oneself in order to contact the springs of bliss and immortality... discard all low desires, like, for a few acres of land or a fat bank account or a few more bungalows and cars. Desire rather the joy that will never fade, that will never cloy: the deep steady and strength-giving joy of divine realization. Discover your truth, your holiness, your divinity. That will be enough to save you, to give you everlasting joy. That is what the Vedas and the Upanishadas teach and that is what the sages and saints experienced."* (Sanatana Sarathi May 2003).

The second teaching I reflected upon was about detachment. It is the most difficult question that faces you – what exactly does detachment mean? Swami often says, "Attach yourself to God and detach from the worldly." This does not mean He says that one should stop enjoying worldly things. We should enjoy them with a spirit of detachment or non-possession. *It is not the giving up things that constitutes* vairagya *(renunciation).* Vairagya *consists in enjoying without attachment, things which were previously enjoyed with attachment.* It also means – *Life is a bridge over the sea of change; pass over it but do not build a house on it.* A doubt that emerges is how does one get detached with loved ones? Is one supposed to stop loving them? Not at all. One is just supposed to love them without a sense of possession as one loves something held in trust. *Nothing in the world is yours and you are just a trustee for the wealth, which belongs to the divine. Developing the feeling of mine and thine people get attached to the unreal and the transient and forget the eternal.* Also, we have to learn universal love. We have to expand our hearts and love all, not just our family members.

Many would presume detachment to be a daunting, if not impossible, task – but there is a way out. When you attach yourself fully to God, the attachment to the world just falls away – there is no effort involved, no anguish. The thing is to love God so much that all else finds it's rightful place – second to Him. However, I thought, but isn't this love of God too, entirely His gift of grace and given to the chosen of Him? The answer I got was that God chooses those who have a sincere desire for Him alone or rather those who have reached that stage of their journey where they have an overpoweringly intense desire for God. They show their sincerity and willingness to let go of the worldly – not only in letter, but in their very deepest spirit. If the worldly yet holds pockets of lure and there is the slightest resistance to the idea of letting-go, the candidate is not yet ready. "Give up the world and gain it", said Jesus Christ. That is the whole truth of the matter – a total and sincere letting-go, a leaving-behind, a moving-ahead, without turning or looking back – in total trust.

Message

Resolve to transform your mind – a bundle of thoughts into a bundle of divinity. You will then be able to live in perfect harmony with this majestic universe created by God as a gift for you... Your eyes will become receptive to the beauty that surrounds you, your ears will get tuned in to the divine melodies that are being sung for you in each moment, your tongue will then taste the ambrosial sweetness of God's words. And your heart, which is His temple, will forever be enshrined with His presence...

22

Four, Go!

"Thus, the world is not to be ignored. God did not create the world for you to ignore it. Be in the world and experience the good things it has to offer. At the same time, do not forget God, do not forget Love."

Sri Sathya Sai

I had read somewhere that a sincere desire always gets fulfilled at some point. As far back as I could remember, I had wanted to travel and see the world. Reading the right books can create an intense longing for travel. Books open up exotic new worlds, all of which can be reached only by travelling. I had made a few trips to England and one to America. Of these, the first one to England before my marriage was more thrilling than probably any book I had read. That first evening in London had been an exhilarating experience. It was not only Shakespeare-country for me but also in varying shades, Enid Blyton, Somerset Maugham, Wordsworth and E.M. Forster country too. It was as if I had entered the pages of a book. Everything looked and smelt fresh and wonderful. On entering a restaurant, one of the first things my sister and I saw was a hat-stand with bowler-hats! That was it! We looked at each other and just laughed in sheer delight!

Though I loved England, my one desire always had been to "do" Europe. I had read fascinating accounts in travel books about the beauty and charm of Europe. However, I now realized that the desire no longer gripped me as before. I was surprised. Now, it would be nice if a trip just happened, but it would not matter if it did not. Then I read another interesting thing – every desire, even if we subsequently relinquish it, was registered in the universe and must be fulfilled at some time or the other. This was to come to me later after our next trip to see Swami in March of 1998. The theory of rebirth rests largely on this premise of unfulfilled desires. *As long as desires remain, rebirth is inevitable.*

The fact is that when you are in Puttaparthi in the presence of Swami, all desires drop away. Except of course, the ones related to His darshan – His glance, His word and smile. On that trip, as we sat in darshan, we had no expectations. Mrs. Shourie, the lady in charge, placed Pammi and one more in the first row and the two of us behind. However, for some reason, she came back and told all four of us to sit in the front row, side by side.

The darshan music started and Swami came into view. We were happy just to see Him. Drawing near, He gave the four of us a pointed look, and said, "Hmm, *char* (four)..." Then, under his breath, He said softly, "Char, *jao*," (four, go). We looked at Him in amazement, "Swami?" We were not sure. Veenu sought namaskar and asked Him, "Swami, padnamaskar?" At that, He turned His face, to look back at her and said in part exasperation, "GO!" (the tone of that 'go' said 'what are you all waiting for'?) We jumped up then and trooped to the verandah. That verandah which had once seemed farther than the farthest star! We were made to sit down in a line to await Swami. There were just the four of us, and one more lady on the verandah. We felt the high drama of the moment. Veenu nudged me and whispered, "Savour the moment".

Finally, Swami came and looking at Pammi said, "Go, go". We went inside. Sunil was standing at one side of the room and we at the other. Swami looked at him with his back to us and jokingly asked him, "Ladies *nahin*?"(no ladies?) knowing that we were all lined up there! Saying that He laughed, His eyes shining with merriment. We sat down around Him and He spoke to Sunil about the green stone ring He had given to him earlier. He said green stood for peace. After a while He looked at me briefly and asked, "Where's husband?" I answered, "Swami, in Bombay." Looking at both Veenu and me, He said, that both Veenu's and my husband were devotees too. About Veenu's husband He asked in a mildly reproving way, "Can't he come?"

When we walked into the inner interview room, He joked, "One Gavaskar – four ladies!" Inside, we showed Him our children's photograph and asked Him to bless it. He took the photograph and looked at it for quite a long while. Tapping it very hard with His hand, He said, "I will bless." He talked about coming to Pammi and Sunil's house in Bombay and how He would bless everybody. We asked Him about what food He would prefer. He stated His non-preference for hot oily food and sweets. He said He loved groundnut chutney, but added sweetly that He would eat whatever we would prepare – "*jo tum khathe ho*" (whatever you all eat). He told the three of us to help Pammi in the preparations. Veenu asked if there was any special *sadhana* that we could do. Swami gave the sweetest reply, "*Mere time* mein? (in My time?) *Kuch nahin* – just love from the heart is enough." As He said this, Swami lightly touched His own hand to His heart. He told my youngest sister to forget about marriage for a while. He said, "Forget for a while, be happy in your own self." He also added that the way He had done for the rest of us sisters, her future had also to be planned. When I asked Him a question on bhakti, He gave a long discourse, of which not a word went into me; He was looking directly at me and I was kind of spaced out! The bottom line, however, which I remember clearly was – 'I am always with you.'

Towards the end of the interview, Swami lightly tapped our heads and blessed us. There was some talk about Kodai, a picnic, and singing bhajans. When we asked Him if we could sing bhajans, He said, "Kody mein," (in Kodai Kanal). We all hoped that Swami would call us to Kodai in the summer. (He did.)

One of the questions in our mind prior to this trip to Parthi was about a proposed trip to Europe for us sisters. We hoped to get some message, some hint in Prasanthi. To get these messages, one has to be alert and often read between the lines. The first hint that we caught was when the four of us were made to sit in the first row in a line and Swami came and said, "Char jao" (Four, go). We decoded that to mean not only the interview room but also the European trip we were debating over. Normally, Swami always calls Sunil in for an interview and then asks for us. This was the first time He directly told the four of us to go in. We felt there was a definite message there for us to make the trip. Any doubts were cleared by the dream Swami gave me in the train on our return journey.

In the dream, *I see that the four of us have been called in for an interview at Prasanthi. Talking and whispering to each other, we go into the interview room. As we go in, Baba says,"I am very happy for all of you." Once inside, we hear some excited talk on the verandah outside. I go out to see Swami standing clustered around in a semi-circle of men. There is excitement in the air. I get to know that Swami is organizing a picnic and is appointing the picnic-manager! I say to myself, "Ah, picnic, how exciting!" Swami appoints Sunil as the picnic-manager! After this, Swami and Sunil walk into the interview room.*

It was so sweet and clear in the dream that Swami was telling us to go ahead on our 'European picnic' and that His blessings were with us. After our return to Bombay, our trip did materialize. Sunil came with us till England and then we sisters proceeded to Europe. We felt Swami's presence right through, on our trip, making it doubly wonderful.

23

European Picnic

"If you develop the inner eye, then walking over the land, or voyaging over the waters is itself a pilgrimage through holy land, giving you glimpses of God in every speck of cloud or patch of green..."

Sri Sathya Sai

In Europe, we took the Eurail pass and covered France, Italy, Switzerland and Austria. I started getting these dream vignettes about our trip, which would later unfold. They were like a subtle guidance from within about where to go, what to do next, and so on. It became a kind of ritual every morning for my sisters to check with me about the dreams of the previous night. On that basis, the action-plan was decided. In fact, this dream process had started just prior to the trip. Even before my plan for going to Europe was finalized, I dreamt that Veenu and me were on a plane to Dubai from where we catch a connecting flight onwards. Later, this is exactly how it worked out. Veenu, Mashu and me went to Dubai and took a connecting flight from there to Zurich where Pammi was to receive us. Before leaving, I also dreamt that somebody in our group loses a camera and then gets it back. Later, in Europe, Mashu lost and then found her camera. This pattern of flimsy dream sequences which would later actuate in some way, continued right through the trip.

One day I dreamt we were on a train to somewhere but it was raining so we couldn't do much. That very morning, we took a train to Florence (Italy) but it was raining there and that was it, there was not much for us to do. On another day I saw a place with green hillsides but not many flowers and Pammi remarking about it. As it so happened, our plans changed suddenly at Verona, and we went to Austria ahead of schedule. Through the train windows, we saw rolling green hillsides but not many flowers and Pammi kept remarking on this. Then I dreamt that we should be careful with money. We started clutching our purses tighter but in Rome, Veenu was given a fake Lira note in change, by a wayside shopkeeper! I dreamt that we shouldn't fly out of Paris (our return was booked from there) and so we flew back from Rome, giving Paris the go-by. Later we discovered, that it was a miserable 4° centigrade in Paris and I was relieved because even 9° and 10° was proving uncomfortably cold.

Wherever we went in Europe, we took Swami with us! We decided that our entry into any new place would be with a signature-tune – our bhajan for Him – '*Hamne apna sar jhuka liya Bhagawan tumhare charanon mein* (we bow and place our heads at Thy Lotus feet). Zooming through the European country-side in a train, or going up a cable-car, to snow-laden peaks in Switzerland, or riding a gondola in Venice, we would break into this bhajan, without inhibition. When people asked us, we would explain that it was a religious song and they would look suitably impressed. In Venice, on our gondola-ride, the gondola-man got so inspired that he wished to sing us a song in his language. It was very charming to have him sing to us like that – standing at the top of the boat, paddling the oars, and singing away.

Our last stop in Europe before our return was Rome. We went to the fountain of Trevi and threw our coins and made our wishes! That day, the 15th of April happened to be Mashu's birthday. We had decided at the start of our trip, that wherever we happened to be on her birthday would be Swami's favourite place in Europe. Well, Rome *is* spectacular and we believe it has the maximum number of Sai devotees. You cannot believe that in the twenty-first century, a city like this can exist. It's grandeur takes you back to the days of the glory of the Roman Empire. We, however, longed to be able to encounter a Sai devotee or see a photograph of Swami somewhere. We went to Roma station for booking some tickets. Outside a bookstore, we saw this bookstand, which was entirely stacked with Swami's books! Swami's photos from the book-covers smiled back at us from every shelf. We were delighted! We took photographs of that bookstand with all of us around it, smiling beatifically. Later, we were lucky to show Swami this photograph in Kodai.

We returned to Bombay thoroughly refreshed. By His grace, after our return, we were even able to make a short breezy three-day trip to Kodaikanal, where Swami was. Pammi got a chance to show Swami our Roma station photo personally and thank Him for being with us throughout.

24

'Hamne Apna Sar Jhuka Liya'

Can there be anything greater than earning the love of the omniscient, omnipresent, omnipotent Lord? There is nothing on earth or beyond it which is equal to divine love. To make all endeavours to earn that treasure of love is the whole purpose and meaning of human existence.

Sri Sathya Sai

Joy alone is ours, not sorrow for we belong forever to Him, who is the Supreme Lord... and we have reached His beautiful flower-fresh feet.

Appar

In August of 1998, we were able to make a trip to Parthi again. Around the 30th, Pammi's in-laws along with her two sisters-in-law and their children also drove down to Parthi from Bangalore. Thirty-first August happened to be her father-in-law's seventy-fifth birthday.

That morning in darshan my daughters, Rubianca and Tia and Nutan's daughter, Salonie were also with us. On the men's side, Sunil, his father, Vishy and even Rohan who had come this time, were seated. We ladies were in bright dazzling silks and for a moment I self-consciously wondered if we were overdressed! Swami came, gave us a pointed amused look and as if reading our thoughts, said, "All *ready*...?" He then softly said, "Go" and continued walking. "All of us?" I asked and He sweetly answered, "Yes, even sisters."

Inside the interview room, Sunil and his father and the other men stood on one side. We ladies of the family, nine in number were on the other side. Swami looked at Sunil. With merriment bubbling in His face, He said, "Large family!" He asked Rohan about 'wife' and mentioned the age of twenty-six as being right for marriage. He then turned to Sunil's parents and materialized a mangalsutra and a ring which He made them exchange and put on each other as a couple. Before this He made note of the fact that in our group were 'nine ladies'. I told Him, "Your number, Swami" and He responded with satisfaction, "yes". He called us the '*navagraha*' – wonder what that meant! Swami materialised a watch for somebody and there was a difference of a few minutes between it and the time showing on the wall clock. He said, "7.27 am is right!" (the time showing on the materialized watch), and pointing to the clock on the wall said, "That is wrong!" There was a very perky Italian lady sitting just by the side of His chair and He had intermittent and indulgent interaction with her. She took every opportunity to open a conversation with Him and spoke with fervour. Her devotion was in full display. Swami was indulgent with her but from time to time seemed to suggest, in a lighthearted fashion, that wasn't she crazy! He spoke of how He had given her darshan in the form of light from a photograph in her house. He also mentioned a particular dream He had given her. "Yes, yes, Swami and you gave me a flower...." (in the dream). Overwhelmed, she looked at Him and said in a torrent, "Swami, you are my everything – mother, father, sister, brother, friend and husband." That last bit hung in the air for a moment or two and Swami made light of it by half-jokingly and half-seriously saying, "Don't *talk* like that – mother, father – yes, but husband – no!"

At one point, when somebody expressed how God had given him everything, Swami smiled and said softly, "Everything is nothing and nothing is everything." He spoke about His own spartan life style – how He possessed five robes at a given time and did all His own work. In connection with that train of thought, Swami said reflectively, "Who can steal or take anything from Me?" (as he had no material possessions with Him) Then in the same breath, in a dramatic reversal of meaning, He said something extremely touching and deep. '*Vaise tho Mere paas sab kuch hai, khali koi lene vala hi nahin hai*" (Come to see, I have everything, My treasury is full, only there are no takers).

He then turned His attention to Rohan and told him to be selective about his company. I asked Swami to give some message to the three young girls (Rubianca, Tia and Salonie) and Salonie's mother, Nutan (Pammi's sister-in-law) asked Swami to grant them sadbudhi (wisdom). Swami said, "Sadbudhi *tho hai par kabhi kabhi misuse hoti hai,*" (sadbudhi is there but it is sometimes misused). Veenu indicated towards my daughters and told Swami how they were weak in maths. At that He indicated Rohan and said, "Aur yeh bhi" (even him). He then teased Rohan by asking him the nine times table at random like – 9x5, 9x7, 9x8, etc. Thank god, Rohan got it right! Swami explained the magic of the number nine – how any product of any multiple of number nine would total upto number nine.

While all this interaction was taking place, the Italian lady started communicating with her son in Italian across the room. This went on for a short while. Swami interrupted sweetly with a cute joke, by himself breaking into a torrent of Telugu, directed at no one in particular, as there were no Telugu-speaking people in the room! We really laughed at that and I think everybody got the message. He then took the Italian lady and her family into the inner room.

After a while it was our turn. Inside, I was sitting at the back, near the door. Swami got up suddenly to go out and get a saree for Sunil's mother. I saw my chance and stood up quickly to open the door for Him. As He passed by me, an aroma of sandalwood trailed the air. After He re-entered with the saree, I shut the door and we settled down again. He spoke about how He had once rushed to help an American devotee, Sinclair, in time of danger, because the devotee had called upon Him with faith. He also spoke a little about Himself – how He doesn't sleep a wink in the night and doesn't feel any hunger at all. He spoke about the present being the most important time – "present is Omnipresent."

He said that every creative talent was a gift from God and should not be wasted. He materialised a diamond ring for Sunil with the alphabet 'S' in diamonds. Swami said, "S for Sunil" at which Sunil replied firmly, "S for Sai Baba". Swami did not put this ring on Sunil's finger but wished to give it to him for occasional use. He looked around the room as if for a piece of paper in which to put the ring. He looked at all of us and asked, "Paper?" Nobody seemed to have that all-important piece of paper just then – except for me! Without a moment's hesitation, I snapped opened my flat purse and whisked out a soft fresh white tissue from it, my purse being usually stacked with enough of these. I checked quickly whether the tissue was fresh and clean before handing it over to Him and I heard Him say softly, "Carries many papers." He took the tissue and put the ring meticulously inside it. Leaning over, He placed the neat packet directly into Sunil's shirt pocket. (Later, after the interview, Sunil immediately handed back the-now-precious-tissue to me as 'consecrated paper').

Swami spoke about the benefits of awaking early in *Bramhamuhuratam* (3.00 a.m to 6.00 a.m) for purposes of sadhana, as it was a purified time of the day. At one point in the interview, He made to get up, as if He was leaving. I immediately asked if all of us could take His padnamaskar. At that He coolly sat back on His chair. He said that He was still sitting there with us and would give padnamaskar later, when the interview got over. Then He said key words, which I felt were especially directed at me and for which purpose this whole little drama took place. Softly, He intoned, "Haste makes waste..." (a month or so back in a dream I had seen myself roller skating zanily and ecstatically down a road only to hear a voice from behind saying, "slow down").

Towards the end of the interview, Pammi asked Swami if we could sing a bhajan to Him. Swami readily agreed. We sang the one we had acquainted all of Europe with! Now we were sufficiently practiced to be able to sing it to Him directly. *'Hamne apna sar jhuka liya Bhagawan Tumhare charanon mein...'* By allowing us to sing the bhajan, I think Swami acknowledged our heartfelt singing of it to Him on our European trip. By His grace, the *bhajan* flowed out melodiously, inspite none of us being great singers. Swami got rapt in the bhajan and listened to it very intently – in His God-like mudra – making gestures with His hands and with a far-away look in His eyes. Turn by turn, He looked deeply at each one of us singing, Himself swaying gently to the rhythm. After the bhajan was over, there was a moment's deep silence. The last line of the bhajan says how *everything* is in the hands of God. Very seriously, with an intense look in His eyes and moving His hand, Swami said, "*Haan, sab hamare hathon mein*" (yes, everything *is* in this hand of Mine).

Shortly Swami got up and gave everybody charansparsh. Outside He distributed the vibhuti packets and gave both my daughters nine packets each. While giving them to my elder daughter, I heard Him say softly, "Study well, talk less." My other daughter, Tia shot some photographs. He joked with her that the photos better come out, otherwise she would be hauled up! (the photos did come out beautifully with Swami looking very vibrant and all of us reflecting His glow!) Later, my elder daughter, Rubianca told me how she had longed for Him to look at her directly and had thought of Shirdi Baba's saying, "If you look to me I look to you". Just then Baba turned and gave her a piercing direct look. Once outside the interview room, a lady came up to me to say how nice the bhajan had sounded. And, could we write it down for her? Though we had sung it very low, the bhajan had filtered out. We felt, it was Swami complimenting us! We went back, singing in our hearts...

25

"*Kabhi Aaya?*"

It is the reaction to restlessness that is bad not the restlessness itself. Restlessness is only the rise and fall of the wave of the ocean that you are. Nothing matters, so long as the depths are secure. Success is not important; failure does not matter. The river of eternity is flowing ever into the ocean of the supreme will. You are a fraction of that will. That is why you are afflicted with the hunger to seek it and find fulfillment and bliss thereby.

Sri Sathya Sai

Sitting in the front one day awaiting Swami, a strange thought came to me. My mind went back to my token line days with their varying fortunes of getting a good token or not and the daily suspense and sharp longing for a good spot in darshan.

What a training ground it had been! To balance out your emotions and get them to that even keel. Of course, on the face of it nobody did. But the work was being done underneath the surface without anyone realising it. But sitting there, what struck me most was how the simple rapture of those days could not be transposed over these. That was a different time. And this, a different one. Then, there had been just Swami and you with only one desire coming in between. To see Him. The overriding concern was not whether Swami would look at me, but would I be able to get a good look at Swami? And of course, there were no further expectations varying from will He talk to me? To will He smile? Because, you wanted less, you got more – one of those eternal paradoxes.

What made those trips, inspite of the roughing out on all levels (no regular meals, no beds to sleep on, being in the twentieth or thirtieth row in darshan) so wonderful? One reason was that there were very few expectations.

The joy of darshan from the remote rows was sharper than from the first or second because sitting at that distance there was less chance for complacency and taking anything for granted. Also, there was no predictable pattern. You could get a 'bad' row one day and a very 'good' one the next. The shifting pattern kept you alert and ever hopeful. You were on the threshold of an experience that felt as if it was going to change your life forever. That first rush of elation at discovering the joy of spirit takes one over all the bumps. Moreover, your tentative steps were guided by some hidden power and everything conspired to draw you in. The smallest of wishes were granted. And every wish granted was but the bait! As Swami says, "He gives us what we want so that we may want what He has come to give." What Swami wants to give us, we learn only later when we are safely too far gone in to think of turning back. Then the real business starts. However tough the process might be, the rewards are richer than any other we can hope for on our earthly sojourn. So, we must keep on at it and every time go, just a little further....

Also, I realized that the closer Swami draws one to the form, maya becomes all the more difficult to contend with. At a distance, the maya factor is diffused. I suppose, maya has to be thickest immediately and around Swami, otherwise how else can He or we, function. There has to be a reasonable meeting point, a plausible platform for such an interaction. That platform is provided by the upadhi of the Lord – maya. Everybody longs for proximity to Swami's form. But the fact is that this beautiful form is not an ordinary one and it does not stop there. It only *looks* like a Form – it is verily That. Many people say that to be close to Him is like being close to fire. And this fire has only one task and that is to burn the ego and cleanse you inside out. The heat of this cleansing gets stronger the closer you get.

That year in 1998, Pammi and Sunil were unable to come for the birthday but for the very day itself – 23rd November. The three of us, however, had arrived earlier on 20th November. Swami, in His inimitable way, made it clear right from the beginning, that He did not entirely approve of the delay in their plan! He ignored us in darshan everytime He came out. Finally, on the 22nd evening, while walking back, He deigned to ask us, "Where is sister – Mrs. Gavaskar?" We said meekly, arching forward, "Swami, sister and brother-in-law coming tomorrow, on 23rd…" Swami asked, "Why 23rd, why not 24th?" Saying which He abruptly turned and walked away. His tone and look conveyed it all. We felt deflated. Pammi and Sunil had to attend a wedding on the 23rd morning after which they were flying to Bangalore and driving down. They could reach only by the afternoon of the 23rd.

Birthday morning, Swami came and passed by with the band in attendance and there was not much chance of gauging His mood vis-à-vis us. We could hardly concentrate on the birthday festivities that morning. We felt distracted. When would Pammi arrive? What if the flight was delayed? We felt worried, thinking of all the snags and delays that could take place.

When they finally arrived in the afternoon, we sighed with relief and told them how Swami had noted and mentioned their absence in darshan. We quickly got ready for the evening function. We decided to wear the bright yellow silk sarees that Swami had given to us during the cricket match the previous year. We walked into the mandir, the rich yellow silk sarees blazing conspicuously. Could Swami miss us in those? We did feel a little anxious about Swami's reception to us that day. Would He acknowledge us with a look or maybe a smile?

As the evening of the birthday celebrations, many ladies in the front were wearing beautiful, purple and gold sarees gifted by Swami, on the Ladies Day. Everybody looked happy and animated. The moment finally came when Swami emerged. He looked as beautiful as ever. We needed His glance, His reassuring word, that day. He came closer and we folded our palms. But Swami had other plans. Just before reaching us, He turned and crossed the carpet over to the other side. Not only that, He walked close to the ladies line on the other side, and kept His head turned completely to our opposite side. It was like a full left-turn and He kept it like that, till He had crossed us. If we had not been so keyed-up, we could have even enjoyed the lila – of how He missed the canarys in darshan that day! We made some weak attempts to joke but our spirits were not in it.

The evening programme got underway. We feasted our eyes on Swami sitting on His chair, a short distance away. In the evening twilight, His face took on shyamal-tones… This made Him more enchanting to the devotees. There was an audio-visual display on Swami. A close-up of Swami's lotus feet, lit up the screen and a collective near-audible gasp rose from the assembled gathering.

The programme got over, Swami took mangal-arati and blessed everybody. He started to slowly walk back. All eyes were fixed on Him. I have always loved these dusk-darshans. On festival days, because of the programmes, darshan lasts late into the evening. By the time Swami walks back, it is past the twilight-hour. The orange of Swami's robe takes on added resplendence and His face exudes a dusky radiance. That evening, Swami turned at the corner and started coming by to where we were seated. He held a rose in His hand. We looked unblinkingly at Him. Would He look – That was the question? He did! The delight of it. He stood before us and gave an appraising glance, one by one, to each of us. He spoke to Pammi saying, "*Kabhi aya*....? (When did you arrive?)" and then gave her the rose! He told her that it had been given to Him by her husband Sunil on the verandah and He was giving it to her! We were all smiles. We gave Him our birthday cards from the whole family, which He graciously accepted. He then said, "How many?" An orchestra of voices rose up, saying, 'four, Swami, four..." Swami walked on. Our faces shone.

We reached our rooms in a joyous mood. We met up with Sunil who had his own story about the rose to tell, the sequel of which we told him! Talking like this and exchanging stories we were moving back and forth between our two rooms. Veenu, Mashu and me were in our room when I decided to get something from Pammi's room. I approached her room and saw they had a visitor – Mr. Chiranjeevi Rao. I retraced my steps. However, a minute later escorted by Pammi and Sunil, we saw Mr. Rao coming towards our room. He had a plastic bag in his hand and a smile on his face. He told us that Swami had sent the birthday sarees for us! He had already given one to Pammi in her room and a suit piece for Sunil. One by one he took out the three gorgeous purple and gold sarees and handed them to us. Affably, he told us that we should definitely wear them for the following morning's darshan. We were only too happy to do so!

26

Splendid Grace

Any moment My divinity may be revealed to you; you have to be prepared, ready for that moment....

Sri Sathya Sai

Our next trip to Parthi would come around at Shivaratri 1999 in a most unplanned and unexpected way. The 'experienced' know that planning trips to see Baba is something best left to Him, for if in any area His control is most manifest, it is this! Nobody can get there without His 'call' – for then, some obstacle or the other foils the best of plans. On the other hand, you may be sitting back with no plans to go and something just happens to arrange a trip for you. Things just fall into the right pattern, when the time is right and one can see Swami's hand everywhere. One of the oft-repeated phrases in Sai-parlance is, "That's Swami!" A phone call, a letter, a song in the air, a butterfly, a seat number, a bell ringing, a message on a billboard or in the newspaper crossword, are all Swami! Devotees have found many ways of drawing messages from Him and this belief is not just fanciful thinking. It is a real line of communication, if you are sincerely open to it. I had read a telling line about this in a book on Baba by a foreign devotee, Matlin. It said, '*when seeking guidance – pay attention. Spirit is infinitely creative, so there is no telling where the next clue may come from.*' God truly is omnipresent, omniscient and omnipotent, but more often than not, this phrase is just a phrase – we are all conditioned into thinking of God as being somewhere else – in heaven, temple church or mosque. For why else do we forget God in our daily activities and join our hands in reverence only when we enter a holy place? It is difficult to be consciously aware of God's omnipresence all the while and its only realized souls who can grasp this reality, moment to moment.

In this instance, none of us had plans to go for Shivaratri, and yet, at the last minute we did! The programme was literally made in a day and everything just fell into place. We got reservations promptly and things on the home front were easy for us to be able to take-off, on such short notice. Subodh was as accommodating as ever, though he did tease me every now and then about my frequent trips.

It so happened that Sunil was in Bombay for a couple of days (a break from his constant travelling) early February 1999. We had learnt that Swami was to come to Mumbai in March 1999. Since, He had mentioned a number of times to Pammi that He would visit her house, she thought this was a good time to make a formal invitation. It was she who told Sunil that he must personally extend the invitation to Swami. With them going, the rest of us got drawn to go along too, especially because the visit coincided perfectly with the Shivaratri celebrations. We had never been to Parthi for Shivaratri so the reason was good enough. This was in 1999. We had no idea what an epic Shivaratri it was going to be.

On reaching Prasanthi, Swami right away told Sunil on the verandah, "Not for Shivaratri, but for invitation – wife *ne bola*" ("wife's instructions!"). Though we all know that Swami knows everything and has demonstrated so innumerable times when He actually does reveal His omniscience again and again, one always marvels afresh! The prabal maya is always at work and one can just imagine how strong it is that it can overpower all the evidence. You need to be very spiritually evolved to have, as Swami says, constant integrated awareness of divinity.

As it was Shivaratri, the crowds of devotees had swelled and the queues were long and winding. These are the times when the sevadals are most taxed having to maintain control and discipline amongst large crowds, with each person urging to get a good place in darshan. They do their task admirably and though sometimes people may take offence at their manner, it should never be forgotten how daunting and difficult their task is. They are forever on their toes, always on duty and have to be constantly alert to many things on many fronts. Like any of us, their main objective too is to please Baba, so their work is their sadhana and obviously Swami has picked them as special instruments with a purpose.

On Shivaratri, Swami is in His Shiva aspect – serious, remote, other-worldly. There is a different charge to the atmosphere. On different festivals, it appears that Baba takes on the predominant aspect of the godhead being represented. Thus on Shivaratri, He is somber and serious. On Krishna Janmashtami, His mood is lighter and more playful. On Ram Navami He drips tenderness and on Guru Purnima He is as the perfect Sadguru. On Christmas, He is mellow yet serious and it is on His birthday, that He is the sum total of all these! The poorna avatar is all of everything and it is only on 23rd November of every year, that all His facets are on stunning display.

During Shivaratri, the nightlong akhanda bhajans, make the mandir reverberate as if with cosmic vibrations. That Shivaratri, when Swami emerged in the early dawn, after the nightlong bhajan, none were really prepared for the extraordinary event that was to follow. The Shiv bhajans had reached a crescendo. The atmosphere was soaked with divine vibrations. Swami sat down in His chair and took a sip of water. He took another sip. And, another, but nobody guessed what was coming. There was something about His facial expressions and gestures that made me nudge my sisters and say, "See, see, Swami...." They too had noticed the same thing and were indicating the same to me. Next moment, even before we had the time to figure out, what exactly was happening, our eyes focused on Swami's face, we saw it happen – by His grace alone – the astonishing spectacle of the divine lingam emerging. It propelled out, as a projectile from His mouth and we gasped in wonder. There was an audible gasp amongst the huge gathering of devotees, as they realized what had happened and now everybody arched forward to get a glimpse...In the moment when it happened, some who were close did not get to see it, others far away saw it, depending on whose glance was fixed on Swami at that time. Apparently, some had, at that very moment turned their glance away or blinked etc. and so missed the opportunity. However, it should all be taken as preordained by the Supreme Will. Those who saw it were meant to see it. Those who didn't were not – just then – but would definitely get a chance later. For, Swami in His infinite compassion was to give many more opportunities in the following years.

In the earlier years, during the Shivaratri celebrations Baba had materialized many such lingams from His body in a spectacular way. The lingam would emerge through His mouth. Baba stated that the elliptical lingam represented the act of creation and symbolized the universe itself in micro-form. However, later when the crowds coming in to see this grand spectacle became uncontrollable, Baba stopped this practice.

After a gap of many years, the lingodbhava – or the materialization and manifestation of the lingam by Swami from within Him had taken place. We had read and heard about it but had never thought that Swami would start it again, in public view, after so many years. And that we would be part of the devotee ranks when He did it. This lingodbhava, Swami says, has enormous spiritual implications for the viewer. It is said to be powerful enough to confer the boon of liberation to seeking souls.

Swami held aloft the lingam between His thumb and forefinger and with a happy smile showed it around to the animated gathering. His face glowed with unusual light. Everybody was quite stunned at this magnificent grace bestowed so unexpectedly. We felt specially blessed to have witnessed this phenomenon on our first ever Shivaratri in Parthi. Feeling deep gratitude we thanked Swami in our hearts. That year Shivaratri fell on 14th February, which is celebrated as 'Valentine's day' in the West. So the date was marked on the calendar as a very significant day for Sai devotees. Maybe, there was some cosmic planning there, for this date was to play a further very dramatic role in my life three years from that time.

On our return to Bombay everyone was keen to hear of our experience. Subodh appeared quite fascinated. He was being drawn into the magic circle of Swami's love. Though he did not reveal much, it was clear that he had developed a strong inner one-to-one relationship with his inner Swami. If uninformed people said anything about Swami casually or dismissively he was there to stand in defence – never abrasive but very firm and coolly reasoned. He even wrote a couple of 'Letters to the Editor' as a fitting rejoinder to careless and unauthenticated reports in newspapers. He had more dreams of Swami and I started seeing Subodh in my Swami dreams. I felt happy. For, what could be better than Subodh turning to Baba?

27

The Supreme Guest

"The Lord rushes towards the bhakta faster than the bhakta rushes towards Him. If you take one step towards Him, He takes a hundred steps towards you!"

Sri Sathya Sai

Around February 1999, I had this dream:

I see in a home the hustle and bustle of some activity as when guests are present. Well, there is a very special Divine Guest – our own Baba. Food is being cooked for Him and my mother is supervising. I am in the dining room and Mashu is with my mother overseeing the cooking. She tells my mother to make the rotis 'mulayam mulayam' ('soft soft') . *I feel happy to hear this because I have the same thought in my mind. Mummy's typical reaction is 'of course we'll send only* mulayam *rotis for Baba!'*

This dream was to be decoded a month later in its own dramatic way.

In March 1999 after the dramatic events of Shivaratri, the city of Mumbai had the tremendous good fortune of Sri Sathya Sai

Baba's divine visit. This was after Swami's visit to Delhi where He thrilled the people of the capital city with darshan and sambhashana after a long gap of many years. Devotees from all parts of north India travelled long distances to get a chance of holy darshan. Swami gave a couple of divine discourses in Delhi. The prime minister of India Shri Atal Bihari Vajpayee was chief guest at one of the functions organized. In his speech, his veneration and respect for Swami and his work was clearly evident. The prime minister displayed no reservations in stating boldly his belief in Swami's divinity.

From Delhi, after a hectic visit, Swami arrived by a special plane to Mumbai. Dharmakshetra, his divine abode in Mumbai was packed with eager devotees keenly awaiting darshan. People were spilling out onto the street. Even the passageways got filled up, after Baba's arrival. I was luckily, already inside the ashram, with other Balvikas gurus and our Balvikas groups of children. Many people got delayed in coming because of the unprecedented traffic heading to Dharmakshetra, which caused a traffic jam. My parents, my brothers-in-law and my sisters got stuck in the traffic snarl. Luckily, they happened to know somebody whose house touched the ashram boundary wall. They took recourse to that acquaintance. The host of the house received them warmly. When Swami appeared on stage outside, all of them crowded the small balcony to get darshan!

When darshan got over and the crowds cleared, Sunil and Pammi got a chance to go up to Satyadeep for an audience with Swami. Swami was seated in a chair on the green lawns of Satyadeep, with a cool breeze stirring the leaves of the trees all around. Swami gave them a warm smile. Sunil took the opportunity to extend a personal invitation to Him for visiting his house in Mumbai. Very graciously, Swami accepted. He told my sister, "*Roti khaoonga.....*" ("I will have roti.") He repeated this "*Roti khaoonga*" and it was telling that he used the term 'roti' which is very north Indian, as against the term 'chapati' used in the south.

The rest of us back at home, were keenly awaiting their return. Would Swami accept? When Pammi and Sunil finally got back, their bright faces announced the good news. What greater news can one receive, than that the Lord himself, is going to grace the threshold of your humble abode? How many lives of accumulated karma is that? Or is it just grace? Nobody can say, but karmic calculations apart, it becomes a high-point of spiritual grace to receive the Host of hosts, as a divine guest in your own house!

A month earlier, I had dreamt specifically about Swami's visit to Pammi's house. *I saw Him coming up in the lift of Pammi's building.* I remember I called up my sister immediately and it made us feel very hopeful! In another dream, *I had seen Swami in her house with all of us assembled there. In that, the scenario was this: prior to His arrival, we are thrown into a state of panic, because we get a call from a mobile phone from a car, telling us, that Swami is arriving early!* Quite stunning, because that's exactly how it happened.

Around this time, Pammi's maid Chayya unexpectedly got her first Baba dream. She recounted it excitedly to my sister and said she was sure Baba would come to the house. *In the dream, she sees that the house is fully decorated with flowers and a red carpet is laid out for Baba's arrival. There are lots of people awaiting darshan. Pammi tells her that she should not take padnamaskar unless Baba allows it. Baba arrives, gives darshan to all and after that comes up to Chayya and indicating His feet allows her padnamaskar.* (This dream too got decoded in an amazing way, down to the last detail). However, when my sister heard it she tried to scale down her maid's expectations. She explained that even if He did not give her charansparsh, she should not be disappointed, because He had already blessed her by giving it in the dream. She knew that even if Swami came, you could never say whether He would grant padanamaskar to anybody. Ultimately, this always depends on Swami's will.

Hectic preparations got underway for receiving Swami. The divine catch, (as there always is) was that Swami accepted but without intimating the exact date and time. It was our job simply to be on the ready. Not so simple, as experience teaches! And especially so, when you are receiving the Supreme Guest! The 14th, 15th and 16th March – three days – one of which would see Swami's divine visit to my sister's home.

The 15th of March, it finally was and we were informed on the day itself that Swami would visit around 5.00 p.m. He would visit on his way to Cross Maidan where a divine discourse was scheduled in the evening, for a large gathering there. Frenetic activity followed. Each and every family member was put on some task or the other – scrubbing, cleaning, polishing, decorating, cooking, etc. The house looked very festive, decorated with flowers (Chayya's dream!) There was so much to do, and nothing less than the best would do. In a way, Swami makes us go through these elaborate external rituals and gestures only so that we may catch their inner significance. All devotees who have had the good fortune of receiving Swami in their homes, go through the same rituals – of polishing their hearths to spitting perfection. But what Swami wishes us to realize is that externals are fine and in their place but ultimately of superficial and passing importance. The real polishing and preparation has to be done within if we wish to receive the Lord as a permanent resident in our hearts.

For the moment, however, external detail had to be attended to and there were numerous. Would Swami prefer juice or coconut water or just plain water? Would it be okay to play soft instrumental music in the background or should bhajans be played? Could onions be used in the cooking? What about the fruit basket? Which fruits did Swami like? Of course, we had done a bit of homework but had received conflicting reports. Some said, "He drinks only plain water". Others, "He takes coconut water". Again, some said, "He does not take fried foods". Others, "But He loves bhajiyas!" We had to sift the information and be guided by our own intuition, which was rather blunted, with our general anxiety about things turning out well. The only option left was to keep all the options ready – coconut water, juice, nimbu paani and plain water! We had deliberated over and over on the food menu and finally settled on the vegetables we were sure he preferred – stuffed bhenda, and groundnut chutney being clear favourites, were first on the list. And, the 'rotis' of course which Swami had made a special mention of. This privilege of making the soft rotis went to my mother and I chipped in with being the one to knead the dough. I am not much of a cook and even now have not had much inclination towards cooking (this is a honest confession, but I am sure that Swami can change my mindset, anytime). Subodh always bore my lack of culinary expertise with tremendous patience and understanding – he never really made an issue of it. On the contrary, he joked and laughed about it, finding it very funny.

Each one of us got busy in our respective tasks, though of course, they were not really tasks but a labour of love. However, we felt a little nervous, something like what a first-time diver would feel before his maiden jump! To add to this, we got a call from Swami's car that He would be arriving forty-five minutes earlier than scheduled (the dream!!). The chaos and panic that followed cannot be described. Instructions were flying from every side and last minutes touches were being hurriedly given. The arati tray had luckily been decorated and set up much in advance and we placed it on the book-shelf near the front door in readiness for Swami's arrival.

In my sister's building, Sportsfield on Worli seaface, word had spread about Swami's visit. Many who got to know lined up downstairs to get a glimpse. In fact, my sister had graciously extended an invitation to the residents of her building to come for darshan. She felt it was a rare chance for certain people to get Swami's darshan. So after debating over the issue, she finally did inform those who she felt would be inclined and who would appreciate it. Since Swami had not indicated to them directly whether it should be just family or not, she thought it better to give as many people as possible a chance for darshan.

Finally, the moment came when Swami's car pulled into the compound. My father, Pammi's father-in-law and Sunil were waiting downstairs to receive Swami. A red carpet had been laid out (Chayya's dream!) and fresh flower and leaf torans had been strung out at the building entrance and the main gate. My father was visibly moved at this grand opportunity of divine proximity after many years of quiet and steady devotion. Could he have ever dreamt that one day he would be escorting Swami in the small 4'x4' lift of his daughter's building? How can anybody know in what ways and in what time his grace will manifest? Had my father but known it, there was greater grace to be showered on him later in the day.

We, the ladies of the house, were awaiting Swami's auspicious entry upstairs. When the lift door opened and Swami emerged in his effulgent orange robe, the threshold of my sister's home and our hearts lit up. As a welcome song, we sang a Sai bhajan – '*Aao aao Nandalala*'. Smiling benignly, Swami entered and my sister did the auspicious arati in welcome.

We had set up Swami's chair in the large living room, which was packed with people. There were all manner of sweet smelling flowers and floating-candle decorations around Swami's chair. After sitting down, Swami cast His eye over all the decorations and even turned His head to study the big painting on the wall. We asked Him what drink He would prefer, "Nariyal paani? Nimbu paani...?" Very sweetly and softly He gave His preference, "Plain water..!" He then spoke a bit about how He did not like to have tea, coffee and other drinks but only plain water. Swami then addressed a couple of questions or so to the gathering. A brother devotee, Pankaj expressed the joy of having Swami over in Bombay and how Swami should come every year. Swami said, "Mumbai or here?" Everybody laughed and there was a symphony of voices saying, "Swami here!"

Two Sai devotee friends, Shanti and Sudha had prepared to sing some Sanskrit slokas composed on Sai and we asked Swami if they could sing them. Swami readily agreed and there was a melodious rendition by them. Swami's rapt mudra showed that He enjoyed the musical offering. After that, we sisters asked Swami if we could sing a Sai bhajan to Him and again He agreed. So, very enthusiastically we started singing. It was the first bhajan that I had ever learnt and the one I sang most often – *'Gopala Radha lola'*. The bhajan started on multiple notes – each one taking off on a different one! Thankfully, with a little correction, it immediately settled down and we got our rhythm. Swami gave us a very sweet patient hearing. It was not so much the taala or the raaga but the bhava and our devotional zest He responded to in His infinite love and compassion. A spontaneous and sincere offering from a devotee's heart is never really rejected by Him, Who is the embodiment of the highest love. However, His acceptance may not always be apparent. Of course, He cognizes everything, even the smallest detail, only He has His own manner and time of showing it. The Lord has many ways not only of giving, but even of receiving.

After that, Swami commented on a painting. Veenu asked Him whether He liked it. Swami appreciated it and mentioned something about the eyes of the subject in the painting. At that, my friend Shanti said loudly, "God is the best artist." Swami, impressed with her comment, turned His head and said, *'Waah, kavi!*" With those simple two words, He blessed her in a stupendous manner that would manifest by and by.

For serving Swami the food preparations, a separate room had been set up. We invited Swami inside. After Swami settled down, the family members scurried back and forth from the kitchen to serve the honoured guest. Finally, however, it was Mashu who did the major part of this co-ordination between the kitchen and the room. My mother remained in the kitchen to prepare our Kanpur-style rotis for Swami! In the meanwhile, Swami interacted with the family members asking the children their names and answering a few queries. It was awe inspiring having Him sit so close to all of us in that small family room. His aura overpowered everything and all most of us could do was to sit and stare at Him. We sat there quietly, delighting in His auspicious presence. To lighten the atmosphere, Swami cracked a few jokes and made everybody laugh. I had prepared a decorative album with beautiful quotes for offering to Him. He took the album and leafed through every page of it. My afternoons of sitting up with the album, bent over it cutting, sticking, pasting, writing was made worth it, every moment of the effort, by His simple gesture.

When the food came, we all got a chance to serve Him personally, which must have been due to the accumulated punya of many lifetimes. Swami very graciously had a roti, as He had told my sister He would, and tasted a bit of every dish that was offered to Him. A family friend had specially prepared delicious badam halwa for prasad and Swami acknowledged her offering by actually asking for it, "Meetha kahan?" (where is the sweet?) Afterwards, Swami again sat for a while outside, where many visitors had assembled for darshan. Some lucky ones got vibhuti materialised by Swami.

After blessing the family, Swami asked about the kitchen. Then, pointedly He started walking towards it. All the servants stood lined up there. They had worked very hard to spruce up the house and get things ready. Very graciously, Swami went up to them and indicating His feet, told them to take charansparsh. "Karo," He said. With beaming faces they bent one by one for the blessing of their lifetime. Chayya was beside herself with joy. Her dream had come true!

After the padnamaskar, Swami interacted informally with the family members and made some lighthearted quips. Swami walked to the large windows facing the sea. For a minute or two He just stood there, looking intently at the ocean's expanse. After that, He made His way back towards the main door, indicating that He had to leave. Pammi immediately lit the arati tray and did His mangal-arati. It was a beautiful sight.

My father and Sunil escorted Swami out and into the lift. My father had a soul-stirringly sweet interaction with Swami in the small confines of the lift, on his way down. As time would show, that special interaction was to prove deeply significant later. For the moment, however, my father was thrilled with the close contact. Apparently, Swami lovingly held my father's hand in His own and my father held it pressed against his own heart, all the way down! We were to hear more about this lovely interaction from my father later. (In his diary, later, my father had this to write about his interaction – "15th March, Monday 1999 – THE GREATEST AND MOST JOYOUS DAY OF THE LIVES OF OUR FAMILY.... After an hour's stay, Swami departed at 5.30 p.m. with His escorts. I went with Him in the lift and HE held my hand in His hands and I kept the clasped hand on my heart throughout the lift journey. This was the MOST BLESSED EVENT OF MY LIFE – rather of several previous lives also!")

After Swami left, everybody was in a happy daze. The maid-servants were overjoyed. For days afterwards, they talked only of that grand moment when Sri Sathya Sai Baba, had granted them charansparsh. They all became ardent devotees and even started getting Baba's dreams. We had to get a constant supply of Swami's pendants, pictures and chains, etc. from Puttaparthi for them and their families!

28

Another Souvenir...

"Women have their strength in their hearts. Every woman must understand the existence of this divine strength within which God has endowed her with. There is nothing a woman cannot achieve through using her inner power. She is verily the embodiment of Shakti, a repository of the divine force and merits highest respect."

Sri Sathya Sai

We got the chance to work on another souvenir – for the Ladies Day 1999. My love for literature and writing, my choice of English honours as a subject in college and my stint with journalism in Bombay, were all coming to good use now. In retrospect, it appeared to be only a preparation for this, to become Swami's instrument and write for Him.

Somehow, my interest in other kinds of writing diminished and I did not feel motivated by any topic, which was not directly spiritual. Of course, as Swami says, everything is God and a distinction should not be made between the worldly and the spiritual. However, one has to be extremely evolved to realize that truth. And at that point for me, the worldly was worldly and the spiritual was spiritual! In fact, this applied to my reading habits also. Having been an avid reader all my life, I suddenly realized that the desire had dimmed. Now, books on Sai, His teachings and on spirituality in general started attracting me more. This was quite startling initially even to me, because literature and the sharp pleasure it afforded had been quite the high of my life. I can only analyse this by saying that the pleasure from my new reading far exceeded the earlier one and so there was no looking back. However, this was my experience and particular to me. Mostly such a dramatic shift does not take place – and neither is it called for or expected. All of this world, with its relative reality, is ultimately His creation. So nothing must be rejected or excluded, for, each thing has its own place, role and purpose. *Do not exclude anything. The exclusive cannot endure. God is all... How can you push God out of His domain? You limit God by your assumption, hence the restlessness... (One Soul's Journey* by Matlin*)*. However, for different people, different things work given the time. What worked for me yesterday may not work for me today but it may work for someone else today and so on. Just as our skin cells keep regenerating all the while, deep within, on inner levels too we must be regenerating and the important thing is to catch the change, and recognize it. *Everything, big or small, every cell and star, undergoes change every instant. The air which one man exhales is inhaled by another and the minute particles of one's system enter the system of the other person. Sea water becomes the moisture in the air and gathered together as rain-clouds, feeds the fields and gardens, with edible sweetness. Matter is but the perpetual communion and separation of particles. The human body has all its component cells replaced by 'new' ones during every seven-year period of time....*

The Souvenir. We wanted to be original. Where to start? Veenu, just younger to me, is a talented copywriter and her husband, Shrikant runs an advertising agency in Mumbai. His office is just down the road from where I stay. Together with his creative skills in designing and printing, we sisters got together the souvenir that was purely an outcome of Swami's grace.

Many days were spent in planning and designing the layouts etc. as also the writing and editing of the material. We decided to use hand-made paper to give the souvenir an exotic look and feel. We then spent many hours debating over the cover. We wanted it to be unique (our previous cover for the Unity Cup souvenir had been a real hit – even with Swami). Finally, we settled for using rich mauve raw silk as the cover material, on which would be hand-painted a golden OM. Shrikant's office staff manually did this painting of the OM on the cover and gold-glitter glue stick was used for this purpose! As this glitter glue took some while to dry, all the office space surfaces were used for spreading out the souvenir copies. Apart from all this, we had to get down to the writing. It was hectic. The loads of typing of our written stuff on the computer, was taken care of by Shrikant's able associate, Harsha.

Even as we were busy in this task, putting all our energies to it, in September '99 we suddenly got a chance to go to Parthi. We hoped to directly seek Swami's blessings for our souvenir-in-the-making.

Pammi and Sunil had their silver wedding anniversary coming up in September. They decided to go to Swami for His blessings. We decided that our whole family from Bombay should go for the special occasion. Luckily, all the children of the family and husbands, could co-ordinate their school and office dates to make it. Subodh and our two daughters were coming along with me this time. I hoped that each of them would get good darshans of Swami that would strengthen their bond with Him further. They all believed in Him but I wanted this belief to be reinforced all the time. When you discover something as wonderful as Sai, you want to share it with all the world but most of all with your near and dear ones – you long for them to experience the wonder as much as you do.

Thus, when Swami most graciously called us in for an interview on 23rd September on the day of their anniversary, it became a very special opportunity for the family to be together with Swami inside. And though Swami did call us in – He almost didn't! That was the day when He had to give padnamaskars to hundreds of sevadal volunteers lined up in rows on both the ladies' and gents' side. Swami had to walk a lot that day in and out of the rows bestowing that grace. When He finished this magnanimous task, He walked back slowly to the verandah and then into his room. He came out again, but by that time, the assembled sevadals had started getting up to leave. They were in a hurry as they had to catch their respective trains back home. The verandah was blocked from view. We kept sitting, feeling just a wee bit dejected. We were quite sure that there was no chance for an interview now. But, with Swami, as we learn, anything can happen at any time! For suddenly, there was a stir and we saw somebody rushing towards us, beckoning urgently. We couldn't believe our ears when the sevadals on duty told us, "Swami is calling your group!" We jumped up and made our way, hurriedly, through the throngs of sevadals, who were leaving after their padanamaskar.

Swami was standing on the verandah, on one side waiting for us. My friend Shanti had travelled with us this time and was part of the group. She was carrying with her a diary of divine messages given to her by the inner-Sai on the inner level. She had been instructed that morning through the inner-voice to carry the diary to darshan. She did, and the diary was now, with its owner, inside the interview room! It had been three months now, since her inner voice experience had started, with clear lucid messages just flowing from inside. She was mesmerized, and so was I, as much with the extraordinary messages as the manner in which they were given. In between the messages, there would sometimes be other instructions and talk, which would completely floor us. It was too amazing and direct a manifestation of His omnipresence, omnipotence and omniscience, that we had only heard about. Like most people who get messages in this fashion, she went through many periods of doubt – is it Him, or me? At such times, I would reassure her firmly for there was not an iota of doubt in my mind, that it was Him and Him alone. In any case, the content, style and wisdom of the messages was such, we knew it could not have come but from the Highest. In her diary, at this point, she had only the first few messages and she felt a bit awkward carrying the diary inside. However, she had to obey the voice within!

We seated ourselves around Swami's chair. There were nineteen of us in all! Swami spoke to Pammi and Sunil and blessed them lovingly. He called them to sit in front of His chair and then chanted auspicious mantras, on the occasion of their silver wedding anniversary.

At one point, I felt Swami look in my direction and say, "*Kya kaam karta hai*?" (what work do you do?). Nobody else spoke in answer, so I presumed it was me, and said, "Me, Swami?" At that He indicated, He was referring to the one sitting before me (Pammi's sister-in-law, Nutan). A few minutes later, the same thing happened. He addressed the question, "*Kya kaam karta hai*" and it appeared as if He was looking at me. Again no one else spoke up, not sure who He was addressing. Again I queried, "Swami?" (Me?) at which He indicated to the person on my left! It was Shanti. I nudged her to answer Him. At that she told Swami about her work with garden – landscaping and He gave a beautiful talk on how the heart should be cultivated into a garden of good qualities. Shrikant had carried a sheet of paper in the hope of getting Swami's blessings and signature, for the souvenir we were working on. At the opportune moment, he asked Swami to bless the project by signing on the title page. Very graciously Swami took the proffered pen and the sheet of paper and signed, "With love and blessings, Baba". We were thrilled. The grandest page of our souvenir was ready – the rest would pale in front of that. At this point, Shanti offered her diary of inner-voice messages to Swami for His signature and blessings. Apparently, He guided her from within to do so. Swami took the diary and very neatly and meticulously signed on His photograph that was stuck on the diary. That precious blessing came to fruition two years later when the messages blessed and the new ones in the diary were published in a gem of a book called, *From Him to me.*

After this, Swami distributed vibhuti packets by the handfuls and somebody clicked a photo just when Swami was giving my lot to me, a photo which is one of the cherished ones in my album.

We began to troop out. Subodh was standing with folded palms near the door. He spoke up. Everybody had taken padanamaskar and he was awaiting his turn. He said softly, "Baba, I am left out". Baba smiled sweetly and said, "take take" and Subodh bent and reverentially took padanamaskar. After that, in a very sweet gesture, Subodh formally introduced the children and me to Baba, saying, "Baba, this is my wife and these are my daughters." At this, Baba gently smiled and said softly, "I know, I know." Baba then spoke in a soft tone with my two daughters telling them to focus on their studies and "talk less!" They were very happy to have Baba address them personally. Swami had agreed to photos being taken to commemorate the occasion. We now crowded around Him, to get into the divine frame. We then left for Bombay feeling truly very blessed.

29

"Saree, *Milla*?"

Work and worship, do and dedicate, plan and protect, but do not worry about the fruit. That is the secret of spiritual success.

"God is also a businessman! What sort of business does He do? Not worldly business but spiritual business. With Him too, it is give and take, not one – way traffic! Give Him love and receive grace from Him. Give up all your thoughts and notions to God and receive ananda from Him. Give to Him your sorrows and exchange them for bliss. This is the business God is in."

Sri Sathya Sai

The souvenir was almost complete but we had to think of a name. Since it was for Ladies Day, some of our initial choices were titles like – *An Equal Spirit* and *A Woman's Devotions*. However, on giving it more thought we felt the former sounded a little feminist and academic whereas in the latter the term 'woman' sounded slightly inappropriate for the occasion. We finally called the offering – *The Spirit Sublime* which sounded both spiritual and sweet. The spirit having no gender, it covered that area too.

The printed souvenir looked quite attractive and we were very pleased. We sent a silent prayer of thanks to our Lord, for clearing the obstacles. There were some hiccups, as there very nearly always are in any worthy enterprise, but the grace of Swami showed up every time to take care of it. In fact, it was only His grace that had accomplished the task. We had simply to go though the motions of effort and worry to completion.

Now that the souvenir was ready, we were looking forward to the birthday and going to Parthi. But this time we were in two minds.

The 18th of November 1999 happened to be our parents fiftieth wedding anniversary – and we had to present the Ladies Day souvenir to Swami on the 19th! Now that was an emotional tussle for all of us, but our parents decided the matter firmly by insisting that we all should be present in Parthi to offer the souvenir to Swami. True to nature, they were foregoing their own desire to spend that special day with their daughters, entirely for our sake.

We landed in Prasanthi on the 17th of November. The little village of Puttaparthi was abuzz with activity. Crowds of devotees from all the parts of the country and the world were coming in for this divine event celebrated by devotees every year.

On 18th morning, as we sat in darshan, our thoughts were only with our parents. We decided that as soon as Swami came out, we would collectively seek special blessings for them. When Swami finally appeared my prayer was that something extraordinarily nice may happen for my parents to make up for our absence. Well, something did happen. Something, we could hardly believe. Of course, we got to know of it only later when we phoned our parents after darshan.

On the phone their voices were ringing with delight. The sweetest thing had taken place. The three brothers-in-law had landed up in Kanpur giving a fabulous surprise to our parents – and us! It had all been kept secret from my parents and us. What a gorgeous surprise! No words can fully cover that gesture of theirs. It took on extra meaning because we daughters, the wives, were sitting in Parthi!

Apparently, it had been Sunil's idea and when he mooted it, both Subodh and Srikanth enthusiastically fell into line. What my parents felt at this marvellous gesture can only be imagined. Even we felt deeply touched and our hearts overflowed with deepest gratitude towards our husbands. And of course to the Prime Mover – Swami!

On the 19th morning, many ladies got wonderful seating on or near the verandah. By His grace, we were part of that group. Swami sat on His swivel chair quite close to our ladies block. He cast His looks around over the sea of eager animated faces. The real 'fun' was to begin later – when He would Himself distribute the sarees to the ladies (He normally does this on Ladies Day, but this was our first experience – our earlier sarees having been sent to us). He came to the edge of our group, with a lady volunteer standing besides Him holding a pile of glossy maroon and gold silk sarees. One by one, He started giving sarees to the ladies present. He would either drop the saree into the hands of devotees near Him or fling to those farther away. I got the feeling that that was the time He enjoyed most – His arm swinging a bit, to throw the saree and eager outstretched hands going up to catch.

I have always been one who can be termed as a 'non-pushy' kind of person. In fact, my mother would always berate the fact of how the world was going ahead and her daughters kept pushing themselves back! Nobody would guess, looking at us though, but it is there in all of us in lesser or greater degree. Even my eldest sister, though extremely bold has never been pushy – there being a very fine distinction between the two things. But then, if you can't make a virtue out of being pushy, you can't also make a virtue about its opposite. I think the Lord was about to teach me a lesson on that. As Swami stood there distributing the sarees, I decorously, and with what I thought was dignity, sat in my place, with my palms reverently joined but not stretching out. Sarees flew in all directions, but mine.

Then, very dramatically, Swami cut a path right through the middle of our group and came right next to me, first before and then besides me! It was thrilling, this sudden proximity. I had my faced arched eagerly towards Him, and my palms folded. Swami picked saree upon saree, flung it to one lady after another, to my left, right, before and behind, but *somehow* He missed me!! What a scenario – Him standing so close, and I looking right upto Him and everybody receiving, but me. Pammi and Veenu got it to my left, others on my right and so on. I started feeling the heat of it, inspite of my most valiant efforts. It was not the saree of course, just the feeling of being left out by Him, a kind of subtle rejection. Also, the whole thing became a mini-drama with everybody egging me on to go up on my knees, lift my hands, etc. to make it one of the more embarrassing moments of my life (in a place and manner where I would have least wanted).

While all this was happening, Swami perambulated the group, going on distributing the prasad (sarees). Everytime He would approach my side, the stage whispers would go up – tell Him, ask Him, etc. and try as I did, in my non-pushy way, to attract Him, He would choose to pretend to miss me! He gave a mischievous turn to it by sweetly asking one or two ladies next to me, "Saree *milla*?" (did you get the saree?). Urgent whispers prodded me, "Stand up and ask Him." Finally, I did. I found He was standing just before me. I said simply, "Swami….." Bhajans were on and Swami looked utterly radiant. As always, that distracted me! Looking at Him, I almost forgot what I wanted to say. This was darshan at its best. Nothing else mattered. Not His snubbing me, not my embarrassment – what mattered was, I was standing face to face with Sai…. As I stood there smiling beatifically, He smiled too (in amusement?) and taking a saree from the pile flung it across to me in a graceful motion. I remember the bhajan playing at that time was *'ras vilola nand lala…'*. What a ras! It had me spinning no doubt!

For the Ladies Day programme that evening, we wore our new sarees to darshan. I got a fabulous place. It was close to Swami's chair near the verandah. I saw Him cast two very deep meaningful glances my way – the kind of looks that are every devotees' delight. Later, in a small ceremony, my sisters Pammi and Mashu made an official presentation of our Ladies Day souvenir – *The Spirit Sublime* – to Swami. Swami received all the books and souvenirs, in a formal ceremony. There were some done by other devotees too. He blessed each one. This time, though we could offer the souvenir personally, we missed the direct and informal appreciation of the last one – the cricket souvenir. Apparently, Swami expressed His appreciation of this one too later, inside but His sharp eye did not miss the fact that the Prasanthi colours on the sketches of the building had not come exactly right! This had happened inspite of our best efforts because of the hand-made paper which made it tough for the colours to come just so. How amazing it is that amidst all His monumental concerns He can take time to make note of such things. It is a lesson for us to try and touch perfection in every task we do – be it a big one or a small one. This souvenir also, by His grace, received a wonderful response.

On the birthday, on 23rd, Swami came in procession, in a white robe. He looks radiant in any colour, but many devotees feel that He looks best in orange. There was a divine discourse in the morning but no musical programme. The morning event for some reason felt a little low key especially in comparison to the seventieth, seventy-second and seventy-third birthdays – the ones we had attended. However, the evening programme made up for it. Many songs were sung which were quite just the best thing as they were the devotional outpourings of devotees' hearts. There were some folk dance performances also with Swami sitting on the swivel chair and watching intently (to all purposes) or sometimes not so, and for that reason swiveling, and casting precious glances at the thousands of devotees sitting all around.

It was dusk when the programme got over and Swami walked back to Poornachandra. Veenu happened to be sitting in the front row. The most incredible thing happened with her. Swami came down the aisle, walking on the carpet in the center, casting a glance here, a smile there, every now and then. When He reached Veenu, He cut across dramatically and came straight to her. With a very soft loving expression He said, "*Karo, bangaru.*" It was overwhelming to say the least. She had not even asked for it. She bent in deep gratitude and love to take the much-cherished padnamaskar of Swami on His 'birthday'. Now, that's really very very special. The seventy-fourth birthday ended for the family on that note and we went back feeling happily content.

30

From Him To Me – To Us

You can benefit from God but you cannot explain Him... Come, take ananda *from Me, dwell on that* ananda *and be full of* shanti.

Sri Sathya Sai

It was around July 1999 that my friend, Shanti started receiving her inner voice messages from within. These messages came to her in such stupendous fashion and were of such amazing spiritual content, it took us a while to digest what was really happening. Could it really be so? I was sure but Shanti would waver sometimes. At such moments, I would try my best to convince her that it could be no other! Apart from the formal messages, Shanti sometimes received guidance on personal and other matters, which became another extraordinary development. Often, I would also be the beneficiary of the guidance.

Even before Swami started giving her these messages, Shanti and I had fallen into the habit of talking on phone at least once a day and the conversation was only and always about Swami. We would also exchange Swami dreams as both of us would have those much longed for dreams of Swami. When either of us were graced with a dream we could hardly wait to communicate it to the other on phone. We also composed an A to Z dictionary on Swami and the spiritual process and the various arduous levels one had to go through. A-levels was the pinnacle and stood for *Atma Nivedanam* which very few reach but all can aspire too. B-levels was the Bhakti-*ras* level representing pure love for God. C-level for Concentrated Integrated Awareness, D-level for Dreams, E for Expansion of the heart, F for Fine-tuning or Frustration (depending on the mood), and so on. I have forgotten most of the others, but remember clearly how V stood for *Viraha* (anguish of separation) level – because we felt it so often! In some way or the other, we would keep in touch with Baba even when the usual day-to-day problems would engulf us and try to snatch our connection away. That one talk on the phone everyday worked like an excellent tonic or the S-Vitamin that carried us through the day.

Whenever a beautiful new message would come forth, Shanti would call me and read it out. We would marvel at the language and the content. The messages were lyrical and packed with deep meaning (*jnana*). Sometimes, for days no message would come and at other times two or three would be given in a single day. It became a unique spiritual adventure to await the messages, which contained the highest jnana in sweet simple language. Shanti started recording the messages in a special diary as Baba indicated that later they would go into a book. As mentioned earlier, Swami blessed her diary when it was just a few messages old, in our interview of September 1999. With this momentous seal on the messages, any doubts Shanti may have harboured about the source of the messages was dissolved. In His own subtle way, Swami showed her where the messages were coming from and that His blessings were with her. After the completion of 108 messages, Shanti got inner guidance to publish them through the Sri Sathya Sai Book Trust, Prasanthi Nilayam, so that others could also benefit. This being a major step, Shanti wished to first have the manuscript blessed by Swami before going ahead with the project.

Would I accompany her? she asked. Ever-ready for a trip to Parthi, I concurred with my husband and happily agreed to go along. It was to be just a short three-day trip and therefore not much of a problem there – or so we thought! One can never afford to be complacent about a trip to see Swami – something or the other will happen, contrary to your expectations. This was sometime in September 2000. As my birthday also falls in September it kind of became an added reason to make it to Parthi around that time.

We reached Prasanthi and very hopefully started carrying the manuscript to darshan everyday. We knew it would not be that easy. We were no longer greenhorns to believe that we would sit in darshan and Swami would readily walk up and bless the manuscript. But we did nurture a definite hope that He would do it sometime in the three day period of our stay, especially because He had guided Shanti to get the manuscript for blessings. Darshan after darshan we sat, with Shanti holding the manuscript, but he chose to ignore, evade, bypass, deflect... whenever those lotus feet came within our vicinity, they would acquire a will of their own and cut across to the other side! It was so studied and systematic, this ignoring, that it did feel like a kind of reverse attention. But, as devotees will agree, the regular type of attention is far more desirable!

We decided to extend our trip by another three days.

Just before all this, came my birthday. This was to be my first birthday in Swami's presence in Prasanthi, and this time too it had happened by chance, because it coincided with Shanti's trip. I wore a brighter than usual saree and carried akshata (rice) in a small silver tray to darshan. I was a bit doubtful about whether I wished to carry the akshata or not, but I finally did. There's always the chance that Swami may or may not come to you – even if you are dressed in peacock plumes – for if He wishes, He will just manage, in a most dexterous fashion, to walk by without noticing you. Anyhow, I thought that whether Swami notices or not (on the form level), we would take our chance, and so I took the akshata along. However, in hindsight I must say that it is not in my nature to do things like that, – I was doing it just for the sake of doing it and really did not attach so much feeling to it.

The music started and Swami appeared. I felt a little tense as it was my birthday and also because of the very prominent akshata tray in my hands. A few paces before He reached me, another young girl sat, coincidently with an akshata tray in her hands. He went up to her and sprinkled the akshata as blessing on her. My heart beat faster – it did appear to be an akshata-blessings day! Swami approached and I looked eagerly at Him. But just as He was nearing me, He cut across to the other side of the carpet! I thought that He would definitely cut across again towards me, but my stunned eyes saw Him walk on, nonchalantly down the darshan lines. I was thrown off-balance. Shanti was equally nonplussed and I looked at her and said, "Amazing Lord...!". However, it was His grace that I almost immediately accepted His action. I was even able to joke about it – though weakly! *You must have not only freedom from fear but freedom from hope and expectation. Trust in My wisdom; I do not make mistakes. Love My uncertainty! For it is not a mistake. It is My intent and will. Be still; do not want to understand. Relinquish understanding. Relinquish the imperative that demands understanding.* Shanti was a little amazed at how I had taken it. Later, after darshan, when we were walking back to the room a little low in spirits, Swami suddenly gave a beautiful inner voice message for me. He blessed me profusely and told me in a very touching manner that it had been a test of devotion and I had passed it.

We continued carrying the manuscript to darshan and Swami continued ignoring it. The last darshan of the extended three days dawned – with a loud clap of thunder and lightning. Early morning around 3 a.m. we woke up with a start to lightning, thunder and pouring rain. It was unseasonal rain, but in Parthi anything is possible. There is really no season there – years ago Swami had demonstrated that with the kalpataru tree from which He had plucked fruits out of season for His playmates. From producing fruits out of season to producing the season itself, is just a short step away for the master of the universe, even from the point of view of logic!

We looked at each other in the room – and laughed. Now what? It was our last darshan of the trip and there appeared to be a big question mark whether there would be darshan or not (considering the heavy downpour). Was this a subtle message from the heavens to postpone our trip? The manuscript had yet to be blessed. We decided that if Swami ignored the manuscript even today, then we would postpone our tickets to the next flight out of Parthi, three days away. By now, Shanti was pretty tense and every passing day of being 'overlooked' by Him in darshan made it worse. She was also concerned about her work commitments back at home. Even my husband and daughters queried me on the phone about our extensions and it took a lot of patient explaining.

Then Subodh gave a valuable suggestion to us on the phone about the manuscript. This gave a surprising new turn to the whole matter. He suggested that on the dedication page, Shanti should add the words, 'with total surrender' to her message. Shanti did that and with those added words of surrender, we waited again next morning with the manuscript in darshan. Shortly Swami appeared. We watched Him intently. Were we seeing right? For He came with a spring in His step, and walking very fast, straight to Shanti! He looked very pleased. She held aloft the manuscript to Him and with a gentle smile Swami tapped and blessed it. We looked at each other in jubilation. He had done it. The title of the manuscript was, "From Him to me". A lady from the crowd, Tara, who had been watching Shanti carry the manuscript everyday came up to congratulate her saying, "Truly, from Him to me takes a very long time."

That little tap of Swami's, that precious blessing, goes a long way. The manuscript was submitted to the Prasanthi Book Trust office for review and later passed and accepted. Through inner guidance, Swami indicated the steps to be taken. This gem of a book was subsequently distributed by the Prasanthi Book Trust.

Of course, the whole process of publishing it took a little while, with the usual hiccups along the way. The final outcome was extremely charming.

There is an interesting story about the book. We sisters gifted a copy of it to our Sai sister, Sarvalakshmi. Veenu scribbled a message on the front flap, 'and now, from Him to you…' On the top of the page, she wrote 'Om Sri Sai Ram'. She signed all our names at the bottom of the page. Sarvalakshmi happened to carry this copy of the book into the interview room once. She requested Swami to sign it. Swami took the book and looked at it with attention, flipped a few pages and then signed on the very page where Veenu had scribbled the message! Swami wrote, 'With love and blessings, Sri Sathya Sai'. We were quite overjoyed to hear this story from her later and promptly got copies made one for each, as also for Shanti to preserve in our treasure chests! Another amazing angle to the story is the observation of another devotee lady of how the ink of the Om Sri Sai Ram and Swami's signature seems exactly the same.

In all the problems we had faced in getting this book ready, there was a lesson to be learnt, which was that just because you are doing 'Swami's work' and with His blessings, it did not mean that problems would not beset you… In fact, you may be given an extra share. But they would, one by one get sorted out too, sometimes in the most miraculous ways. If there were no problems, success would hardly hold the luster that it does. It is the difficulties that we berate, in reaching our goals that lends worth to our final achievement. Viewed from this perspective, everything in life is perfect and in its place – a vast jigsaw where every piece eventually does fit in. Puzzling yes, but in the end it all falls into place. Faith would hardly have value, if there were no doubts…

31

Where The Dew Is Green

Love sprouts, peace descends like dew... foster love, live in love, spread love – that is the spiritual exercise which will yield the maximum benefit...

I will always be waiting for you at the end of the path...

Sri Sathya Sai

The year 2000 dawned. It was wonderful to see the annual New Year card from my parents (from our business firm in Kanpur) arrive in the post. My father had started this firm, 'Mazz & Co.', fifty years back and it was a flourishing business concern. It was running solely and singly on the strength of my father's unique business acumen. It was literally, a glorious one-man-show. Though my father had tried to get us interested in the business, we never really did. Then, one by one we got married – except for our youngest sister, Mashu, who was still too young.

My father was a uniquely loveable soul and it had always been my wish that he should draw closer to Swami and rediscover his bhakti anew. It was through him that Swami had come into our lives and initially it was my father whose current of bhakti was the strongest. Though this love for Swami stayed with him through the years, family responsibilities and business commitments as also his worry and concern for his wife and daughters kept him from really 'letting go' in this regard. He held himself back, and it was here that his practical and scientific temper came into the picture. He had immense love and regard for Swami but he maintained a fair balance between that and his worldly life. Yet, he always joked with us that, though we were the ones running off to Parthi all the time and talking constantly of Swami, it was he who had a deep special connection with Him, which we knew nothing about. He would lightheartedly say that we could check it out and decide the matter once and for all by putting chits in front of Swami's picture and seeing whose name came up! "*Parchi nikal ke dekh lo*", he would tease us. After the experience he had had in the lift with Swami in Pammi's house, he told us, with a twinkle in his eye – "Now we know, who is the *asli* (true) one!"

My father had a special name for me – *Ginthi.* (translated it means someone who is short) Till standard five in school, I was apparently very short, compared to the other girls in my class. Once at a sports event in school, I was partaking in the baton relay race. My parents watched me from the guest stands. All the other runners were tall and lanky. I was the shortest. Yet, I managed to run fast and overtook the tall ones! They told me later how they had been amazed with my looking so small – '*Ginthi*' – and yet running so fast! That day my father gave me that name and it became his term of endearment for me. All his love for me was packed into that one word – *Ginthi.* He would use it when he was feeling exceptionally indulgent and affectionate towards me. Well, I can hardly ever remember him calling me by my regular name. It was always *Ginthi.*

My mother's approach to Swami was and remains her own! She is not ritualistic and is rather fearless by nature. She feels nothing should be done even in matters of faith and religion out of mere superstition or fear. Having a very strong mind, she is, without realizing it herself, very evolved spiritually, being extremely self-possessed. But above everything else, she is the most lovable person, with, as we children say, the softest hands in the world! People often take her to be of royal lineage. That is not surprising. She is a natural royal – queen of hearts! (my father often called her that!). She draws constantly from within and is not overly dependent on external support or situations. However, when things don't go right she is ready to fight with Swami, question Him and so on! Overall, she has a deep feeling for Him. In darshan more often than not on facing Swami, tears have sprung unbidden to her eyes. Swami has, on and off, through the years given her some wonderful dreams. In one such dream, *Swami flings a ruby necklace in darshan straight to my mother, which garlands her neck. In an other significant dream my mother saw Swami sitting informally in a room with our whole family...Someone comes in and questioningly looks at Swami and the informal ambience of the room. Swami smiles at that person and dismissing his doubt says, "these are My own people.."* (*yeh tho apne hain*). Around the world, devotees experience Baba's omnipresence, omnipotence and omniscience in many ways and dreams is one of them. Sometimes non-devotees or people who have never seen or heard of Baba get a dream experience, which marks the beginning of their journey to Sai.

My father – what can I say about him – he merits a biography of his own.... I hero-worshipped him for a number of very good reasons. When I got married, I hoped and prayed that, I could give my children even a bit of the kind of unique upbringing our parents had given us. I look back and marvel at my childhood, adolescence and youth and if I cherish my memories, it is all thanks to them. I don't ever remember him lecturing to us on anything and yet, subtly, all the important values of life were transmitted to us.

The new year card that I received was a plain white one, with the year 2000 embossed in gold on the top. Every year, the same style of greeting card – with just the changing year embossed in gold on top, each time – would be sent out by my father to his friends and business associates. It was a simple but elegant card. On receiving it, a silent prayer of gratitude went up from my heart to the Lord. It was sixteen years since my father had suffered a massive heart attack, which he had miraculously survived, by Baba's grace. It was as if he had come back, from the edge, and every year after that was perceived as a bonus of grace. During his illness, at the moment when my father became most critical, he had an amazing experience. In his hospital room, he saw a tall old man, like Shirdi Baba come to his bedside and rub '*malham*' (healing ointment) on his heart. At that very juncture, I was sitting outside the hospital room with the rest of my family, praying urgently to Sri Sathya Sai Baba. That was in the year 1983 when I had not developed that close connection to Baba, which was to come later. I had read somewhere in a book that in a moment of severe crisis if you mentally sent a telegram to Baba by calling out to Him thrice and giving the local address of where you were, 'He would come' immediately to help. It was a kind of prayer technique for SOS situations and I resorted to it in full sincerity. I called out to Baba urgently, in the manner recommended. And sure enough, He responded. For even as I prayed outside, my father had his incredible vision and experience inside, after which, he turned the corner miraculously – and recovered. Sixteen years went by, and my father lived a relatively healthy life, doing all the things he most loved to do – working ('work is worship' was his favourite Baba quote), gardening, reading, vacationing in the hills of Mussoorie, visits to his daughters homes in Mumbai, and of course, pampering us all!

Our garden in Kanpur was always the pride of our home. Whoever visited us, first made a special mention of the garden. It was my father's sacred grove in which he invested deepest devotion. Maybe because of this, it became a magic circle of delight that attracted everyone. Apart from the exotic array of flowers, seasonals and otherwise like petunias, phlox, asters, zerberras, verbena, sweet pea, there were fruit trees too – a lemon tree, an orange tree and a beloved *narangi* tree (kind of tiny Chinese oranges) with small white flowers exuding an enchanting fragrance...

In winter, the garden was a colour-riot of chrysanthemums – yellow, mauve, white, maroon. The bigger single varieties of this flower would be in separate pots lining the entire length of the garden. The other smaller varieties were planted with flowerbeds – masses and masses of them, slightly stooped with their own weight! It was as much the flowers as their unique arrangements in the garden that captivated everybody. If my father worked on the flowers outside, my mother made the most exotic arrangements of them in the flower vases inside the home. In fact, my mother's name '*Pushpa*' means flower – undoubtedly the best flower in our garden!

There were loads of potted plants of all exotic varieties (cycus, aricaria, adenium, begonias etc) and my father would shuffle these pots around every week to create new aesthetic arrangements in the garden. Mornings, we would see him in the garden with the maali, arranging and re-arranging. There was a wheelbarrow for moving the plants. Seeing the maali wheeling the barrow from one corner of the garden to the other was one of the most familiar sights for us.

In fact, it was my father's belief that freshness could be brought to life by a dash of creativity. Like a kaleidoscope, which can create endless beautiful patterns with a fixed number of glass pieces, he taught us that life too can be made attractive. Even within the house, the arrangement of the furniture was never allowed to stagnate! The paintings, the sofa arrangements, other decorative pieces were constantly shuffled. In this way, old things looked new! He would often tell us children to view things differently and not in the usual way. "See a spoon bent", he would say, and break through the pattern of accustomed thinking and preconceived ideas.

My father was an intellectual but a delightful one! We would have these brain-storming sessions with him and explore new concepts and ideas. He would outwit us easily and we would be awed by his knowledge, command over the English language and his overall felicity with words. He had knowledge about almost everything under the sun. He was an M.Sc. in Physics but he subscribed to the TLS (*Times Literary Supplement*) too! Thus, we grew up with both Shakespeare and Newton in the house! My father's writing style was exquisite. I have yet to come across that style and grace in anyone. To give a sample from his letters, he once wrote to his daughters in Bombay tongue-in-cheek – "My dearest ones, So, what is the pilgrims' progress now. Having arrived at the destination, I feel like guiding those who are still engaged in the ascent. Keep up and when you feel you are fit to open the *parchi* (chits), let me know...." Another time prior to a vacation in Mussoorie, he wrote: "So the joy and thrill of Mussoorie has begun. Am getting visions of the cakeman on Dick Road, Mr. Baretto's soul in some form near the Tibetan Coffee House, the flowers on the horsechestnut tree facing the study. This time though the study would be purely mine and entrance would be permitted on scheduled days to those of literary bent! I am thinking of Landour and the tea shops where democracy reigns supreme and one sips tea with the rickshawpuller alongside hot jalebies on the plate.... Hoping to see you all there, so help us Baba. Your, Papa." Even Swami once told me in a dream about my father's writing abilities. *In the dream, Swami says about my father very longingly, "he writes so well...." At that I tell Swami, "I know, but he feels we write well....!" Swami dismisses that with a hhmmph! which suggests that there was no comparison!* I often told my father to write a book on Swami in his unique writing style, but he would joke and dismiss the idea and tell us to do the writing!

Since our childhood, there was one tree in the main garden that we all loved – the oleander tree. It had a green canopy under the shade of which we had many good breakfasts and brunches down the years. This tree was part of our garden-lore. It had conical yellow flowers, with soft curling petals that exuded a pungent fragrance. As children we would string these together in garlands or just throw bunches of them into the air and see them fall in a shower all around us. Every morning the green lawn would be strewn with these bright yellow flowers.

In March 2000, my parents were in Mumbai visiting their daughters. When they returned to Kanpur after a couple of months, there was distressing news. They were pained to discover that the oleander tree had fallen – a squall had uprooted it.

The minute I entered my house in May 2000 for the summer vacations, I saw this vacant gap in our garden. It looked so empty. I felt deeply sad. However, I tried not to show it. A small bit of the tree had survived and we hoped to nurture it back to full strength again. What was more touching was that my father had used the yellow flowers of that bit of the tree to decorate a big potted plant near the verandah, for my welcome! It was always something unique coming from him.

This was on May 22nd. Veenu with her kids had already reached there. Subodh, our daughters, and I had now arrived. Pammi, Sunil and Rohan were in England. We were to be in Kanpur only for a few days this time. So, every day was precious. This time, however, so much more precious, if only we had known…

One morning on that trip, my father strolled with me in the garden, proudly showing all his plants and the fruit on the jackfruit tree. This jackfruit tree had its own story. Fed on a diet of Enid Blyton, we grew up with a fascination for earthy adventure. We were always looking to create simple joys in our lives. It was more an adventure of ideas than external heroics or dare. The idea of a tree house caught our imagination. My father heard us out and the next we knew, a tree house came up on the jackfruit tree! This became a happy platform for both family members and guests. In fact, many Test cricketers both from India and abroad, have been entertained there during a cricket series. An English writer, Frank Keating was so charmed by our tree house and that particular evening under the stars, that he mentioned it in a cricket article that he wrote in *The Guardian*.

Now, we stood under the jackfruit tree, admiring the fruit. My father looked happy and relaxed. Looking around fondly, he said that later, his soul would breathe through every leaf and blade of this garden. As usual, we dismissed his statement by countering that, 'that' was a long way off... He laughed mischievously and asked, was he immortal?

That morning – 29th May – the household awoke to the usual morning rhythms and activities. On the verandah, the slight tussle for *The Times of India* took place. I was reading it when my father came, peered into it and teasingly said, "I *only* read the Speaking Tree" (an oblique reference to my reading tastes!). As Veenu was vying for the paper, I dodged her and went and handed it to my father, with a smile, before she could lay her hands on it! I clearly remember that small act of mine even today...

There was nothing in the day – in the blue sky, in the morning air, in the general look of things, to suggest anything. To suggest that in a matter of few hours, my dear father would be passing on to newer vistas, and more sacred groves.....

Sixteen years had passed since he'd had his heart attack. Sixteen wonderful years, bonus years, in which he finished a lot of undone work, completed many tasks, set things right, into as perfect an order as he could, for his wife, daughters and grandchildren. All that done – the pain struck. Except for Pammi, Sunil and Rohan, we were all by his side. Rubbing vibhuti, praying. Even at that point, he looked at me and said feebly, "*Ginthi*, you'll get tired..."

There was a big, framed photo of Swami facing him. This photo had been there from the very beginning. Raising his hands, best as he could, he folded them into a namaskar and pointing them to Swami's photo, he said, "Sai Ram..." Soon after, he was gone... to Swami, to His divine arbour of love and peace.

The oleander tree had preceded him – maybe to receive him there...

32

'Sai Ram'

Do not be concerned with who I am! Concern yourself with who you are and how you can be aware of your Truth. I will lead you if you rely on me. The alternates of the world will not bring you happiness, for the mind which revels in alternates (alternate states) is but a will-o-the-wisp flitting before your vision along the marshy wilds.

Sri Sathya Sai

After a long wonderful association of fifty years with my father, my mother suddenly found herself alone. Though initially shaken and near-broken by her loss, she bounced back, with her indomitable spirit coming to the fore. At the point, when she was feeling her lowest, the priest from our Radha-Krishna temple from Kanpur, walked into our house. This was Swami's timing! The priest gave us, not so many words of consolation, as an amazing discourse (*pravachhan*) on the *maya nagari* (this world) and its evanescence; how the atma was the only reality and eternal. The rest is all a passing show. He also gave our spirits an immense boost by disclosing that my father had left on a very auspicious day and at a moment when, as he said, "*Brahmand ke charon kivaad khule the,*" (all the four doors of the heavens were open).

However, spiritual consolations apart, the ache of absence, was very real. To alleviate the sudden loneliness that descended after years, a dog was kept as a pet – as a salve and also to provide the much – needed watch-dog protection to the house. A jet-black labrador with honey-gold eyes he was called Charcoal. Pets, especially dogs, come closest to giving the unconditional love, all humans are even seeking and very soon Chiklum (Charcoal's pet name) became a cherished and much-loved member of the household!

In 2000, only Pammi Sunil and I came to Puttaparthi for Guru Purnima. Mashu decided to stay back in Kanpur, with my mother.

Veenu too stayed back in Bombay and did not come to Parthi this time. She was booked to come with us and packed, but last minute she cancelled her plans because of an inner 'message' she got. The message simply said, "forfeit" and though she felt distressed about missing the trip, she complied. In a way, it was the best thing. She was still struggling hard to overcome the loss of our father. She was in deep anguish and needed some more time – to restore her inner equilibrium and fully accept what had happened.

We arrived in Parthi on the eve of Guru Purnima. Swami came by in darshan and spoke to Pammi. He asked after Vishwanath, who was sitting on the verandah. Vishy's wife, Kavita and son, Daivik were also present but were sitting a little away from us. On the verandah, Swami spoke to Vishy and patted him affectionately on the head

Guru Purnima morning, Swami gave a discourse in which He used the word '*kritagya*' three times. Now this deeply touched us. My father had uttered this very word to Veenu, just a few days before his passing away. The word denotes gratefulness. In what subtle ways, Swami shows His compassion and all-knowingness! He also hinted that we should not regret or rue what had happened but accept it as the will of God – and count our blessings. Or, in other words, be grateful (*kritagya*).

Walking back after the discourse and arati, Swami put a special smile on little Daivik's face! Daivik had written a heartfelt letter to Swami and specially prayed that Swami take it in darshan that day. Kavita was sitting with him in a little out-of-the way spot. Yet, Swami took a detour and came to them. With a loving smile, He took the letter and patted Daivik on the head. Was he over the moon! As also his parents, Kavita and Vishy.

After darshan, we phoned Veenu and Mashu to tell them about darshan and how Swami had used the word kritagya. We knew that would make them feel better.

On Guru Purnima evening, I was placed in the first row next to Pammi. On my right, was seated a dear Sai friend, Sarvalakshmi from the USA. She had just arrived. Swami came out and gave her a fabulously warm welcome. Rarely have I seen such a 'cute' interaction between Swami and a devotee in darshan. He looked at Sarvalakshmi and going back a step expressed happy surprise. Smiling broadly, He said, "Lakshmi… Lakshmi… Lakshmi.." thrice. The tone denoted surprise and welcome in the manner of 'look who's here'! However, the sweetest was He pronounced her name as 'Laschmi' in the rustic accent because apparently she had just finished a major stint of village or gram seva!

After this Swami circled His hand, materialized vibhuti and gave it to her. I was sitting to the left. He looked at me then and indicated for me to stretch my palm. I did. He gave me the vibhuti and then to Pammi sitting beside me, wiping the remnants of vibhuti on His finger lightly on her palm. "Where is Gavaskar?" He asked Pammi. She pointed to the verandah and said, "Verandah, Swami."

Next morning, Swami came into darshan looking ebullient. He patted a devotee on the head, jauntily. He walked on and came to Pammi and asked, "Where is husband?"

"Swami, on the verandah."

"Hoon?" He said. Pammi repeated, "On verandah."

"I know that!" He rejoindered. As all this was happening, He was standing right in front of me and talking to Pammi, at an angle. I got a chance to take a beautiful padnamaskar. Continuing to stand there, He asked a lady besides me, "When are you leaving?" Even before she could answer, He started materializing vibhuti. I thought it was for that lady. But, no! He stretched His palm towards me. I immediately raised my palm and He poured vibhuti into it. He then gave vibhuti to Pammi. He looked searchingly behind us as if looking for the other two sisters. After giving the remaining vibhuti to the lady next to us, He enquired, "*Sab* sisters *nahin ayya*?" (all sisters haven't come?)

That evening in darshan, Pammi had a thought. She wondered if it was possible for Swami to give me vibhuti again, third time running! Darshan music started and a wave of anticipation ran through the crowd. Swami came in with a serious expression. Pammi had letters in her lap. He came to her and she offered the letters. He took them from her and asked her, "Sisters, *kahan*?" Pammi answered, "Swami, only two have come." Then He said, "*Verry* happy", giving His approval to Mashu's and Veenu's decision to stay back this time. All the while, Pammi was secretly hoping and wondering if it was possible for Swami to materialize vibhuti again and give it to me! Swami spoke in Telegu to a lady next to us and then materialized vibhuti! Pammi's eyes widened – will He, can He? she wondered. But Swami gave the vibhuti to the other lady! After giving the lady vibhuti He sprinkled the remains onto Pammi. Pammi thought, regarding her wish for me, "oh well, twice is stupendous enough..."

If she had but known! Swami walked onto the verandah and the next we knew was that Sunil and Vishy were standing and looking towards us. Swami had ever so graciously called us in for an interview.

We felt deeply touched by this gesture of Swami. We had hardly expected it, feeling that our father's passing away being so recent, He may not call us. When one is emotionally overwrought, one may ask awkward questions and be out of one's depth. But, Swami called us in and I prayed that He be in charge of the proceedings. We decided to employ as much restraint as possible.

And once inside, the first thing Swami did was materialize vibhuti (as is His norm) and give it to the ladies, including me! So, Pammi's wish was fulfilled – in its own way – of Swami giving me vibhuti in three consecutive darshans in a row!

We sat down around Swami's feet. We told Him about our father's 'passing away'. Swami's response to that was unusual and striking. Very forcefully, He said, "No, no, *not* passed away....". Swami's eyes had that faraway look. In that godly mudra, He continued, mentioning how my father had said 'Sai Ram' in those last moments. That He knows everything we know, but that He should *show* it at such a time, moved us deeply. It gave us the assurance we needed. That image of my father raising his hands in a namaskar to Swami's photo and saying 'Sai Ram' is imprinted in my mind. And now, this acknowledgement coming from Baba Himself put that all-important seal of total grace on my father's going.... Swami's emphatic words had conveyed that my father had not passed away, only moved on....

It was a short interview. At one point, Swami picked up His handkerchief and showed it to the gathering. He marked the colour as being pure white. He then called Sunil to His side and pointing to him said how Sunil too was pure and spotless.... That was not all. Looking happy and pleased, Swami said about Sunil, "Others see Me and feel happy, but *isko dekh kar, Main kush hotha hun*...!" (when I see him I feel happy). He then said, "He is *My* Bharat Ratna...." Later, one of the people who had been witness to this said, "When the Lord Himself gives such a certificate, what praise does one need from anybody?" Sunil smiled happily. His face glowed even more than when he had scored his record breaking thirty-fourth Test century!

33

Does Anything Else Matter?

Do not ask for things. Aspire for God.

Sri Sathya Sai

By His grace, we were able to attend Swami's seventy-fifth birthday. Big crowds were expected. The main function was to be in Vidyagiri stadium, which could accommodate the large numbers of devotees. We reached Parthi on 17th November. On our very first darshan Swami gave us a welcoming smile.

On 18th morning, we saw a very sweet interaction. This was between Swami and His devoted elephant – Sai Gita. Tales of Sai Gita's affection for Swami are legendary. When you see Swami showering love on her, you can understand why. In the earlier days, when she was younger, Sai Gita would garland Swami on festival occasions and even go down on her knees and do loving namaskars. When Swami would leave Puttaparthi on visits to other places, big fat tears would roll down her eyes. That day, we saw a caparisoned Sai Gita being regally lead into the mandir grounds. How grand she looked. Swami went up to her and stroked her trunk. She curled it and through the 'loop' Swami's face was clearly visible as in a frame! It was radiating immense love. With His own hands, he fed her apples. He caressed her and patted her, as if to say, 'good girl'. No wonder that she almost embraced Him. It was a most endearing sight. The devotees watched this interaction closely and with joy. Whoever got the chance to see this mudra of the Lord of Parthi?

The 19th was Ladies Day. Bedecked in Swami's sarees, many lady devotees got their special seating on the front verandah. After the morning programme, Swami distributed the new birthday sarees, green in colour. But this year He did not give with His own hands. He only supervised the distribution. We too were blessed to receive these sarees. After the sarees, other gifts were distributed. There were these small red fibre suitcases and the *sevadals* had some time in trying to 'negotiate' them over the heads of the ladies. This is the moment when one has to really watch oneself. How strong is the desire to get the article/gift? How grasping is your hand? And is it really that important? Also, what is the real reason for our wanting it? As *prasad* or ....? What about so many others sitting way back, with no chance? Aren't we lucky just to be close to Him, to see Him so clearly? Does anything else matter?

The thing is that when you are sitting there, it is difficult not to want. It becomes almost an ego thing. The 'I' rears its big head – "I got it – I didn't". It is possible that in such a scenario, one may lose the focus. And even take one's eyes off Swami – all for a suitcase! Would Swami perform this ritual of giving sarees and other gifts like this year after year, just for nothing? Can we forget that it is the avatar's action? And so bound to have some deep meaning and purpose? Both, for those who get and those who don't.

The convocation on the 22nd was, as always, a grand affair. Swami came in the procession looking resplendent in a maroon robe. It touches you deeply to see all the students lined up there taking the pledge. Their voices ring out loud and clear and vibrate with sincerity and love.

However, the birthday celebrations were a little uncharacteristic. There was a slightly subdued atmosphere. An element of uncertainty hung in the air. Many programmes were cancelled and Swami kept everybody on their toes. Nobody knew till the last moment whether they were performing or not.

I think one of the main lessons Swami keeps driving home is of '*samadristhi*' or equal vision in all situations – to be able to view all things with an even gaze as a witness. This training is important because it gets us closer to our reality – our *atma* – which is always the pure witness. By exposing us to these situations time and again, Swami 'beats us into shape' as it were. It is tough going because we are too attached to notions of self and what it can 'do'. We are terribly attached to our own sense of identity. If we are thwarted in our expression of this identity, we feel negated. If we were to only loosen our egos, we would be freer of negative emotions like depression and disappointment. It would not matter. Or at least not matter that much. The only workable way to do this is to forget the self and gain the Self....

34

White Diamond

There can be no greater blessing than to have the love and grace of the Lord. No one can know what He will give to one who has earned His grace.

Sri Sathya Sai

The Lord's favours cannot be forced out of His hand: Some even when awake attain them not; on others, he confers these, shaking them awake...."

Adi Granth

The heartening thing for me was to see Subodh's growing devotion to Swami. In his own way, he was drawing closer every day, growing as much in love as in reverence and respect. He developed a very strong inner connection. This helped him a lot in his professional life as a lawyer. The stress of the profession was telling on him and being basically a 'free soul' who had no material desires or career aspirations, he was as if, stuck in a rut. Somehow, this frustration was very deep and for that reason maybe Subodh was unable to give up his habit of having a drink every evening.

His,one dream was to teach village children and since our farm was situated at Panvel, a short distance from Bombay, he hoped to fulfill his ambition there one day... Weekend visits to this farm became the balm for his soul, and he went around telling everybody blithely, even his clients and colleagues, that he would retire at fifty and settle down at the farm. This became a kind of mantra for him, and he made it a point to repeat it every now and then. About me, he would laughingly say that it would not be a problem because I would anyway be in Puttaparthi! I would retort that all these things were in the hands of God (Swami) and He would decide. In any case, I said, it was to be His plan not ours. But Subodh stuck to his ground and merrily kept announcing his decision to retire at fifty. Since I try not to cross any bridges before they come, I simply laughed it off and thought to myself, "He'll think differently then." If only I had known...

Once, on a trip to Pune, an old aunt of Subodh's mentioned her desire to get darshan of Sri Sathya Sai Baba, at least once in her lifetime. A pious simple-hearted lady, this aunt had done almost all the other pilgrimages, to the prescribed sacred '*dhams*' of India. Being a frail old lady, not in the best of health, her wish seemed rather improbable. None of the other members of her immediate family were devotees of Baba and did not have any similar inclination. Also, she was not a devotee as such but had heard a lot about the holy personage of Baba. She merely had a simple-hearted curiosity to have darshan once, as one would of any renowned much-talked about 'holy shrine'.

Anyhow, we came back to Mumbai and I forgot all about the matter. Not, Subodh. He had already decided in his mind that he would take his aged aunt, Shashi Tai for Baba's darshan at the first given opportunity. He mentioned this to me once or twice but I did not take him very seriously. Subodh's sense of humanity was such and so all-encompassing, it would not have surprised me if he had included a few others too in the list for darshan – his legal colleagues, some judges, friends, his peons, etc. Subodh had, I think what is called, a unified vision – a deep sense of the kinship and unity of all beings. His natural goodness flowed out to everybody who came in his path. His aunt had expressed the desire just once and he wanted to fulfill it. However, I knew that it could not happen unless Swami willed it and there, conveniently, I let the matter lie.

By and by the idea of another trip to Bangalore came up. Excitement started surging through my veins. I asked Subodh to join us. Breezily he informed me "Yes, I'll come, and we'll take Shashi Tai and Aai (his mother) along too." He said he would speak to the travel agent and do all the bookings. I was zapped. It was not a simple procedure. For Shashi Tai had to be brought to Mumbai first, to catch the flight onwards with Subodh and his mother. However, Subodh arranged everything to the last detail and along with his mother and Shashi Tai, they boarded the plane to Bangalore. All I could think of was – 'What a call,' – for Shasha Tai!

As for my dear mother-in-law, the purest gem of a lady I have come across, Subodh had already made a special trip earlier with her to give her Baba's darshan in Bangalore. On that trip, my mother-in-law had an amazing spiritual experience during darshan. As darshan music started, she saw clearly a beautiful vision of Lord Shiva and Goddess Parvati. She saw a *'vahan'* (plane) high up in the sky slowly descending on to the darshan ground. And from it emerged the resplendent forms of Shiva and Shakti – the cosmic whole. This coincided with Swami appearing in darshan. Swami has declared that his earthly manifestation is of the Poorna avatar, combining both the Shiva and Parvati aspects. My mother-in-law knew nothing about this, but her pure hearted devotion to Lord Shiva over many years probably made her the beneficiary of such a blessed vision.

Many have had such experiences while sitting in darshan. In a recent experience, a Westerner saw a dazzling light descend from the heavens just at the moment Baba came out for darshan. He was bedazzled in more ways than one! Of course, not all get to see this, or even get the same kind of experiences. Baba gives each one what he/she needs and is ready for. That readiness is something that relates not to just this one life but is maybe the ongoing work of many past lives. There are manifold experiences that keep happening and are a source of ceaseless wonder and inspiration for devotees round the world. My mother-in-law felt extremely uplifted by this intense spiritual experience.

We had already gone ahead to Bangalore. We awaited Subodh's arrival over the weekend. Their plan was to stay for a couple of days, take darshan and fly back. Subodh had booked two rooms in a club in Bangalore. He felt his mother and aunt would be more comfortable in the club and also provide good company to each other in the period between darshans. We were staying at Gokulam (ashram complex) where, by Swami's grace, we had a room. Sunil would stay with Kavita and Vishwanath at Bangalore and we sisters would occupy the room. At darshan we would all meet up.

Shashi Tai arrived and got her darshan! She was truly pleased. One final darshan of Sunday morning was left before their departure. We were already seated in the mandir when they arrived that day. I was hoping they would get good places, as it was their last darshan of the trip. In my heart, I also hoped that there would be some small interaction – a look, a word, a blessing – for my husband and his mother and aunt, which they could fondly carry back home. However, when the darshan music started, I had no clear idea of where they were seated. Swami came gliding looking radiant and fresh. He walked to the men's side and all eyes followed Him. Taking letters, speaking to some, blessing others, he slowly moved on. And then, we saw something we couldn't quite believe. Sunil and Subodh were both standing and then walking respectfully out towards the interview room. Swami had called us for an interview! We gasped, as much for ourselves as for Shashi Tai. This was her first ever trip to

Swami and her last darshan and she would soon be with Him in the interview room!

Marvelling at the ways of the Lord, we made our way to Swami's lovely garden en route to the interview room in Trayee Brindavan. The walk to the interview room here is very pleasing. To get to the inner chambers, one has to walk through the garden and it is enchantment at every step. The emerald green lawns are skirted by varieties of tall trees and the neatly tended flowerbeds flaunt colour and fragrance. As you wait in the picturesque arbour for Swami to arrive, you may hear a koel breezing though the trees. In such a setting, Swami arrives after completing His round...There is a charming little bridge in the Trayee garden which one has to cross to reach the interview room. Swami came and walked towards it after giving us a look. Before I knew it, I was exclaiming in a stage whisper, "So sweet.." Everybody heard it, even Swami! The sevadals present cringed and scowled at me but my gaze was fixed on Swami. He stopped in his tracks, turned His head to look directly at me and then gave the sweetest smile of exasperation which said, "What to do with her?" ***In a dream once, I had told Him not to walk barefoot on the hard ground as it might hurt His lotus feet and he had looked indulgently at me and said with loving exasperation, "this one..." (suggesting, what to do with her).***

Before Swami's arrival, as we stood in the porch, a stunning thing took place. Kavita suddenly exclaimed, looking up at a window in Swami's Trayee house. She stared fixedly for a moment and then in a tremulous voice said, "I just saw 'papa'...in a white kurta pyjama and he even had his specs on..." We stared at her not immediately comprehending the magnitude of what she had said. She told us in a stunned voice that she had just seen our father at the window upstairs... She too called my father, 'papa' and my father had always harboured a special affection for both Vishy and Kavita. Vishy had got his first ever Test hundred in Kanpur at Green Park stadium and that too after scoring a duck in the first innings. After that poor start,

Vishy had come over to our house, a little crestfallen with some other cricketers for a meal. My father confidently told him that he would go on to score a century in the second innings, giving examples of great cricketers who had done so. And in the next innings Vishwanath did score a century! That was, much before Vishy came into the family – yet the bond had already been forged. Now, as we stood in the porch in Trayee, we were overwhelmed by what Kavita saw and experienced. She was blessed to be the instrument to reveal not only to us, but to all who ponder over these imponderables of life that 'papa' was still there (and with Swami) and had not 'passed away'... (in fact Swami Himself had ticked us off in the interview room when we conveyed to Him the news that our father had 'passed away'. He had said strongly, 'not passed away' emphasizing the 'not'. Also, had one of us sisters got this experience it would have been dismissed as a fond hallucination. But Kavita getting it gave it a different seal of credibility altogether. Of course, the rest of us could not 'see' anything, but we could feel the wonder of it. It is a measure of His inexhaustible grace that He takes care of the subtlest needs of His devotees.

In a happy daze, we walked over the bridge in a single file. Swami stood near the door watching us as we approached. What do His eyes see I wondered – His vision must be so different to ours. Inside the interview room, we ladies sat around His feet with the men a little on one side. Subodh chose the farthest spot at the far end of the room! There was a foreigner sitting on a chair. Swami spoke to him and then took him inside. After a while, the curtain between the two rooms was pushed aside and Swami emerged. One waits for Him to do so. There are periodic brief disappearances of Swami behind the curtain into the inner room with different groups of people. It is the sudden appearance each time, after a short gap that the devotee ardently waits for. Swami was in a wonderful mood. He came out in a graceful swaying motion, softly singing a bhajan under His breath, looking at Pammi as He did so. The bhajan was about '*madhusudana*...' It was one of the first bhajans, which caught my sister's imagination, and it was probably the only one she fully knew! Swami looked at her with an angled glance and smiling sweetly said, "*Bhajan malum hai*?" (do you know this bhajan?) Smiling beatifically she said with folded palms, "Yes Swami, *malum hai*!"

He indicated that our family should go into the inner room. I looked at Shashi Tai, frail and innocent, as she walked in with us, and thought if she would ever know the grace upon her? Her very first visit to see Swami and here she was in His direct presence. Wonderful and inscrutable are the ways of the Lord. Subodh again seated himself at the back and Sunil sat on one side. After we were seated, Swami looked straight at Shashi Tai and said, "*Kya naam hai*?" (what is your name?). This was so unexpected that for a moment nobody responded. Swami repeated the question and immediately we prodded her and she answered in a slightly high-pitched voice, "Shashikala". Compassionate Baba was giving her not only darshan but *sambhashan* too – and *sparshan* was to follow!

Swami then looked across the room to Subodh seated at the back. He asked him, "*Kya kaam karta hai*" (what work do you do?) Subodh answered that he was a lawyer. Swami then told Subodh that he was not very happy in his profession and that there was a sense of disappointment in him, which was true. He said, "Money comes, but goes." At that Subodh smiled and pointing to me said, "Thanks to her!" As usual, Subodh was teasing me even in the interview room and I fell to the bait! Turning to him I said a little aggressively, "ME?" It was funny and everybody laughed at that interaction. Swami looked at Subodh again and said, "if I make something for you, will you wear it?" (*kuch banayga tho pehenaga*?). Swami reveals his all-knowingness even about little little things. Subodh was never one to wear rings, chains, etc., so the question from Swami. There was a short pause and then all our voices, except Subodh's telling Swami, "Yes Swami, yes". We couldn't rely on Subodh to give the right reply!

He could easily have said, "But Swami, I don't wear rings, etc." So, to be on the safe side, we answered on his behalf!

Swami got up from His chair, circled His hand in the air and materialized a huge and glittering diamond ring. Swami looked at Subodh indicating that it was for him. Since Subodh was sitting way back, Swami had to bend forward a little and extend His arm even as Subodh came forward to receive his gift of grace. I don't think I can ever forget that splendid moment. There was something in Swami's expression as He made Subodh wear the ring that caught at my heart. Swami's face was a-lit with what I can only call pure love. His eyes sharply glinted as He put the ring on Subodh's finger and He said softly, "White diamond…pure, puure..", with prolonged emphasis on the word 'pure'. It was so clear that the 'pure' covered not only the diamond but also the recipient of it. We were so excited, but we heard Subodh's voice from behind, "Swami, can I wear the ring only on the weekends?" That was a typical Subodh-classic! We had to quickly cover up for it. Swami said, "*Haan*, all the lawyers will see it otherwise." In one voice, we started telling him how of course he must wear it everyday.

We sisters always had the dream to say something to Swami in Telegu. I had parroted one or two lines in the hope of being able to say them to Him. Now seemed the best time. I expressed my gratitude to Swami in a well-rehearsed line in Telegu. Swami looked at me with an amused smile and then at the others saying, "New Telegu!" Everybody laughed and so did I. After this Swami gave Shashi Tai and my mother-in-law padnamaskar. He also lightly touched their heads, blessing them. Subodh's effort in getting Shashi Tai for Swami's darshan was richly rewarded. After taking *charansparsh*, we sailed out of the interview room feeling truly elated.

35

Summer In The Hills

Always at every time, at every place, I am where you need Me...

Sri Sathya Sai

A month or so later after I returned from Bangalore, the summer vacations commenced for my children and husband. Summer was on its way – temperatures soared and tempers rose! There was nothing else to do but head for the hills – to Mussoorie to our own little cottage nestled there on the mountainsides. Love for the hills flowed in our veins and I think this came from our father who was a true nature lover. He fostered this love in us too and we grew up venerating the natural beauties of creation. We were truly nature worshippers, very like our ancestors! Our life at home in those days was one of deep unity with nature – which was our singular paradise.

As children, we tuned in to the changing rhythms of the seasons and appreciated the moveable feast provided by nature. Winter with its sharp cold air, chrysanthemum blooms, sun-drenched days on the verandah and tea-inundated evenings was a favourite time of the year. The rainy season with its cooling showers of grace soothed our spirit after the long hot summer. Being rain lovers, we would sit on the verandah and gaze at the falling rain exulting in the particular smells of wet dampened earth. Only summer posed a bit of a problem with its scorching dry heat called 'loo', which sweeps through the northern planes in summer. It was the only lack-luster season, which we couldn't get poetic about. The hot summer afternoons were spent in the house with the cooler droning and whirring its khus-cooled air into every corner. My mother would prepare iced rose-milk for us. I still remember the way the ice cubes clinked in the steel vessel as she stirred the milk and we hovered around expectantly, waiting for the refreshing milk sherbet. Another way to beat the heat was gorging on slices of green juicy melons!

In those hot summers, the nights were a reprieve when a semblance of coolness descended on the earth. We used to sleep outside under the sky with all the night sounds of insects buzzing in our ears and the damp smell of the garden as also the dark looming shapes of the trees and bushes. We would stare at the star-filled awnings of the sky and weave dreams. Scents of jasmine and other summertime flowers would assail us and the night dew gently falling would keep us cool through the night.

Now, I cannot imagine such nights. They seem to have melted into the past. Who would today consider moving out from their urban air-conditioned interiors to sleep out in the open anymore? And isn't this the root of all malady of modern man – this moving away from nature, which is the very crucible of life. The concrete and mortar world can never satisfy the longings of the spirit. Why else do we see people today struggling to find meaning in their lives even though they have 'everything'? As Baba once said, "everything is nothing and nothing is everything." Spirituality opens a door to that inner truth where 'nothing is everything'.

Plans for the summer vacation to Mussoorie got underway. After attending the Easwaramma day celebrations on the 6th of May, I rushed home to leave for the station, with the family. Veenu, her husband and kids, Subodh, our daughters and I were travelling together. Mashu had already reached there from Kanpur with my mother. Pammi too was already in Mussoorie; so we had quite a welcome party awaiting us. Pammi had spent a lot of time and energy in the previous months in getting our Mussoorie cottage renovated. There is a saying in English often used to express praise for a woman having handled a demanding task very well – 'she worked like a man'. I say, she worked – like only a woman can – when she has set her mind on a certain task! She put all her intelligence and creative talents to their fullest use. The new-look cottage was to be 'unveiled' to us on our arrival. We loved it right away. Swami of course, had preceded us – and had found His way into every room of the house! My sister had not overlooked that all-important detail. Lovely framed photographs of Swami smiled or blessed us from every room. However, the old Lynwood with its blue windows and rough-hewed rustic furniture was very dear too, being wrapped up with memories of summers spent there with our father. I will always remember those mist-laden dawns broken by the tuneful trill of the blackbird's song, something in which my father and I especially delighted. It was – alongwith some other things, like the horse-chestnut tree with its dainty flowers, facing our study – our special association with our summers in Mussoorie. Now, the blackbird's song and all those other things, would cause a pang...

Subodh very proudly showed his diamond ring that he had received from Baba to my mother. His affection for my mother had always touched me but this time he outdid himself! He wanted to give the ring to my mother! Now, this will appear very strange to those not acquainted with Subodh's personality – but those who have known him will not find it the least surprising. When he first expressed this wish to me, I laughed at his innocence telling him that my mother would never take it considering it was Swami's gift. He mentioned it to me a number of times and I simply wondered at him. I realized in a flash that though Subodh loved his ring (he would often just look at it from every angle and marvel over the different colours in the lights beaming out) he had no attachment whatsoever to it. His willingness to let go of it so easily threw me into a spin of admiration for him. Was this not a divine quality that he was demonstrating?

When he offered the ring to my mother, she laughed and declined firmly saying that it was Swami's gift to him and he must keep it. In any case, she said, her joy was in seeing him or any of us receiving such gifts and what more, apart from that, could she want? However, she agreed, on Subodh's insistence to wear it for a while, sometime during the vacation.

Shortly, afterwards, my mother's health became a cause for concern. Always having been asthmatic, she contracted a severe respiratory ailment, which compounded with her asthma, made it all seem rather serious and disturbing. Medicines seemed to have no effect and my mother could hardly stir out of bed. This was very depressing. We called out and prayed to Baba. Subodh felt that the ring could help. He put it on my mother's finger saying it would confer the healing touch of Baba. It is faith that works wonders. My mother's health starting improving almost immediately. Very soon, she was up on her feet. Not only that, she became so remarkably fit that she could even walk up the steep hillside, something she hadn't been comfortable doing for a long time. It was a joy to see her joining us on our outings and climbing up the slope from our house to the road above. Earlier, she was mostly forced to be house bound, her asthma preventing her from venturing out too often. Things were set right in a wonderful way. We smiled again.... The diamond ring sparkled brilliantly on my mother's finger....

While in Mussoorie, though involved in all manner of holiday activities, my mind was mostly fixed on Swami ...."like a bee poised on a dawn lit honey rose..." (Sri Anand Acharya). I could not shake off thoughts of Him even if I tried. It was not that I did not enjoy myself – I did, but the innermost core of me was tuned only to Him.

Maybe for that, in His supreme compassion, He gave me some very sweet dreams during my stay in Mussoorie just to show me how He was very much there with us.

In the first week of June, we returned to Bombay – with Swami's ring back on Subodh's finger. Though it had been a very relaxing break for all of us, there was a nagging worry about Subodh's health at the back of my mind. He had had his routine medical tests before our trip and they had been okay, yet, I felt anxious. Whenever I brought up the topic, he dismissed it saying the tests were okay. His habit of having a drink in the evening was very worrisome to the family and me. How I wished he would give it up. However, that was not to be – maybe because it was simply not meant to be. Sometimes, with a problem, however hard you try, it seems a case of shoving and pushing a boulder but it does not budge an inch. This is because it was never meant to budge. You were nevertheless meant to go on pushing all you could and get yourself stronger in the bargain. This boulder is like our past karma – we feel so outwitted sometimes when certain problems never seem to go away. There is only justice in God's darbar and this world is only a platform. This justice may not be apparent because it operates over many lifeimes which none of us remember. However, once you accept this law then acceptance of the vicissitudes of life becomes a trifle easier.

36

The Avatar And His Ways

You will not know me in a trice, or even in days. It is something that has to be realised in stages, in due course, through viveka *(discrimination),* vairagya *(non-attachment) and* vichakshana *(clear sightedness)*

Sri Sathya Sai

Though gurus and saints are many, an avatar is a separate and singular phenomenon comparable to none other. It is important for spiritual aspirants to understand the fine distinction between a human guru and avatar. Though an avatar is always the Guru, all gurus are not avatars. The human guru is a realised soul – on the ascent. An avatar is the highest soul who chooses to descend into the human form for the welfare of mankind. The function and workings of an avatar can be very different from those of a saint or holy man. His methods of teaching his disciples may be varied and sometimes inscrutable and baffling. Total trust and surrender becomes a primary need for followers because direct access to Him may not be easy. Even if it is available, an avatar chooses to allude and hint – He never gives direct guidance on a platter. As Baba says, He wishes to steer you to your Self – the guru within. For this, he must awaken your intellect and intuition, so that your own light stands revealed. He is here to take away your dependence on all external forms and support systems – even that of the external guru. For that alone is true self-realization.

One special aspect little known and lesser understood, is the '*kshobana*' factor, whereby an avatar willfully confounds His followers. The Lord creates confusion in the mind of the devotee by some word or act, which clouds rather than reveals His omniscience. This is a test of faith and devotion for the avowed. The devotee flounders and gets muddled. Is He God? The question torments Him. Sometimes, the avatar may go out of His way to say things, which on the human level of understanding do not bear out. Yet, you have to hold fast to your belief in His supreme wisdom. Such instances are meant to strengthen your faith – after testing it. Being aware of this, one can guard against falling victim to confusion and doubt.

In fact, even if once the Lord has proved Himself, it should be enough. The devotee has to store the divine revelation deep inside him and remained fixed in it, no matter what further evidence or events may manifest. This becomes the truest test of faith and surrender, which all devotees are subjected to at some point of their journey towards the goal. Even Jesus Christ chided his close disciples for their wavering faith in the face of enigmatic events, and their wanting more proofs of divinity all the time.

The lesson is to develop such an unwavering faith in His word that whatever He says and does is taken as Truth, even if it appears to the contrary. Once Krishna and Arjuna were going together along an open road. Seeing a bird in the sky, Krishna asked Arjuna: "Is that a dove?" Arjuna replied, "Yes, it is a dove." Krishna told Arjuna, or "Is it an eagle?" Arjuna replied promptly, "Yes, it is an eagle."

"No, Arjuna it looks like a crow to Me, is it not a crow?"

Arjuna replied, "I am sorry, it is a crow beyond doubt." Krishna laughed and chided him for agreeing to whatever suggestion was given. But Arjuna said, "For me, Your words are far more weighty than the evidence of my eyes: you can make it a crow, dove or an eagle and when you say it is a crow, it must be one."

Also, the idea is to annihilate the ego and reach a surrender where worldly matters and their arrangement or disarrangement – ostensibly by the Lord, as all comes from Him – does not upset the fine balance between God and His devotee. Let things go topsy turvy, says Shirdi Sai Baba in *Sai Satcharita*, but you remain unconcerned and fixed in your devotion. Obviously, a very high level of faith and devotion is required to be able to reach such an exalted state and it probably cannot be attained but by the grace of God.

The avatar will not offer Brahma *Jnana* on a platter but He will show you the way and make you work for and reach it. For ultimately, in this whole business of life, the journey appears to be the goal, and the striving, the very purpose of existence. The processes, both on the material and spiritual plane are the very summum bonum of the whole drama of life; it is not so much the reaching as the reaching out that defines our existence.

Also, the avatar hints and speaks in riddles so that the disciple hones his own intuition and intellect, and doesn't become a slave to external guidance, from a guru. "Seek the Sadguru within," exhorts Baba. Were an avatar or guru to spoon-feed direct and clear guidance to his disciple, he would lose his faculty of discrimination and become mentally sluggish and soul-lazy. Baba stresses that life is an ongoing struggle, a continuous saga of challenges. Each and every human being, whether a spiritual aspirant or not, has to be ready to face these [on their own] and grow in the bargain.

Realizing that nothing, not a single moment of agony, goes waste on the path – is also spiritual growth. In fact, one of the greatest realizations is that whatever is – or is happening – is most perfect, as is stated in the *Bhagawad*. In our limited understanding we rue many things, not realizing how these may just be the perfect pieces in the larger jigsaw of our lives. It is difficult, of course, to apply this logic to our complicated life situations when they actually crop up. At that point, it takes all our spiritual strength to hold our own against the onslaught of circumstances. However, we have to keep training ourselves to that faith, which knows and believes that God is always there and always does help, though it may not always be in a manner apparent to us.

The amazing thing is that *each* devotee from the millions around the world has had a personal experience that has brought him to Baba and kept him there. Most of these experiences are profound and powerful enough to change a person's life – sometimes turn it right around. Grace acquired is commensurate to the effort made. Grace can be bestowed on many levels. External grace is physical and evident, related to the outer and the worldly. Internal grace is not evident but has a vaster reach relating to the inner spiritual landscape of a person. It all depends at what stage of the journey one is at. However, this journey, though it begins with the outer for each one of us, it must proceed to the inner – for that is why the avatar comes down – to show us the way back to the self – our real home.

37

Ups And Downs

Play on the strings of the Lord's Name and concentrate on the Lord in Kailasa. This is the main door to the mansion of the Lord. Our hearts filled with love and ananda is really the Kailasa and the Lord has all the right to move about in our hearts.

Let it go. I am all there is. Everything around you will change, except God. Hold on to Me. Don't worry...

Sri Sathya Sai

Opening the newspaper one July morning (27th) Subodh got a wonderful surprise. It was the 'Speaking Tree' article in *The Times of India* that caught his attention. It was by his wife! He called out to me. I was in the kitchen making our morning cup of tea. Excited, I scanned the paper. An article by me, '*Nama Japa – the Yoga of Chanting*' had been published. 'The Speaking Tree' is a spiritually-oriented column, which was started a few years ago by the paper and has become extremely popular. It struck a responsive chord in the heart of many a reader. Some articles are brilliant having rich spiritual flavour and content. In the murky climate of daily news, this column is like a breath of fresh air. For a long time, I planned to write for this column, but my instinctive laziness came in the way. Also, I wondered if I was competent enough especially since I had not written for a while now. My few attempts at writing 'Middles' for the *Times of India* had not borne fruit. Maybe the thought of the rejection slip deterred me from picking up my pen. Whatever it was, I took my time to put pen to paper. My father loved reading the column and sparking off a discussion on it. Whenever a good article would appear, everybody in the family would get into a discussion over it. In this matter, Subodh and my father took a lead in sparking off contentious discussions. As for Subodh, he simply enjoyed stirring us up a bit with his healthy counterviews on things!

By and by, I gathered material (mostly from Swami's books) on the topic of '*namasmaran*' and culled it into an article. Swami has repeatedly emphasized the importance of *nama japa* in our lives. *The Name is enough to give you all the results of every type of* sadhana.

This article on *namasmaran* was ready with me in the beginning of the year 2000. It was at the back of my mind to edit it and send it to *The Times of India*, but that's where it remained – at the back of my mind. It was only in April 2001 that I finally sent the piece, prior to my Mussoorie vacation. Three months later, the article saw the light of day and was published. In the middle of the excitement, my thoughts went to my father – how he would have loved to see his *Ginthi's* article in that column! I felt an acute pang, more so at the thought that had I sent the article earlier, he too would have got to read it. I like to believe, however, that he did read it from wherever he is right now...

The day my article appeared in *The Times of India*, I was flooded with phone calls – mostly from Sai devotee friends. Everybody had woken in the morning to the pleasant surprise of seeing Swami's name in the article. In fact, my prime motivation became just that – To see His name and quotes in my published articles, (they were entirely His – every bit of the matter coming from Him). I sent a few more and each one was published by Swami's grace. However, in one of the articles, an editor deleted Swami's quote. That piece gave me no joy. I decided to write an *entire* article on the teachings of Sri Sathya Sai Baba for the column. I wrote the article and sent it with the specific request that it should be published on 23rd November – Swami's birthday, which was round the corner.

We started making plans for the birthday. The months preceding that had been beset with problems on the home front. I felt stressed out and my connection to Swami felt weak. I felt sure that seeing Swami would set things right by recharging my spiritual batteries.

The 21st of November found us in Parthi again by His grace. I wondered if my article on Baba would appear on the 23rd. How exciting it would be if it did.

This time, however, the whole birthday feeling was a bit different. Mashu had been unable to come being in Kanpur with my mother. For some unknown reason, our spirits were low and our customary zest toned down.

On the day of the birthday, Pammi was placed in the group of ladies near the verandah. Veenu and me were in the regular line. The students' band started and Swami came with regal tread in procession. Showering benediction on all He glided through the darshan crowds. There was the divine discourse after which prasadam was distributed. At the conclusion of the morning programme, aarti was done and Swami started walking back. Everybody sat up and adjusted themselves. So did we. The boys were holding a '*chatri*' (a decorative umbrella) in regal style over Swami's head. But He didn't appear to be too comfortable with that! Smiling gently, He tried to wave them off. He came closer. We folded our palms. Then, He looked at us and stopped in His tracks. We couldn't believe it – turning full to us, He spoke to Veenu, "Saree *nahin mila*?" (you didn't get the saree?) (having arrived after Ladies Day we hadn't got the birthday sarees.) Veenu was so excited at His talking to her, she said something unintelligible – maybe,

"*Milla*!" We were so touched by His gesture – that He should take note of such things even on a day like this.

After morning darshan on the 23rd, I procured a copy of *The Times Of India* hoping to see my article in it. However, on opening it, I discovered that they had not used it. I felt disappointed but only to a point. I knew it is all to His plan.

I would always break a coconut at the Ganesha shrine just before we are leaving Parthi after every trip. I also do a fixed number of parikramas each time. Ganesha is the darling God of all Baba devotees! It is understood that to reach Baba, Ganesha gets us there! He smoothens the path and clears the obstacles. This Ganesha shrine at the entrance of the ashram in Parthi is a most potent one. The intensity of prayer and yearning brought there constantly by devotees infuses the atmosphere with divine vibrations. A huge peepul tree, (one of the five sacred trees of India) and a neem tree spread their green canopies overhead to add to the holy atmosphere. Early morning the nagarsankirtan rounds start from there – after obeisance to Ganesha. Standing there in the early dawn silence, in front of the shrine, it seems as if your soul breathes.

That day, I went as usual to the Ganesha shrine with a coconut. I did my namaskars and parikramas. I stood in front of the shrine and prayed. Raising my hand, I brought the coconut down to the wet stone to break it. Now, I am quite practiced in this. For years now, I have broken a coconut every Thursday. In fact, I felt I had acquired a certain felicity in the matter. That day, a most unusual thing happened. As I brought the coconut down, it just slipped out of my hand and rolled away whole. I got a start. That had never happened. I felt out of my depth. What did it mean? The sevadal on duty there kindly picked it up and gave it back to me. I took it and broke in on the second attempt. But that didn't help. I kept thinking and worrying about why the coconut had slipped out of my hands. Veenu reassured me by saying, "Why, it must be a very good thing – it means He has accepted your offering in full…." With great mental effort, I shook it from my mind.

I had to pick up some bhajan cassettes and books from the new shopping center. So I went there and tried to forget about the matter. Walking back with my packets after a while, I passed the board, which puts up a 'thought for the day' from Swami's teachings every day. Most devotees make it a point to read these in passing. I too stood there and read the message. I thought it may cheer me up. It was a long one and it far from cheered me. The last two sentences shook my equilibrium. They read something like this –"Happiness and sorrow are two sides of the same coin. Where there is happiness, grief too follows. This is inevitable."

I was leaving that day. The coconut had slipped out of my hands and now this. For some odd reason, I felt disturbed. I hurried back. I childishly rued the fact of having gone that way. If I had gone from the other side, I would have missed the message... Of course, it was just a general message. One of the many similar ones, that Swami keeps giving. It had nothing to do with me specifically. Yet.

I returned to the room. Everybody was busy packing. Spirits were generally low. And in that general frame of mind, we returned to Bombay.

38

Holding Tight

Worldly life is transient, like passing clouds... joy, sorrow, everything will pass by. Our highest endeavour should be to attach ourselves to the one unchanging reality – God. This relationship with God is the only permanent one, being the eternal relationship between Atma *and* Paramatma...

Sri Sathya Sai
(in an interview to
me in October '96)

It was sometime after my Mussoorie vacation (May '01) that I had awoken with this unusual line echoing in my head – "*dukha sukha ban jayega sihahi mein daal ke...*" I had felt a little startled and wondered what it meant (in translation it would roughly mean – sorrow will turn to happiness when transcribed into ink or in other words, putting down your sorrows on paper will ease your pain...) The words of the message had flowed in *shudha* Hindi – where had they come from? And, what did they mean? What sorrow? That bothered me for a while. 'Sorrow' appeared to be a very heavy word. Yes, life is a continuous challenge with its ups and downs but the word 'sorrow' appeared out of context to me... I rationalized that it must mean, 'viraha' or the anguish one feels at separation from Him. What else could it mean, for wasn't sorrow the last thing on my mind?

A month and a half after my return from the birthday trip to Parthi in November – it happened. The even tenor of my life was shattered. The 5th of December 2001 was the day – how can I forget it. It was the day Subodh awoke feeling distinctly unwell. He felt weak and looked pale. I urged him to immediately see a doctor and get all the tests done. I gave him vibhuti water. Though I tried not to show it, I was feeling far from calm. I silently chanted Swami's name. I now understand why the Name is called 'the raft that saves'. It is the only thing one has in moments like these to bank upon. And if you hang on it, it gets you across. More than anything else the constant repetition of the name keeps other thoughts out.

We went to the doctor who sent us to the pathologist. Subodh had his sonography done. The reports were to come only in the evening. I felt worried but tried not to let it show. Every time a negative thought arose, I cancelled it out with a positive thought. I looked at Swami's photos in my house and told Him to take care.

The reports finally came. Subodh had jaundice. Though that was bad, it could have been so much worse. Both Subodh and I felt vaguely relieved. Jaundice could be set right with adequate rest and diet control. With that pattern being set, in a couple of months or so, things would be right back to normal – or so we thought.

For a while, we went around thinking it was jaundice. But why then was he not showing signs of improvement? We were told jaundice takes a long time and recuperation is a slow process. Pammi, Sunil and Mashu were going to Parthi for Christmas. Subodh typed out a letter to Swami on the computer and sent it with them. In the interview room, Swami took the envelope with Subodh's letter and without opening it said, "*Malum hai*, brother-in-law's health not good....".

Subodh was on enforced leave and had to be house-bound. He spent a lot of time on the computer doing his legal work from home. He also surfed the net for latest pictures and news of Swami. He would make printouts of the pictures he particularly liked. He would then show them to me and ask, "Have you seen that one before?" Even if I had, I would pretend I hadn't. It gave him childish joy to feel he had chanced upon new pictures and quotes. There was one particular picture of Swami, which was truly enchanting – and I had really not seen it before. Even Subodh just loved that one. He took a printout, made colour xeroxes and then had six or seven laminates made. One each for the four sisters and the rest were given to his close friends. He even took some quotes of Swami and made them into laminates. Visiting one of his dear friends from the legal profession who had become a high court judge recently, he took this as a gift. Subodh also downloaded many songs from the net which he loved hearing. It was an assorted collection with some devotional songs also. He downloaded some bhajans sung by Baba and spent a lot of time trying to locate his favourite – '*Chitchora Yashodha ke bal*'. Whenever the bhajans would come on, he would shout for me to come across and hear them too.

Apart from all this, there was one more activity that kept him preoccupied. Thinking and dreaming about the West Indies! He had made two trips to the West Indies with Sunil during cricket match time and had fallen in love with the place. If there was heaven on earth for Subodh, it was the West Indies. He took to that place like a fish to water. His pure carefree spirit, I think, felt at home in that simple informal honest-to-goodness atmosphere of that country. And now with another cricket event coming up Subodh wanted to go again. Both Sunil and Subodh would often tease me about the West Indies trips, with them secretly plotting and planning with me saying, "No way, would I let him go!" Well.

However, Subodh's health did not show signs of improvement.. We decided to go in for further tests. The sonography now showed up some newer disturbing findings. But nothing could be said for sure. Subodh went for further check ups at a good family friend doctor's pathology lab. The reports were to come on 14th February – Valentine's day. I felt tense about the new findings. I couldn't wait till we reached the clinic to know the reports, so I quietly called the doctor. He spoke very gently but did not divulge the reports and said that we should come there and he would explain. That made me more concerned. Subodh kept his calm right through in a most distinctive way. The doctor's face and voice showed concern. He told us that he had sent the samples for tests to two more pathology labs just to be sure. "Sometimes, there is a mistake….", his voice petered off. He had to finally tell us – and we had to hear it. The worst. That dreaded word, which you want cancelled out from human destiny. But which persists – as only a cancer can – cancer itself. One reads about it and it happens all the time but still one never thinks it will happen to one's own. My mind felt blank. Subodh, true to nature, took it in a very clinical fashion. He made some queries, etc. but it did not look at all as if the ground had shifted from underneath his feet. It had, underneath mine.

We drove back home. Subodh tried to make normal conversation but I couldn't really respond. There was only one thing to do. Go right away to Parthi – to Baba. He would take care of it. I felt lucky that at such a moment I had Him to turn to. His thought consoled me, fortified me. Otherwise, I would surely have been bereft.

We reached home. Of course, I couldn't tell my daughters anything. I didn't even tell my sisters. How could I? How does one tell such a thing? I thought I'd wait till the following day's report.

The next day, anxiously I phoned the doctor. His voice said it all. All the reports said the same thing. My heart sank. I had to tell Pammi now. How I did it, I'll never know. But I couldn't really finish speaking on the phone – my voice kind of broke. She was shattered. She rushed over immediately. Our first thought, of course, was

Swami. Without wasting any time, we coordinated the dates and booked our seats to Parthi. The thought of Swami gave us a lot of strength.

We took the flight to Bangalore. Sunil, Pammi, Subodh and me. Swami was in Parthi. We took a taxi from Bangalore airport. Halfway through we were informed, there was some trouble with an Andhra strike and roadblocks further on. So one would have to take a diversion. The new route was much longer and round about. It took us almost an extra two hours extra to reach Prasanthi. Under normal circumstances, that would have hardly mattered. We would have sung a few extra bhajans and talked a bit more of Swami for the extra time. But this time it was different. Subodh looked tired and drawn. Our anxiety showed on our faces.

Next morning we sat in darshan and awaited Swami. I felt relieved that we had made it and were in Parthi – under His shelter. Just reaching there made it feel better – like reaching a safe harbour. I found that I was able to put my worries at His feet. Swami came and spoke to Pammi. He asked about Subodh's health. He then completed His round and came to the verandah. We watched Him. He spoke to Sunil. Next moment, we saw Sunil and then Subodh getting up. In His compassion, He had called us in. Pammi and I got up immediately and walked to the verandah. We had walked that walk many times (by His grace). But never with such a heavy tread. We went in and awaited Swami's next cue.

Swami came in and immediately materialized vibhuti. He gave some to Pammi and me and then the balance to Subodh telling him to eat it up. We sat down. Swami looked at Subodh and said, "*Diya tho tha*," (I had given him....). Subodh stood with his hands folded in namaskar and said in all humility, "Mistake *ho gaya*....." Swami called him to His chair. He waved His hand and materialized a silver *dibiya* full of vibhuti for Subodh. There were letters lying on the table next to Him. He picked out one, removed the letter and used its envelope for placing the *dibiya* inside. He neatly folded the paper flap around the *dibiya* and handed it to Subodh. He then got up to go to the inner room. He called Subodh inside alone for about five minutes. After that, He took the three of us inside as Subodh waited in the outside room.

In the inner room, Pammi and Sunil sat on each side of His chair and I in the middle just in front of Swami. Pammi and Sunil both started talking immediately about Subodh. Swami looked very godly. He went into that 'far away' mudra with hands circling the air and His eyes distant. In fact right through that interview, He did that – going into those mudras. At one point, He looked heavenwards, His lotus shaped eyes narrowed and glinting with unfathomable depths.... Even in that moment of extreme pressure, I felt stunned at this vision of Him. Those eyes – it felt that the cosmos' were swirling in their depths.

Swami did not give any specific assurance. On the contrary, He told us that Subodh had come very late and that it had spread a lot being of the galloping sort. He looked at me directly and asked, "What do the doctors say?" I said, "They say it is very bad."

Then He asked me, "What does he eat" I answered, "Swami, mainly fruit, light non oily food, etc." Swami advised, "Give him Viva and one apple everyday." He further said that I should give the vibhuti in a glass of water twice a day. He said I could give the Viva either in milk or water. He advised rest and half day work (to keep his mind occupied.

Later outside, when Subodh asked if he should return the huge pile of long standing briefs to his clients, Swami said, "*Karo*". But the manner in which He said it created a bit of confusion in us as to what exactly He meant. Half of us thought, He meant 'return *karo*' and the other half that He had meant 'work *karo*' (do your duty, do your work). This confusion I think was clearly intended by Him. Swami indicated to Pammi for the vibhuti basket and distributed vibhuti to all. He allowed no one else a padnamaskar except Subodh. (It had been a year since Swami had announced His decision to stop giving padnamaskar). When Subodh sought it, Swami graciously assented and lovingly pressed His head down to help him take it. As we left the interview room, Swami gently stroked Subodh's arm and smiled. In the course of the interview, He had also put His hand on Subodh's head and blessed him. Each blessing counts. However, only God knows, the true nature of that blessing.

As I was leaving the mandir that day, before our return to Bombay, an old inmate of the ashram accosted me to hand a xerox sheet being circulated. It was a message on surrender. The words were beautiful, no doubt. But, for some reason, they gave me a start inwardly – true surrender was way beyond what we thought it to be. Why was this message given to me, just at this moment? I shut my mind to thought and mentally clasped His feet, tighter…

The kind of belief in Me, I ask of people, is more, much more than most people think is love or faith. I ask you to give me everything: not fruit or flowers or money or land, but you, all of you with nothing held back, your mind, your heart, your soul...

39

An Auspicious Day

Pray... from the heart...pray until God relents...

Sri Sathya Sai

Twenty-seventh March '02 – will go down as a very auspicious day in the lives of the Vishwanath household, Bangalore. It was Kavita and Vishy's wedding anniversary, but on this occasion, something even far far more. For years now, Swami had told them that He would grace their home in Bangalore. Many devotees know from experience that when Swami says, "I will come to your house" it could mean, a day, a month or even many years before the promised visit materializes. It could also mean that He would come in another form (dream, vision, vibhuti materialisation, etc.). But yes, the word given would be kept. Your job was simply to keep praying...

That morning of their wedding anniversary, when Kavita and Vishy sat for darshan in Brindavan, they had reason to feel both anxious and excited. Swami had been sending feelers to them that He may come anytime. They had to be ready. Kavita, prudently, had spruced up everything and was on 'high alert'. All she would need now, she thought, was a day's notice...

Swami came up to Kavita in darshan and gave blessings for the occasion. He hinted in an enigmatic way, that He may come to their house anytime today... We too were in Bangalore at that time, staying in Sai Gokulam, near the ashram. In fact, we had prevailed upon Subodh and Shrikant to come to Bangalore too for darshan and they were with us. We were hoping that Subodh may get a chance to secure further blessings of Swami.

However, in darshan, that day when Swami hinted about His visit, it was presumed that He would come only in the evening, as He was otherwise engaged in the morning.

So, after darshan, we went back to Gokulam and Vishy, Kavita, Daivik, Pammi, my mother, Sunil and his parents drove back to Bangalore city. Before leaving, they all told us to be 'on the ready' for the evening. They would intimate us as soon as they got to know.

Swami of course, had His own plans. Very different to what anybody might have imagined. When Vishy, Kavita and the rest of them left the ashram that morning, they could never have dreamt that they were being followed – by Swami's car! Swami had given instructions to follow their car (without informing them) and so give a surprise visit.

Barely having entered the house, they got a call from the mobile phone from the car. Swami's car was five minutes away from their house and He was arriving! Surprise! Surprise! Only the kind that can make you faint! Forget a day's notice, it was not even an hour's notice. Just five minutes. That surely must have been a first, in the matter of Swami's house visits!

It was pandemonium. Luckily the basic things had all been taken care of, yet. There were *only* a million things to do! Even the daily domestic for cleaning and mopping had not arrived. Every member of the family got frenziedly busy in some activity or the other. In the middle of all this mad running around, Pammi was dialing us frantically in Gokulam, where we were lolling after morning darshan. "COME FAST", she said...! We jumped up and in five minutes, five very chaotic minutes, were racing out of Gokulam. But in this context, five minutes was a very long and crucial time. Remember, Swami was just five minutes away from their house and we were a good forty-five minutes away. And the first thing we encountered as we left was the closed railway crossing near the ashram!

Well, Swami came. It must have been one of the most informal visits ever – and Kavita and Vishy can always remember that with extra fondness and gratitude. Formal visits Swami has made a-plenty. But, to 'drop in' like this, that makes it very different and special. Apparently, Kavita had seen the scenario in a dream a month back. *In the dream, she gets news that Swami arrives suddenly without notice, to her house and His chair is not ready for His use.* After this dream, Kavita made *sure* to see that the chair was made ready and kept waiting for whenever He should come. However, when Swami came, and was led to the chair, He opted not to sit on it! The sunlight streaming in through a skylight fell directly on the chair and so Swami decided to sit elsewhere. He went and sat down like any visitor on the regular sofa in their drawing room. So the dream decoded perfectly!

Kavita, Nutan, their mother and Salonie were busy in the kitchen preparing food for Swami. Vishy, Sunil, his father, Pammi and my mother were sitting outside with Swami. And we – we were speeding down a Bangalore highway, praying fervently to make it on time! There was heavy traffic on the road, there were the traffic signals to contend with and we didn't even know the exact directions to Kavita's house. There was nothing else but to place the matter at His feet. We did. And broke into bhajans, as a form of prayer calling out to the Sai Deva, Parthi Natha. Another matter, that the bhajans came out in the croakiest tone possible.

I realized with a start that I had seen this whole scenario of Swami's visit to Kavita's house in the year 1999! *In the dream, I see that we are all in Bangalore and speeding from the ashram to a devotee's house for a special audience with Swami. The car in which I am in has to wait at the railway crossing near the ashram. While waiting, I see from my car window a woman in a casual kaftan, busy in some work. For some reason I notice her as she is very striking. The railway crossing opens and we proceed to the house. I have not been able to comb my hair before leaving so I take out a comb and brush my hair in the car. As we are approaching the house, I see something written in the Kannada script in big bold letters in the sky. I cannot understand what it says. When we reach the house, people are already assembled there for darshan and in this group, my sister Pammi and my mother are also there.* This dream decoded stupendously in every minor detail. The wait at the railway crossing, the speeding to Kavita's house in the car, combing our hair in the car because we had no time to do it earlier and even the bit about the lady in the casual kaftan. That was Kavita, who after reaching home had got into her nightie when the call had come, saying that Swami was coming in five minutes. Another unbelievable aspect was my mother being there. She hardly travels out of Kanpur and if so, it is only to Bombay or Mussoorie. When I had got the dream, I had wondered as to how I saw her in Bangalore and I remember it even niggled my mind as to why my father was not present in the dream... (That was in 1999 and my father passed away in 2000). And yet, my mother had made it to Bangalore, last minute. Her programme to come to Bombay was made suddenly in March '02 and we asked her to join us on our trip to Bangalore.

In the car ride to Kavita's house, I buoyed hopes somewhat by recounting this dream in bits. All this nervous chatter and bhajan singing was basically by us ladies with Subodh and Shrikant sitting quietly most of the way. They too felt the tension of the moment, but they kept silent whereas we didn't stop talking.

Somehow, we managed to reach in about twenty-five minutes. We saw the security vehicles and personnel at the gate of their residence and heaved a sigh of relief. That meant Swami was still there. But every moment counted. We made a dash for the gate but the security had to do its job – they stopped us! We felt frantic. Luckily, just then, somebody from Swami's entourage recognized us and came to our rescue.

We literally ran in – Veenu, Mashu and me. Subodh and Shrikant followed far more sedately behind. The french windows leading to the garden were open and we rushed into the drawing room, to see Swami standing – that heartening flash of orange – at the far end behind the dining table. What a sight that was to our eyes!

It was as unconventional an entry as any one could ever hope for into the august presence of Swami. Of course, Swami did not bat an eyelid. It must have been a change even for Him! We just went up straight to Him, without any protocol, folded our palms and said with feeling, "Swami, we have come..." The informality of the encounter was entirely in keeping with the whole theme of Swami's visit.

Swami in His compassion must have waited for our arrival, so we could get a glimpse. For, very soon He made to leave. We accompanied Him to the door. We felt elated to have got there on time for His darshan. However, when He started to leave, I realized there had been no chance of any talk about Subodh's health. In fact, we had barely entered and now Swami was leaving. I couldn't restrain myself from mentioning Subodh's health even as Swami was walking to the door. Swami said a little sternly, "*Malum hai*" (I know) but gave no reassurance. (Subodh later chided me for mentioning the matter of his health to Swami. "He knows everything," he said, "so where was the need?")

Later, we got the whole account of the visit from Kavita and Vishy. Swami had spent a long time in their mandir, which has very powerful vibrations. Swami's presence must have heightened these further. He had sat on their regular sofa and looked most comfortable doing so! As for little Daivik, he had a field day! He was thrilled to have Swami over to his house and sat glued to Him right through.

A very blessed day for the Vishwanath household!

40

The Golden Lingam

Mahashivratri is sacred for it is the day on which Shiva takes the linga *form, for the benefit of seekers.*

Sorrow and pain are caused by desire. The cure is to use the same desire and turn it to God, to desire God...

Sri Sathya Sai

Back in Bombay, my main concern was to ensure Subodh's having the apple, Viva and vibhuti regularly as Swami had instructed. All my hopes were pinned on that. And for a while, things did seem to look up, with Subodh's energy levels improving dramatically. In fact, amazingly, he was doing all those activities which a person in his condition could not even dream of. He was driving every day, going for walks to the seaface, making weekend visits to the farms, and even swimming – twelve lengths of the club pool. That baffled everybody – and also gave us a lot of hope. Sometimes he would have a very bright look and we would feel very confident but at other times he would not look so good. I held firm to the belief that he would be fine. Some strange power had gotten hold of me where I could not believe that anything negative could take place. In a way, this strange experience of mine was a miracle of sorts. In a situation, where I should have been sick with worry and concern and totally depressed, I found myself shielded from all such negative emotions. I could not figure it out myself, but I knew that I was being protected. It was as if I was held aloft in that whole period and carried across the turbulence. It was grace of the highest sort. I experienced it but I don't really have the words to describe it. Whatever it was, it had everything to do with my faith and love for Baba.

Shivaratri was round the corner. With Subodh looking better, we decided to make a short quick trip for blessings. Pammi, Veenu and I landed in Parthi, a day prior to Shivaratri. However, this time, it was with a very different kind of feeling. Our hearts were heavy. We hoped for some further assurance from the Lord...

One day, I was feeling particularly low in darshan. Everything looked bleak. Suddenly, during bhajan time, the students burst into a heart-stirring soulful rendition of Subodh's favourite bhajan – '*chitchora yashodha ke bal.*' The student singing it that day put in extra *bhav* (feeling), or so it seemed. That immediately lifted my gloom. I took it as a sign that I should not worry and that everything was going to be set right.

On Shivaratri day, Pammi was given seating in the aisle, just in front of Swami's chair. Veenu and me were in our regular places in the line. Just a few minutes before Swami emerged for afternoon darshan, Pammi got up from her vantage position and came hurriedly to me. She told me to go and sit in her place. She got a strong feeling to do this and she followed her heart. I went and took her spot. It was so close to Swami's chair! I gasped! I would have the most clear and direct view of Swami. I was sure Swami had drawn me close to shower the blessings I especially needed in my situation. Of course, He could do it from anywhere, far or near, but being near to Him would give *me*, my human heart, the consolation and hope it needed.

Being in the aisle seat, there was a thin strip of red carpet between our ladies line and the students line on the other side. Would Swami choose to walk down through that aisle to the verandah? That was the one thought in our minds...

And when Swami appeared for darshan, He slowly came to that very spot. He stopped for a while and then turned to walk through that narrow aisle where I was seated. It was an overpowering darshan. His presence felt stunningly immediate as He glided nimbly on the carpet, inches away, His robe gently trailing. It felt awesome.

After a while, Swami went and sat on His chair. The Shivaratri discourse was followed by the Shivaratri bhajan. Nobody really expected the lingodbhava right away. In fact, you could never say, in any case, whether Swami would display it or not. His actions defy any sort of a pattern. However, everybody was alert and kept their gaze fixed on Swami. Sitting very close I had an unobstructed view. The lingodbhava was not really on my mind – Swami was. In any case, whatever He can create, however magnificent, can it compare to the Creator? Sitting there, I realized that everything – everything – was secondary to Him. Everything dropped away – all thoughts, all worries. A feeling of total trust and surrender overpowered me.

My eyes were fixed on Swami. He took a sip of water from the silver tumbler placed near Him. After a minute, He took another sip... and another. Now that is always a signal to devotees to remain alert. It often heralds the lingodbhava. The bhajans were picking up tempo and reverberating in the mandir. There was a sharp expectation in the air. I realized that even a blink of an eyelid could make one miss it – for it took just a moment for the *lingam* to emerge into view. Swami took successively more sips of water and from His bearing and general demeanour it became clear that the lingodbhava was about to take place. The students were singing impassionedly – "*mrutyuanjayaya namah Om...*" On the notes of that bhajan, the golden lingam emerged in all its glory in dramatic fashion. Swami mopped His mouth and held the lingam aloft between His thumb and forefinger for the crowds of devotees to see. A wave of excitement ran through the thousands sitting there. Everyone wanted to get a glimpse of this supreme act of creation. I too feasted my eyes on the golden lingam. And I wondered what mystical qualities it might contain. Considering the exceptionally unique way it was created, surely it must be extremely potent and powerful. Who knows, what grace was bestowed on those who looked upon it? Not to say of those who would get a chance to touch it? But one thing was clear, it was a blessed opportunity to just be there at that moment, as a witness to the event. I felt extremely grateful.

Swami placed the lingam on a small silver plate, atop His tumbler and it remained there for the whole night in display for the Shivaratri bhajan gathering. I too sat up the whole night, for the night long vigil singing bhajans, which is customary for devotees. The Shiva bhajans resounded in the mandir. The golden lingam on its silver perch glittered splendorously sending rays of light all around...

At the break of dawn, Swami walked into the mandir again. Fresh and aglow. The devotional feeling had swelled and spiritual vibrations were strong.

Swami gave His discourse and later took arati. Prasad was distributed... We wondered if the glorious lingam too would go as prasad to some lucky devotee as we had heard that Swami sometimes blesses a devotee in this stupendous way... Shivaratri celebrations came to its conclusion. We came back to Bombay with, I'm sure, the blessings each one needed.

41

'Mrutanjayaya Namah Om'

The lingam is the fittest symbol of the omnipotent, omniscient and omnipresent Lord. Everything starts from it and everything is subsumed in it...

Remember: what is transient is not important; what is important is eternal.

Sri Sathya Sai

Why do you stay in prison when the door is so wide open?

Rumi

I returned with a lot of hope. I enthusiastically recounted the lingam story to Subodh. I felt, just by hearing it, he would be blessed. As yet, he had not ever got the chance to set his eyes upon the lingam. Well, if only I had known… Subodh looked intrigued. The lingam story always fascinated him. As for his overall health, it was the same. The reports were all the same, showing no improvement. BUT – he was defying all norms of his condition. He was even driving to the farmhouse on certain weekends. He had increased the number of laps in the swimming pool and the doctors had no explanation for that. Maybe I thought, it was just a question of little more patience, before the light appeared at the end of the tunnel. In fact, an unbelievable development now took place. Subodh started planning a trip to the West Indies with Sunil who was leaving for a tour shortly. Subodh felt he could do it and appeared firm on his decision. He told me that he had thought over it and that though I might feel upset at his decision, he had decided, "to go"… I now think, with hindsight, that it all had a very symbolic connation..

Subodh downloaded some new pictures of Baba from the net and especially had sticker sheets prepared of them in my brother-in-law, Shrikant's office for use on his travel bags. When we expressed our acute reservations and distress on the issue he simply said, "trust and surrender..." Then one day, amidst all the fret and worry, he brought home a laminated sheet of the Gita-saar and pasted it on our wardrobe. He particularly drew my attention to it and made sure that I took note of the words – how, whatever happened, happened for the best – by the will of God. And that since nothing was ours in the first place, and we had no claim on it, nothing could be taken away from us. It was all God's. Of course, he – and He – were only preparing me.

And sure enough one day, his condition suddenly deteriorated. It all happened so fast after that, like something skidding. A dark cloud was now above us. My daughters felt pained and distraught – they could not understand what was happening. My elder daughter, Rubianca wrote a poem from the depths of anguish in her heart. This poem along with the touching 'get well *very* soon, Papa' card from his Binka and Tippy (Subodh's names for them) brought a tear to their Papa's eyes – ever a man, ever strong, yet in that moment, overcome with deep emotion.

I CAME TO YOU

I have looked and looked, You are nowhere to be found,
My heart is sinking deeper into the ground.
I am crowded by worries and I'm filled with fear,
You've left me alone, you aren't even near!
I am drowning in sadness and floating in sorrow,
You aren't here today but I am expecting You tomorrow.
The next day has come and I've sunk into depression,
You better come now, You owe me an explanation.
I trusted You when You said those words to me,
'Wherever you go there I shall be'.
'Have faith' You told me. 'I am always around'
Then how come right now You are nowhere to be found?
All I can do now is sit around and mope,
I've given up now; I've given up all hope.
You said, 'Call out to me and I will come'
But You didn't, see now what I have become.
Where else can I look around for You?
How much I have searched but yet have no clue.
Where have You gone? Oh why did You hide?
Can't You see how much I have cried?
Looked everywhere but You weren't there.
No more of this now can I bear.
I am angry and hurt; to me You have lied.
All He said was, 'YOU FORGOT TO LOOK INSIDE!'

First July '02. The sky had an unusual bright colour. Both Pammi and I felt that it was a positive sign and Subodh would surely turn the corner.

He did – but in a very different way. He left – on a very different kind of a journey. And his going was not ordinary. In fact, it was extraordinary. Swami's grace saw to that. He went, with the golden lingam (*hiranya garbha*) Swami had materialised that Shivaratri, now beside him, in my hands. The very one I had seen Swami manifesting that year in darshan, during Shivratri, with me sitting a couple or so feet away. It had come to us miraculously a day before, given by the devotee to whom Swami had entrusted the lingam to. That morning, the devotee had awoken with a clear instruction inside her head to bring the lingam to me – for Subodh. That moment of extraordinary grace, when she handed the lingam into Subodh's hands, is one to be never forgotten. Subodh was always considered to be a very good-looking man, with the most amazing eyes. But the way he looked at that moment, when he received the lingam in his hands (even in his illness) surpassed everything. His face was radiant with light and his eyes beamed something inexplicable. Never had I found Subodh so good looking as on that day and his eyes so brilliant.

We had the lingam for one whole day. It arrived on 30th June. Subodh got the greatest delight in making sure that the doctors, nurses, and all who visited him got a chance to see the lingam and get the blessings. All those people, who got a chance to do that, must have done so from the accumulated merit of many past lives – without even knowing it. It was total grace of course for Subodh. Everybody has to go, but how many can go like this?

The family was anguished. And most worried about my daughters and me. The love of all our family members, husband's side and parents side surrounded us in a protective cocoon. They all felt extremely worried as to how I would take it and how I would react. For hadn't I been sure and confident in my faith, that nothing would happen?

How did I react? And was it me? No, it was only Him. 'I' reacted only as came from Him. Also I understood a key thing about the spiritual life. There are two climates – outer and inner. Spirituality strengthens the inner climate, which gives you the resources to tackle the vicissitudes of your outer life in the world. *Swami had once told me in a dream enigmatically,* "andar ka mausam bahut bhadia *(the inner climate is very good)...* I wondered at that time, why is He saying that and, what about the outer climate?

At that moment in my life, when I should have been completely shattered, if anything saved me, it was my inner climate, which was full of Baba. I realized then that grace has many faces... and faith and surrender have a meaning far beyond our ordinary understanding.

42

On Subodh

Pure...white diamond...

In the song 'Chitchora Yashodha ke baal', *God is called a thief. God is called a thief not of worldly things or pleasures but only of pure hearts. Make your heart pure so He can steal it.*

Sri Sathya Sai

Can I capture Subodh's personality in a few lines? I will try... Subodh had entered the legal profession primarily because his father was in it and it seemed the most natural thing to do. My father-in-law, Mr. M.V. Paranjape was an eminent lawyer who had distinguished himself in the legal field in many ways. He was one of the leading lights of the profession in his time. He was appointed as a High Court judge in Bombay but after a while he voluntarily resigned from that esteemed post for personal family reasons. His brother passed away suddenly, at a young age leaving his wife and three small sons with no real means of income. My father-in-law had carved an honoured niche in the Bar. As much for his sharp legal acumen as for his inviolable sense of ethics honesty and fair play. He felt compelled to resign from his High Court Judgeship – which though one of the most prestigious posts in the country did not afford the kind of income, he felt he would now need to support his brother's family alongside his own. Subodh looked up to his father and respected his ideals and aspirations. Subodh's elder brother had already gone off to the States on a ten-year stint to pursue his Ph.D. in Physics. Subodh and his sister, Snehal both decided to join the legal profession and keep the tradition going.

However, though Subodh distinguished himself in the legal field, his heart was never in it. This was mainly because of the nature of his profession. The unseemliness of life manifests itself too starkly in the law courts. The frauds, the deceptions, the greed, etc. that overtake life and even the best of human relations – all this disillusioned him.

He had an innate nobility and certain convictions. I will not even call them principles because principles are something that one sets oneself to follow – Subodh didn't have to try. He was just 'naturally good'. His amazing humanity flowed to the world at large. I would marvel at him and so would my family. My father once saw Subodh's palm and having some knowledge and felicity in the art of palmistry told me confidentially that there was something very extraordinary about him. All of Subodh's ten fingers had 'circles' on their tips, which is very unusual. Most people have one or two, if any at all.

However, being in the legal profession caused a degree of distress to build up in him over the years. He carried the stress and worry of his clients (mostly from the rural areas of Maharashtra) on his shoulders. At night, he would sometimes talk in his sleep and talk about the cases pending in the court. The result was like many lawyers, he too started resorting to a drink for relieving the tension. By and by this habit increased to become a daily one. I nagged him about it but nagging never produces any positive result. Also, every now and then the newspapers would come up with some new findings, which said that a moderate amount of alcohol or red wine could actually be healthy for a person. I would prop my hopes on that. However, as the saying goes, there is no right way of doing something wrong. And the wisdom of that was to hit me later.

Since he was in the habit of regular exercise – swimming and yoga, his face always looked bright and healthy in the mornings. On days when I refused to talk to him, he would respond with some sweet gesture that would melt my heart. The fact that his drinking never once interfered in his duty either in the court or at home (he would often remind me of this), kept me from getting paranoid about the whole matter. I never thought that it could ever cause any major problem. Also, I always hoped that he would give it up and when he started drawing closer to Baba, this hope became a beacon light – now he would definitely give it up I thought. My mind charted the course of events to follow, something like this – Subodh meets Baba – Subodh is drawn to Baba – Baba's magic works on him –Subodh gives up drinking (overnight) – takes up Baba and we live happily ever after.

Most of the above happened by His grace except – 'Subodh gives up drinking' and 'the *ever after...*'.

As a husband, he was God's gift to me. I cherished his care. He was an unusual man and gave me some unusual compliments. Never would he say it in the clichéd way! Even the messages he wrote in birthday cards etc. were highly original with an apt message for the recipient. As there was nothing so remarkable about me that could have cast any kind of spell, I presume it was entirely the grace of my Lord, Baba. Maybe, he was just the answer to my sincere prayer for a 'good man' above all else, for a marriage partner. If anybody epitomized the universal love that Baba often speaks about, it was Subodh. One can have that feeling only if one has deeply understood the oneness and unity of all life. To Subodh, this understanding came naturally. So I conclude that he was a realized soul 'undercover'. He had come to earth for a fixed tenure to finish off some left over karma and having done so he left – without looking back.

He was in fact, a bohemian in spirit having very 'little baggage' of possession, attachments, desires, etc. Being entirely without ambition for status or wealth, he travelled light. I had to beg him sometimes to buy a pair of new shoes or trousers. His wallet was weather-beaten and old and when I would buy him new ones (his birthdays gave a pretext), he would not switch to the new one but keep using the old! I gave up on that front! His watch was probably from the last century – and the new ones given on birthdays kept piling up in the cupboard and this was not because he was tight with spending. He was one person from whose wallet money came out most easily (if it was there of course). Spontaneous charity came very easily to him. He would give without any thought of getting it back. Money was for convenience and for comfort but never for luxury and display.

He had a way with people. He attracted friends and people just got drawn to him. Maybe this was because he never flattered and always said it as it was. This endeared him a lot to discerning people, especially those surrounded by a lot of flattery. Sunil and he shared a very special relationship. Sunil would love talking to Subodh about cricket matters and loved Subodh's frank opinions. This frankness covered Subodh's opinion of Sunil's views too, in his columns! My other brother-in-law, Shrikant and Subodh also got along famously. The three brothers-in-law shared a wonderful rapport and had some very good times together. Subodh's going has left a very painful gap in many areas and that is one of them.

Subodh always had something new and unexpected to say on any matter. We sisters felt it was just his habit to take the opposing stand – a natural fall-out of his being a lawyer! He would laugh right through the argument and that would rile us even more! In fact, we would be a little keyed up on 'important' social get-togethers as to what he might say next, to whom! Yet, the surprising thing was that nobody ever took offense at his candor. His words had a soft honest edge to them. People recognised this by and large and so took him on his own terms.

It could have been picture perfect – but nothing in life really is. Can one put the blame on his drinking and smoking? One can never say. For who hasn't heard of the Churchill syndrome? Britain's famous prime minister drank and smoked heavily throughout his life and lived to beyond the age of ninety! Maybe, it was just destined to be and all our actions are 'set up' as causes.... Who knows?

Whatever it may be, I think back today with love and gratitude and wonder if I just a little bit took it for granted – his unique love and caring and his uninterrupted support of all I was and am. I also think, is there anything I could have done more or differently to have made him happier? Who can answer such questions? All I know is that were he to answer that question, from wherever he is, he would laugh, in that lovely way of his and say, "Yes, you could have given me that extra beer, without the nagging!!"

43

Touching Base...

Let go. Don't cling. Be still. Establish yourself in the homelessness of the mind. Physical homelessness will not earn the victory. I prescribe homelessness of the mind, mind abiding nowhere.

When devotees surrender their lives to God and obey Him, He takes the full responsibility and cares for His devotees even to the smallest details.

Sri Sathya Sai

For Swami's seventy-seventh birthday celebrations, we reached Parthi on 21st November. Everything was the same – and yet not. Sitting in darshan, I couldn't help but feel the intense poignancy of my situation. Year after year, darshan after darshan, I had sat in the same way and there was nothing to show that today was any different. On the face of it, no.... But in reality, between the last birthday and this, my world had turned upside down. Was it real? In any case, what was real? The dream-like nature of our existence in this world came home to me with renewed force. There were moments, I could actually feel the truth of the statement, 'it is all a dream'. Also, that everything was only a play of consciousness and the individual dramas of our lives were just a ripple on the lake of this vast consciousness. All our experiences were only a super-imposed reality, temporary, passing, evanescent, like the flickering play of sunlight on water. Wherever we came from, THAT was the reality – all else was a passing show, the dance of maya. If so, then the question was, how much importance to give what? I realized more than ever the need to seek out the Source, my source, and attach myself to it. I could see it clearly for the drama it was – everything – the joy, the sorrow, the laughter, the tears. This, I thought, must be the beginning of *samadristhi* (equal vision) – feeling detached. The world and all its doings began to appear like a cardboard cut-out. The sense of identity and ego disengaged and for a flash of a moment I felt I touched infinity. *Wisdom flashes like lightning amidst the clouds of the inner sky; one has to foster the flash and preserve the light...*

Twenty-third morning, Swami surprised everyone by coming out in His usual orange robe. This was a change from the past years when He would either wear yellow, maroon, or white on the birthday. We wore sarees given by Swami on the previous birthday. We saw that Swami had given attractive new sarees to many lady devotees on the occasion of Ladies day. Some of the ladies got red silk sarees, others a lush yellow. Like always, the sarees were beautiful!

There was a divine discourse by Swami filled with gems of wisdom. Down the years, Swami has been showering this divine nectar, and like a loving parent who never tires or gives up on his own child, He has not given up on us! What more can one say of His love? Over and over He has been repeating the simple verities and truths that can change our lives – if only we will listen. These truths appear deceptively simple in language – help ever, hurt never, love all, serve all, – but are so difficult to translate into action. We all go around mouthing these truisms but how far will just uttering them take us? It would do well for us to understand that these sayings of Swami apply not to other people, but to ourselves. We have to be scathingly honest, which requires courage and character. Can we summon that? If we wish to make real and not imagined headway on the path, then we have to summon up these qualities that Swami requires of us. If we don't, the glory will be brief. If we do, its radiance will only grow. They say that Swami gives a very long rope! Many chances. But when inspite of His indulgence, there is no desired change then one fine day, He snaps the bond – just like that. We can never forget that we are here in Parthi, a remote village of south India, not for trivial gains or petty satisfactions. Not even for big material gains and big worldly satisfactions. We are here only for one thing – to march on straight to the goal of self-realisation.

Afternoon darshan, something happened! Just as we were leaving our rooms, we saw Mr. Subramaniam hurriedly approaching us. He was smiling broadly and had a newspaper in his hand. He waylaid us and flashed the paper – the Speaking Tree column of the *Times of India* of 23rd November 2002 had carried my article on Swami on the auspicious occasion of His birthday – the same one I had written for the previous birthday. To say we felt thrilled is putting it mildly. It had been my dream for over a year now to see a full article on Swami's teachings appear in the column on 23rd November.

As mentioned earlier, this published article had a long story behind it. After I had sent it to the Delhi edition for publication for Swami's seventy-sixth birthday, Swami had given me a dream, which clearly suggested that my article would get published. The dream was this: *I am sitting on a chair at a corner spot somewhere in the open. I have got a diary and pages of my written stuff on my lap. Swami suddenly comes right up to me, and starts asking me for something from my sheaf of papers. I immediately spring up from my chair, feeling quite delighted at His proximity wishing to thank Him for everything and tell Him how much I love Him... But His interest mainly seems to be in the written stuff on my lap. He picks up one sheet and looking at it smiles, as if He has got the right one. He says He will take that since He wishes to show it to His students.. His exact words are "students* padna chahta hai" *(students would like to read it). At that I look at the sheet in His hand, and see that it is a rough draft full of untidy scratches and corrections. So I tell Him eagerly not to take that one but how I would make a neat fair draft and send it to Him. He readily agrees, gives back my sheet and tells me sweetly with a smile as He is walking away,* "haan, aur 'get-up' achha karna, ***Main dekhega...***" *(do it well, I will see it).*

However, when on Swami's birthday the previous year, the article had not been published, I felt a little perturbed. Hadn't Swami given me that dream? How could His dream go wrong? Had I misinterpreted it? Of course not. Swami's dreams never go wrong. They only take time to get decoded. For later, after the previous birthday, when I had checked with the Delhi editors they coolly informed that they had not received any such article by me. I was baffled. I had couriered it to them and had the receipt. Anyhow, I immediately sent them another copy with some changes for their reference. This time I emailed it. On receiving it, they informed me that it was fine. So, the article with some corrections – like in the dream! – was kept in the cans for one whole year before it saw the light of day.

Now the published article was in our hands! In Parthi, on 23rd November! I realized with a thrill that Swami's dreams are foolproof... only one has to glean the hints and read between the lines. The fact that He had given back my first draft to me in the dream meant that I had to further improve it and send it again and as for the '*Main dekhega*' – the evening darshan would sweetly unfold even that!

Sunil, who came out just then to go for darshan, saw our excited faces. He heard the story. He got the idea to carry it as a newspaper cutting to show Swami in darshan. Sitting on the verandah, he felt he could get a chance to offer it to Swami. We quickly made a neat cutting of the article and gave it to Sunil. After that, we all went for darshan.

Shortly the music started and Swami emerged. It was birthday time and the whole walk from Poornachandra to the mandir was beautifully decorated with flower-awnings and arches. The auspicious mango leaf torans fluttered in the breeze, at the gate entrance. Swami came slowly in that majestic way of His. How His appearance lights up the space!

Showering blessings all around He reached the verandah. Would Sunil get a chance to offer the article? It was not a question of chance, of course. It all depended on Swami! So we waited and watched. Luckily, we could see Sunil clearly from where we sat. If Swami decided to talk to him, we could not miss it. Shortly, we saw Swami approach Sunil's side. We saw Him stop. And look at Sunil. My heart beat faster and I watched them intently. I saw Sunil half rise-up and then extend the newspaper cutting to Swami. My heart in my mouth I wondered, if Swami would take it. He did! The cutting must have been upside down for I saw Him turn it around and then look at it for a long moment as if reading it ("***Main dekhega***!"). He then made as if to give it back to Sunil. Sunil said something and Swami kept the cutting with Him. (Apparently as Sunil told us later, this is what transpired – Swami came to Sunil and he offered the cutting saying, "Swami, sister-in-law's article on you…." Swami took it and scanned the title, 'Touch Base With God Through Atma Vidya'. He uttered the last two words of the title loudly and reflectively, "Atma Vidya… hmm…" When He started giving back the article, Sunil told Him, "It's for you Swami." At that Swami kept it with Him!)

What a balm it was for my soul. After all that had happened, this one small gesture of Swami's soothed me no end. It also gave me the necessary encouragement to keep on writing… for Him.

For the evening programme, Pammi was seated in the group of ladies up close, in front of the verandah. We sat in our regular darshan places. The fact that Pammi was wearing a different saree from the others in the group was very noticeable! Most of the other ladies were donned in Swami's new saree. A Sai friend from the block told Pammi that Swami would surely make note of the fact and give her a birthday saree too! Swami often does this, giving sarees subsequently to some who may have got left out. Another matter that those who get left out, do so in perfect accordance with the Master Director's plans! Pammi was seated in a very conspicuous corner spot just where the student ranks started. It would be difficult for anybody – but Swami – to miss her there! He did – and sailed on to the verandah.

After the interaction with Sunil about the article, Swami came to the edge of the verandah and started looking around. He suddenly started making elaborate long distance signs to some lady in the crowd. It could have been anybody! Swami wanted to give her a saree! When it was identified as to which lady it was, the matter was sorted out by Swami graciously coming half way to hand the saree to her. This happened for a couple of more turns, with Swami picking out ladies to give sarees to. He would make the barest of indications and within a minute a boy would run into the interview room and would be back with the required bag with the saree. I am sure those fleet-footed students who do this are blessed by *vaayu-putra* Hanuman – they go about their task at the speed of wind! After this, Swami stood on the edge of the verandah looking happy and pleased and kind of scanned the ladies group again as if to check that nobody had got left out. He even asked some, "Saree *milla*?" The lilas of the Lord!

Pammi sitting in her corner spot was suddenly nudged by her Sai friend neighbour. "He's asking for you." Swami was looking towards their side and softly asking for someone. Pammi looked at Him but being at a distance could not clearly make out whom He meant. She kept sitting. A flutter then, as Swami repeated the name of the person – "Mrs. Gavaskar..." This time Pammi could not miss it. It was her! She got up at once, her face glowing. She was wearing a rose pink silk saree that evening. I will never forget how she looked that day as she walked up that whole centre aisle to where Swami was standing, waiting. The soft evening light filtered through the acrylic dome, and fell on and all around her, as with folded hands and smiling face, she walked to the Lord! We watched her as in a trance! It was like a dream sequence!

Swami looked at her and asked softly, "How many?" And then, "*Char hain ki panch*?" (how many are you, four or five?). Her face all lighted up, Pammi answered, "Four, Swami....". Immediately Swami made the sign, and in a moment, a bag of sarees was in His hand. For some reason, there were five sarees in that bag. Swami took out the extra saree and sent it back to the room. The rest, He handed to Pammi – for the four of us! The bounty of the Lord! That extra saree must surely have been for a Sai sister somewhere! Also the message from Swami that we were not just four sisters but there were many more Sai sisters now in our fold...

It was the rich yellow and purple combination saree that Swami gave us and very happily we wore them to darshan next morning. We felt *that* saree was a very special blessing, the manner in which Swami had given it to us.

23rd NOV 02

Touch Base with God Through Atma Vidya

By Shammi Paranjape

Sri Sathya Sai Baba is among those realised souls whose wisdom cuts across all barriers of race and religion, aimed only at restoring dharma and establishing the unity of faiths and peoples under the common banner of universal love and brotherhood. *Manasa bhajare guru charanam, dushtara bhava sagara taranam* — O mind, chant the glory of the Guru's feet, which can take you across the treacherous ocean of samsara — exhorts Baba. However, to widen spirituality's reach beyond retreats and rosaries, it has to be made to touch all of life and divinise every activity. For this, the quest for *atma vidya* or self-knowledge is essential in a human being, for it awakens him to his inherent divinity and also promotes reverence and respect for all creation.

The *Bhagavad Gita* tells us that it is more important to be an *atmavan* or rich in atma shakti rather than be a *dhanavan*, materially rich or *balavan* or physically strong. Atma shakti confers everything on an individual. The real purpose of life is to make contact with God within, who is *satyam, shivam, sundaram* or truth, goodness and beauty and to draw from that supreme source the inspiration for an ideal life. This can be achieved by building on the foundation of *satya, dharma, shanti, prema* and *ahimsa* or truth, righteousness, peace, love and non-violence.

THE SPEAKING TREE

"If there is righteousness in the heart, there will be beauty in character. If there is beauty in character there will be harmony in the home, if there is harmony in the home there will be order in the nation, and if there is order in the nation there will be peace in the world", says Baba. "Where there is love, there is peace, where there is peace there is truth, where there is truth there is bliss, where there is bliss there is God." Baba says, "Let the different faiths flourish. Let the glory of God be sung in all languages. Respect the differences between faiths and recognise them as valid, so far as they do not extinguish the flame of unity." The Vedas, repository of the highest knowledge, declare: *Sahana vavatu, sahanau bhunaktu, sahaveeryam karvavahai, tejasvinaav dhitamastu maa vidvishavahai* "Let us live together, struggle together, grow together, in joy and harmony."

What is dharma or righteousness? It is essentially purity and unity in thought, word and deed — *trikarna shuddhi*. No man can claim to be religious if he observes the sacraments but fails to be upright and compassionate. The end of all education is character and selfless seva is more beneficial to spiritual development than japam and dhyanam behind closed doors. 'Help ever, hurt never' is the highest religion endorsed even by the Vedas, for hands that help are holier than lips that pray, and service to man is service to God.

Wasting of food, money, time and energy have to be studiously avoided and a ceiling placed on desires. The Vedas lay down the four goals or purusharthas as *dharma, artha, kama, moksha* — righteousness, wealth, desire, salvation. Sri Sathya Sai Baba says, "Since the first and last are difficult to attain, man has given them up as impractical and is struggling with the middle two, wealth and desire. All the misery and fear of life can be traced to this monumental mistake. The four should be taken in two inseparable pairs, dharma-artha, kama-moksha. That is, earn wealth through righteousness and let your primary desire be for salvation."

Baba asks seekers to distinguish between the momentary and the momentous. He asks us to be constantly aware of three things: Faith in God, the illusory and ephemeral nature of the everchanging world, and the imperishable nature of the atman within. He also asks us to banish two ideas: The harm that anyone has done to us and the good we have done to anyone.

(Today is Sri Sathya Sai Baba's birthday)

http://spirituality.indiatimes.com

Sacred Space

Good Health

Health is better than wealth... and stealth.

Anonymous

Sickness tells us what we are.

Proverb

What destroys one man preserves another.

Pierre Corneille

Look to your health; and if you have it, praise God, and value it next to a good conscience; for health is the second blessing that we mortals are capable of; a blessing that money cannot buy.

Izaak Walton

Much of the world's work, it has been said, is done by men who do not feel quite well.

John K Galbraith

Our body is a magnificently devised, living, breathing mechanism, yet we do almost nothing to ensure its optimal development and use... The human organism needs an ample supply of good building material to repair the effects of daily wear and tear.

Indra Devi, Russian-born US yogini

I don't have ulcers; I give them.

Harry Cohn

If you start to think about your physical or moral condition, you usually find that you are sick.

Goethe

Illness is in part what the world has done to a victim, but in a larger part it is what the victim has done with his world, and with himself.

Karl Menninger

44

(Rohan and Swati's wedding) Rohan's Nakshatra

Be happy... there is no need to worry about anything...

Sri Sathya Sai

If Swami has displayed great love and affection for Sunil, his son Rohan has not been far behind. Though outwardly, Rohan is like any other young man of his generation – outgoing, fun-loving, – he has a very deep spiritual side, of which not many are aware. Even Rohan himself was not aware of this till recently! However, after he started coming to Swami, this part of him was awakened and he even had some stunning experiences. Like a true initiate, he never spoke or discussed these too openly or too easily. In fact, his reticence in this matter, underlined his spiritual orientation. His specialty is that he carries his 'spirituality' very lightly – like everything else.

Swami had once told Rohan that twenty-six would be the right age for him to get married. Immediately after he completed twenty-six, things fell into place, clouds if any dispersed and suddenly the 'nakshatra' was just right – for a wedding, to his long time sweetheart Swati.

The wedding was fixed for Guddipadwa of 2003. This was the only day (from the auspicious days marked out for weddings), that saw Rohan free from his cricketing and other commitments at that time.

In March '03, Pammi and Sunil made a visit to Bangalore to give Swami the wedding card and seek His precious blessings. In the interview that Swami very kindly gave them, Pammi was able to personally hand over the wedding card – designed by her. (It was a scroll with a gold tie-up thread placed in a pouch).

Swami materialized a gorgeous piece of jewellery for the new bride-to-be – a chunky gold necklace studded with emeralds. It matched perfectly with the bride's yellow and green wedding saree. How does Swami know these things? Just as He knows everything – even things that we may not know about ourselves! For when Swami asked the bride's name, and Pammi said, Swati – Swami revealed that 'swati' was Rohan's nakshatra!! (hardly any of us, including Rohan was aware of this).

The wedding went off like a dream – by His grace. In every function, for five consecutive day, Swami's chair was placed at the venue and His auspicious Presence sought.

Message

The morning sun spreads his golden rays across the skies and awakens the entire world to start their day... In the same way, the Atma *within is waiting for you to shake off your slumber, so that He can engulf you in the golden rays of His love. From out, turn in. Open the eyes of your mind. In that darkness, you will see the soothing* Atmajyothi, *its soothing flame will lighten up your path and guide you through this journey of life; it will enrich you by bringing out the best in you and it will humble you by its majesty and splendour... Then you will become a perfect divine instrument, worthy of His grace...*

45

The Only Reason

"Resolve to carry on the quest for your own reality. Resolve to live in the splendid inspiration of the constant remembrance of God."

"The purpose of living is to achieve 'living in God'. Everyone is entitled to that consecration and consummation."

Sri Sathya Sai

As for me, everything was a total turnaround. But I did not analyse too much. I thought it best to place even my mind into His hands.

In an important interview, in July '02, Swami called us in. I had no intention of saying anything specific. In any case, one could not use the term 'passing away...' Swami had once chided us about that with reference to my father. So frankly, I did not know what to say. When the time came, He must have put the words into my mouth. I told Him about my young daughters and how now, there was nothing for it, but that we were entirely in His hands and in His care... Swami heard me out. Something had made me speak in a very emphatic way. He made His Godly mudra with His hands, and looking up, His eyes enigmatic and deep, said just three words.... Small words but they covered everything for me. He said simply and emphatically, "Okay, okay, okay...."

I have experienced the inner voice directly in my life only twice. The first time, I awoke in the morning with this voice speaking rapidly in my head. The voice went so fast that I was unable to record the whole message on waking. The one line I could recapture was the first one – "God made this world so that He could love all of mankind...". There was much more on the same theme and how important love was, for then, every small gesture got transmuted into the highest sadhana that melted the heart of God. When I got this experience, I felt truly amazed because I knew hundred percent that the voice was not a conscious thought of my own volition. It just poured in from somewhere....

On 7th March '01, I again got this experience. I awoke to this voice, running rapidly in my mind. I realized with a pleasant start that it was the inner voice again. The message the voice gave me seems to epitomize the entire theme of existence and my life – as I see it.

"To offer our cups up to God that He may fill them with the nectar of divine love.... This and this and only this is the reason for our lives..."

Amen.

OM SRI SAI RAM

Glossary

Abhayhastha: conferring the boon of fearlessness with raised hand of blessing.
Agarbatti: incense stick
Ahimsa: non-violence
Akhanda: non-stop, continuous
Amrut: divine nectar conferring immortality
Anandam: divine bliss
Atma: soul; Self
Arati: waving burning camphor in front of deity as conclusion of worship; symbol of total annihilation of ego in front of God
Ashram: spiritual retreat; abode of peace
Avatar: incarnation of God; descent of God on earth in a form.
Bhagawad Gita: the principle holy book of Hindus, meaning song of God; expounded by Lord Krishna on the battlefield to Arjuna.
Bhagawan: God
Bhajan: devotional songs
Bhajiyas: deep fried Indian snack
Bhaktas: devotees, worshippers
Bhav: feeling
Chamatkars: miracles
Chattai: folding rattan mat.
Chitchor(a): stealer of hearts-God.

Dandam: staff carried by ascetics.

Darshan: sight or vision of a holy being.

Dharma: right action; action in consonance with conscience.

Dharmakshetra: the abode of virtue—the name of Baba's ashram in Mumbai.

Dhyan(am): meditation; unbroken concentration on an object for stilling the mind for spiritual communion.

Dibiya: small container

Gayatri mantra: an ancient vedic prayer that invokes the supreme intelligence to Illumine the intellect.

Gopi: female cowherd devotees of Krishna, examples of supreme devotion.

Halwa: Indian sweet

Hamne Aapna Sar Jhuka Liya: we bow our heads at Thy lotus feet.

Kaliyug(a): the current age of strife and dissension.

Kalpataru: wish fulfilling tree

Kalpavruksh(a): wish fulfilling tree

Kamandal(am): the vessel in which sages carry drinking water.

Krishna: an incarnation of God who took birth roughly 5000 years ago.

Jagat: cosmos; world

Jai: folding hands in reverence.

Jap mala: rosary; prayer beads.

Japa(m): constant repetition of the Name of God.

Jhula: swing

Jnani: sage or person possessing unitive spiritual knowledge and experience.

Likhita japa: repeatedly writing the name of God.

Lilas: play; diversionary sport of the Supreme Lord.

Lingam: sign; ellipsoid shaped stone. Symbol of Shiva; symbol of that from which everything has emerged and into which everything merges.

Lori: lullaby

Mahashivratri: 'the night of Shiva'; big Indian festival.
Mandir: temple
Manjira: cymbals
Mantra: sacred syllables or mystic formula for spiritual enlightenment or achieving desired results.
Maya: veil of illusion; the mysterious, creative and delusive power through which God projects the appearance of the universe.
Milla: got
Mrityunjayaya: name of Lord Shiva, meaning the One who is victorious over death.
Mrityunjayaya Namaha Om: Shiva mantra
Mudra: expressive pose
Mulayam: soft
Murali-lola: lover of the flute; Krishna.
Nagarsankeertan: devotional singing at dawn by people walking through the streets.
Nakshatra: constellation of stars; one of the many which according to Hindu astrological belief govern human destiny.
Namaskar: folding palms giving respect and reverence.
Navratan mala: necklace of nine gems.
Nityanutanam: ever fresh and new.
Om: sacred primordial sound of creation.
Omkar: letter in Sanskrit alphabet representing Om.
Pallavs: the part of a saree that covers the shoulder.
Parmatma: supreme Soul; God.
Poorna: whole; complete.
Prasad(am): consecrated food or article.
Prem(a): unconditional and ecstatic divine love.
Puja(n): worship.
Raag: composition of musical notes in Hindustani music.
Ragi: coarse nutritious food grain.
Rangoli: coloured powder used for making decorative patterns on floors during festivals.

Rig Veda: first veda; oldest religious scripture.
Roti: Indian wheat bread.
Saburi: patience
Sadbuddhi: wisdom; clear intellect.
Sadhan: tool
Sadhana: spiritual discipline aimed at God's realization.
Sai Ram: a manner of greeting among Sai devotees.
Samadhi: super conscious state of oneness with God; final merger with the Supreme Soul.
Sambhashan: dialogue
Samsar(a): worldy life; the objective material world which the human soul experiences through repeated births and deaths; liberation means freedom from this cycle.
Satsang: the keeping of elevated and sacred company.
Satya: Truth
Seva: selfless service
Seva dal: volunteers at the ashram.
Shakti: divine energy
Shamiana: colourful tent used for large functions.
Shanti: peace
Shishyas: students under the tutelage of a guru (teacher).
Shradha: reverence/faith
Shubha: auspicious
Shyamal: the lotus blue colour of Shyam or Krishna.
Sindoor: vermillion powder worn on forehead by married Indian women as an auspicious mark.
Sloka: Sanskrit hymns in praise of God.
Sparshan: divine touch of spiritual preceptor or holy personage.
Taal: rhythm that accompanies musical compositions.
Tapas: austerities or ascetic practices.
Telegu: south Indian language.
Tulsi: basil; holy plant in Hindu belief.
Upadhi: title of honour.

Vedas: oldest Hindu scriptures; divine revelations given to sages meditating on the mystery of life. The four Vedas — Rig Veda, Sama Veda, Yajur Veda, Atharva Veda are a profound and comprehensive body of all kinds of knowledge both temporal and spiritual.

Vibhuti: holy ash

Vivek(a): discrimination

Vrindavan: historically the place where Krishna sported as a child; also name of Baba's ashram in Bangalore.

Yogi: an equal minded person who seeks union with the divine.

Yug(a): age